# PLAYING FOR KEEPS IN STARR'S FALL

## KATE HEWITT

Boldwood

First published in Great Britain in 2025 by Boldwood Books Ltd.

Copyright © Kate Hewitt, 2025

Cover Design by Head Design Ltd.

Cover Images: Shutterstock and iStock

A CIP catalogue record for this book is available from the British Library.

Paperback ISBN 978-1-83603-251-9

Large Print ISBN 978-1-83603-252-6

Hardback ISBN 978-1-83603-250-2

Ebook ISBN 978-1-83603-253-3

Kindle ISBN 978-1-83603-254-0

Audio CD ISBN 978-1-83603-245-8

MP3 CD ISBN 978-1-83603-246-5

Digital audio download ISBN 978-1-83603-247-2

This book is printed on certified sustainable paper. Boldwood Books is dedicated to putting sustainability at the heart of our business. For more information please visit https://www.boldwoodbooks.com/about-us/sustainability/

Boldwood Books Ltd, 23 Bowerdean Street, London, SW6 3TN

www.boldwoodbooks.com

*Dedicated to the Tedanator, thanks for all your gaming advice!*

# 1

The turkey sat in the middle of the table, cooling and congealing and generally looking unappetizing. It wasn't even a real turkey, just a pre-cooked turkey crown that had come with shrink-wrapped veggies on the side, an all-in-one Thanksgiving dish that looked like she'd bought it at a minimart. She should have done better, Maggie thought with regret. It was just that neither of them had really cared about Thanksgiving this year, and she hadn't had the energy for anything more. But now that she and Ben were sitting in front of it, she wished she'd gone to a little bit more effort, tried to make this something like the Thanksgivings they remembered.

"Shall we say what we're thankful for?" she suggested brightly, and her son simply stared at her.

Maggie opened her mouth, closed it again. The trouble was, she was just so *tired*, and all the truisms for this situation—*time heals all wounds, it's okay to feel sad*—had been said and done to death. And really, that was what this was about. Death.

Thirteen months on, they still hadn't gotten past Matt's death. And why should they? Thirteen months, Maggie had learned, was pretty much nothing when it came to grief, especially when you had lost someone as vital to your life as your husband or your father. Thirteen months was just the beginning, the veritable tip of an enormous iceberg that stretched coldly and darkly *miles* below the ocean, seething with all sorts of emotions that were so utterly exhausting to acknowledge, never mind examine and process. Grief, she'd discovered, was far more complex than she'd wanted it to be.

"Should we just go?" she asked instead, her words falling into the silence of their yawning dining room like tiny pebbles into a pond. They were seated at one end of a table that could host fourteen, the house echoing emptily all around them.

Ben looked up, which Maggie told herself was a win. Hours, even days, could go by without her son looking her in the eye.

"What?" he asked.

"Should we just go?" Her voice came out stronger; she was getting into this. "Forget the turkey." Turkey *crown*. "Let's do something different today. We can drive to Starr's Fall and check out the new house."

Ben shook his head slowly, skeptical, even suspicious of such an idea. "But we're not moving till January."

"That doesn't mean we can't look at it now," Maggie argued. She had a sudden burning desire, a *need*, like an itch all over her skin, to get out of this house with its eleven-foot-high ceilings and cathedral foyer, its sweeping double staircase and its kitchen that was as big as a basketball court. Well, pickleball, maybe, but still, it was huge and full of Carrera marble and gleaming chrome, everything look-at-me shiny and unrelentingly hard. She'd loved the house, or thought she had... once. She didn't anymore.

"Let's go," she said again, and for emphasis, she slapped her hands on the dining-room table, hard enough for her palms to sting.

Ben simply stared. Her son was good at staring. He had several different kinds. Like the blank-eyed I-absolutely-don't-care look that made Maggie shrivel inside. Or the narrowed death stare of doom for when she was embarrassing him, which was, Maggie had discovered—to her regret, shame, and exasperation—very easy to do. And worst of all, the one that cut her to the heart every time, the silent swamped stare of misery, when she knew how wretched he felt and that there was nothing she could do about it.

Except she *had* done something about it. In the last month alone, she'd withdrawn her son from school and bought a house in what he'd insisted was his favorite place in the world, Starr's Fall, Connecticut. She'd also sunk a hefty chunk of Matt's life insurance into a business she really had no idea how to run.

Whether she *should* have done those things was another matter entirely, but she had, and now they were here, waiting out the rest of the semester before their real life in Starr's Fall—whatever *that* looked like—could begin.

"Let's just go," she said again, and for the first time in longer than Maggie cared to remember, a light sparked in her son's eyes.

"What... just *drive* to Starr's Fall?" he asked incredulously. "Today?"

"Why not? It's only an hour."

"An hour and a half," he corrected her, and she gave a grimacing nod of acknowledgment. Fine, an hour and a half. An hour fifteen if she drove fast, not that she *ever* would, considering how Matt had died, but...

"Let's do it!" Now she was starting to sound a little manic, like an extra on *Mickey Mouse Clubhouse*, or maybe like she'd inhaled helium. Either way, she knew she needed to moderate her tone. "Seriously, why not?" she said in a quieter, more reasonable voice. "We don't need to stay here if we don't want to, Ben."

"Isn't Thanksgiving, like, the worst day of the year to drive?" Ben asked as he hunched his shoulders. "For traffic and accidents and stuff?"

"Well, yes," Maggie allowed, because she was determined always to take her son's concerns seriously, especially around driving. He hadn't gotten into a car for weeks after Matt's death, save for the limousine they'd taken to his funeral. "But I think it's the Tuesday or Wednesday before, or the Sunday after, that are the trafficky days. On the day itself, most people aren't driving. They're eating turkey." Cue them both glancing at the turkey crown in the middle of the table, uneaten and looking even more unappetizing. The once-golden skin on top had started to shrivel.

"We could be there before two," Maggie continued as she glanced at her watch. If they'd left five minutes ago.

A minute passed while Ben simply stared. This stare was yet another in his repertoire, the vacant I'm-acting-like-I'm-not-really-here one that Maggie still hadn't figured out how to handle. "Ben?"

"Okay." He nodded slowly, his shaggy hair sliding onto his face once more. "Fine. Let's do it."

"Great." Maggie jumped up from the table, glad to be in motion. She grabbed the turkey in its foil tray and dumped it, soggy veggies and all, straight into the trash. "We can get something on the way, your pick."

"Really?" A faint lilt of interest in her son's voice had her smiling.

"Absolutely." Then she grabbed her coat, her shoes, her keys, while Ben stood by the front door, looking like he was debating whether he should actually get into this idea.

"What are we even going to *do* there?" he asked.

"Look around the town?"

"Everything will be closed—"

"Check out the house," Maggie suggested instead. "Choose paint colors. Walk up to the waterfall." She was starting to sound desperate, but she really wanted to go now. "I don't know, Ben. We'll find something, I'm sure."

And anything would be better than staying here, in a house that felt like a mausoleum, a testament to what had once been with no hope for the future. "Let's go."

* * *

It was, Maggie realized, a nice day. She hadn't noticed the weather this morning—she'd tended *not* to notice a lot of things about life lately—but today was one of those late autumn days where everything was cold and crisp and clear. As they drove north toward New Haven, the highway sparkled under a wintry sun. When they turned off I-95 for Route 8, the scenery became more pleasant—trees and fields rather than the occasional eighteen-wheeler and endless billboards.

The very last of the leaves were clinging to the maples and birches that lined the road, ragged scraps of scarlet and ochre fluttering in the autumn breeze. The grass was tipped with frost, making the meadows rolling by glitter with silver. Maggie took a deep breath, letting her lungs expand along with her fledgling hope. She could *breathe* out here, under the autumn sky, with the world seeming so wide open, not like back in Greenwich, in a house that felt like a tomb, with all the memories pressing in on her all the time, which was part of the reason they were moving.

The other far bigger part was because of Ben.

Maggie slid her son a sideways glance, as ever trying to discern his mood. She took mental readings of his emotional state as circumspectly as she could because Ben hated it when she asked about his feelings. He called it creepy; she saw it as essential. Her son had been through too much, and had too many dispiriting and frankly frightening lows, for her not to do a daily, and sometimes hourly, check-in.

Now she kept her voice light, almost playful, as she asked, "Are you glad we're doing this?"

Ben shrugged in reply as he turned to look out the window. All right, well, that wasn't a no. Maggie turned back to the road. Ten more miles to Starr's Fall. Was it silly, she wondered, far from the first time, to move to a place you'd only been to twice, three if they counted the day they'd looked at the house and bought it in the same afternoon? Was it *stupid*? Her sister certainly had thought it was.

"Maggie, you don't move to where you've vacationed," she'd stated, like it was a universal principle that everyone instinctively understood and followed.

"Tell that to everyone who retires to Florida," Maggie had shot back with a smile. Lynn was just about the only person who didn't pussyfoot around her since Matt's death, and she appreciated that. Mostly. "Anyway, I thought you'd be a fan," she'd continued. "We'll be closer to you in Boston."

"Yes, but... you don't actually *know* anyone in Starr's Fall," Lynn had replied. She'd always had a gift for pointing out the obvious.

"We'll get to know them," Maggie had insisted staunchly. Although since Matt's death they had not been exactly the most social of people, but they would *become* such people... in Starr's Fall. They'd have neighbors over for cozy suppers, and walk the dog they didn't yet own down quaint, tree-lined streets, and invite friends over for a movie night, everyone curled up on the sofa with a giant bowl of popcorn, and generally live life like it was a rose-tinted montage on a soppy romcom. It was going to happen. She had to believe that, because otherwise what she'd done really was not just silly, or stupid, but certifiably insane.

And she was doing it anyway.

"Mom," Ben said suddenly, "you're going to miss the turn."

Maggie came out of her reverie to find she was about to pass the right turn to their future. She hit the brakes with a squeal, causing Ben to inhale sharply as he clutched the door handle, his face paling.

"Sorry, sorry," Maggie said in a rush, and she slowed down to turn onto the road at a more sedate speed.

Tall, straight evergreens stood like sentinels on both sides of the road, the Litchfield Hills rising up in dark green humps above as they drove the last few miles into town. They'd been to Starr's Fall for two vacations—once, when Ben had been nine, that Maggie recalled with dreamy, rose-tinted fondness, when they'd taken long walks through the woods and gone to the nearby lake to canoe and swim. She remembered Ben lying starfished on the sand, giving her a gap-toothed grin. "Can we stay here forever?" he'd asked, and she'd laughed and ruffled his lake-damp hair and told him she wished they could, but three more days would have to do.

The second time had been when they'd gone back to Starr's Fall two years ago, a vacation that she recalled with less rose-tinted fondness and more quiet regret. Ben had been on the cusp of teenaged angst and glumness; seventh grade had not been a great year. Matt had received his promotion a year before and had grumbled about being in Connecticut when they could have afforded the Maldives.

It was only after he'd left, four days in, to respond to a work crisis, that she and Ben had started to relax. They'd gone back to the lake and canoed all around, and once again, when they'd been sitting on the sand, watching the sun set over the placid water, Ben had asked her the same question, but this time sitting with his head lowered and his elbows resting on his knees, in a voice that had been touched with despair.

*"Mom, can we stay here forever?"*

Finally she was able to say yes.

Their third visit to Starr's Fall had been two months ago, when they'd bought a house there in a matter of hours. It had been a snap decision that, Maggie hoped and prayed, had been the right one.

"Does it look the same?" she asked lightly and got yet another one of her son's stares—the well-duh one which meant she'd asked a particularly stupid question that was usually undeserving of a reply.

"It was summer then," he said, as if that explained everything, which maybe it did. Starr's Fall at the tail end of autumn was, despite the bright blue sky and sunshine, not the same as in the high heat of summer. Now, the streets were empty, the stores shuttered, the planters that had been bursting with flowers holding only a few dead-looking chrysanthemums. The trees lining the street were devoid of leaves, their branches dark and skeletal against the bright sky.

Still, Maggie told herself, it was beautiful—it was cold enough that the lampposts were glittering with frost, and she passed a sign for Max's Place, a pet store and bakery, that looked cute before she pulled into the empty space in front of their home and hopefully, one day, café.

"Here we are," she sang out just a little too cheerfully. Ben scowled. Maggie knew what happened when she went too hard on the Pollyanna act; her son shut down. She took a steadying breath and then got out of the car.

A couple were coming out of the pet store a few doors down, balancing several pies as well as a small dog while the woman locked up. Maggie thought about saying hello, decided she wasn't that brave—*yet*—and headed for their own forlorn-looking storefront, just as Ben finally slouched out of the car.

"Hello," the woman sang out, and Maggie turned, startled. She still wasn't used to people talking to her without knowing her history. She wasn't used to people talking to her, period. Since Matt's death, she'd gone into hermit mode, and the twin awkwardnesses—because that was how people viewed grief, she'd come to realize, as *awkward* —of Matt's death and Ben's difficulties had kept any well-meaning acquaintances away. She hadn't minded that much, because she hadn't been craving chitchat, and she'd never been particularly adept at it, anyway.

But now this woman—she couldn't be more than twenty-five—was beaming at her, while the dark-haired man behind her tried to keep hold of a small, and very cute, wiry-haired dog.

"Are you new here?" the woman asked. "Are you moving in?"

Maggie glanced at the man, who smiled and waved. "Yes," she said when she realized belatedly that it was her turn to talk. "We're moving in." She nodded toward the shuttered storefront. "We're... we're hoping to start a boardgame café here, actually." There. She'd said it out loud, so now it had to happen, right?

"A boardgame café!" The woman sounded delighted, far more than Maggie might have expected. "That's amazing."

Maggie managed a smile. "Well, I hope so," she said, mainly because she really did. She'd never started or managed a café, or even worked in one. She'd never so much as operated a cash register. She could play Scrabble and Monopoly when pressed, but not much else. Yet here she was, doing this crazy thing, this so very stupid thing, because it just might be the way for Ben to find his way back to himself. She hoped. Oh, Lord, how she hoped.

"I'm Laurie Ellis, and this is Joshua Reilly," the woman continued, introducing them both. "I run the pet store Max's Place, and he has the bookstore across the street."

"Oh." Maggie couldn't help but be a little startled by so much overt friendliness. "It's very nice to meet you. I'm Maggie Parker, and this is my son Ben." She put a hand on Ben's shoulder, a gentle reminder for him to actually speak, like pulling a string on a talking doll.

"Heynicetomeetyou," Ben said, his greeting one long mumbled word that Maggie was pretty sure neither of her new neighbors caught.

"Nice to meet you, too." Laurie Ellis looked between Maggie and Ben, her hazel gaze seeming to take in too much. Could she see how battered they'd been by life, how bruised they both still felt? Maggie had wanted to start her new life in Starr's Fall as someone happy, healthy, and whole. At least, she wanted to give that impression, but she had an uncomfortable feeling she'd failed at the first test. "I'm so glad you're here," Laurie continued, sounding like she meant it. "Welcome to Starr's Fall."

"Yes, um, thank you." Now was probably the time to admit they weren't actually moving here until January, but Maggie couldn't figure out a way to say it that made sense, and in any case, it was too late, because with a friendly wave, Laurie Ellis and Joshua Reilly had moved down the street, to their own car.

"Mom, it's freezing out here," Ben said. "Can we go inside?" He jammed his hands into the pockets of his jeans, looking like he'd rather be anywhere else.

"Yes, sure." Maggie fumbled with the key and then unlocked the door, stepping into their new home. They'd settled on this place because it was right in the middle of Main Street, with some lovely old-fashioned details —a corniced ceiling, wide floorboards of golden oak, a deep bow window that was perfect for displaying boardgames. Plus, it was large enough for the sofas and tables they'd need for the café, and it already had a small kitchen in the back, for when they were ready to provide their own food. "Just the basics," Ben had told her. "French fries and nachos and stuff like that."

Looking around now, though, all Maggie felt was overwhelmed. Last May, she would have promised Ben anything—and she basically had. Starting over in Starr's Fall, selling their house, and buying this place, agreeing that he could finish the school year online... she'd said yes to it all. Now she had to turn her rash promises into reality.

"Shall we look upstairs?" she suggested. Ben's response was a shrug.

Maggie headed up the staircase in a separate hallway that rang alongside the store to the apartment above. The whole place was about the size of the kitchen in their old house, but the few rooms possessed a certain cozy, quaint charm. The second floor was just one big room, with windows at the front and the back and a kitchenette tucked into the back right corner, a fireplace at the front. Up another flight of stairs were two bedrooms, both small, and a bathroom, even smaller. Considering they were moving from a house that had twice as many bathrooms as bedrooms, all of them enormous, it was certainly a step down, but one they'd both agreed they wanted.

Now Maggie wasn't so sure. Truth be told, she *liked* her sunken marble tub with its profusion of jets. And, reality check, she and Ben were going to be able to hear *everything* in each other's bedrooms. Not something she'd relish, and she doubted he would, either.

Never mind. They went back down to the living space, and Maggie sat down in the window seat overlooking the empty street below. She could see herself curling up here with a book and maybe a cat. They didn't have a cat, not yet anyway, but that could be on the list, maybe instead of the previously fantasized dog. Ben was more partial to cats, anyway, as she recalled. "What do you think?" she asked Ben, who was standing at the bottom of the stairs, looking a little lost. "Family room sofa or living room sofa in this room?"

Ben glanced around. "Family room, definitely."

Maggie gave a decisive nod. "I think so, too." Their family room sofa was made of deep, squashy leather, while the living room furniture was modern, incredibly expensive, and even more uncomfortable. The interior decorator her mother-in-law had insisted she hire had told her it was how everyone who was anyone was styling their living rooms, and Maggie had been too meek to refuse. But now they could sell it all or leave it on the curb for the trash, because since Matt's funeral her mother-in-law had more or less stopped speaking to her, and after sixteen years of a decidedly tense relationship, that was a somewhat welcome change. So really, no sofa and no mother-in-law could be considered a double win, although she hoped Matt's mother stayed in touch for Ben's sake. She knew it wasn't a guarantee.

A sigh escaped her before she sucked it back in, not wanting Ben to see her falter for a moment. She could worry about her mother-in-law and their lack of relationship later. "We could move here early," she ventured. They'd promised Lynn they'd go to Boston for Christmas, but nothing was keeping them in Greenwich except a sense of duty, or maybe propriety. Maggie hadn't wanted it to look like she was running away, even if on some level she knew that was exactly what she was doing.

Ben looked tempted for a moment, but then he shook his head. "Nah, let's keep it to January," he said. "I've got the RQ Con, anyway."

Maggie gave a mechanical nod. "Of course." How could she have forgotten the weekend online conference, where Ben played the fantasy roleplaying game RainQuest for thirty-six hours straight? He'd done it for the first time last year, just a few months after Matt had died. Matt, Maggie knew, had been more than a bit dismissive about playing a game so obsessively, which Maggie sort of understood. But Ben didn't consider Rain-Quest merely a game; it was something of a lifestyle choice, and it had become even more of one since his dad had died.

Maggie looked around their new home, the sunlight streaming through the window as the sky went white on its edges, the sun starting its inevitable descent to the dark horizon. "January it is, then," she said, and her voice echoed through the empty room.

## 2

___

### SIX WEEKS LATER

"I thought global warming meant it didn't snow anymore."

"*Mom*," Ben replied in the tone of someone who has felt he's had to say it a million times, "it's climate change, not global warming, and it means the weather is *variable*."

"Right." Maggie had meant it as a joke but clearly it had sounded like a grumble, which, truth be told, it probably was. Driving her ten-year-old station wagon through six inches of slushy snow wasn't high on her bucket list, but here she was. They were finally moving to Starr's Fall.

The last six weeks had been a blur of getting things organized for the sale of the house, the move to Starr's Fall, and the start of their business... as well as freaking out internally while trying to remain manically upbeat for the sake of her son. She didn't think she'd fooled Ben, and certainly not her sister Lynn.

"You don't have to move, you know," Lynn had told her over Christmas when Ben had been in the basement gaming and Lynn had broken out the bottle of Baileys Irish Cream. "You can unwind all of this, if you want to. It's still possible."

Maggie had taken a slug of Baileys, trying not to be insulted by her sister's canny intuition. Now that their move was getting close, she had been experiencing a tiny frisson of cold feet. "What makes you think I don't want to move?" she'd asked, a bit truculently.

"I just mean... it seemed kind of sudden," Lynn replied, which was more diplomacy than she'd exhibited in some time.

Maggie had stared into the depths of her drink; one gulp of Baileys had sent her head spinning. "You know I have to do this for Ben," she'd said quietly.

Lynn had been silent for a long time. She'd been on the receiving end of Maggie's angst and worry for long enough to take her time with her reply. "Yes, but you know," she'd finally said, gentling her voice, "this isn't necessarily going to be a magic bullet for Ben, or for you."

Maggie had taken another slug of Baileys. "I know," she'd replied, but the fact remained that she *wanted* it to be a magic bullet, a fix-all for all that was wrong with her—and Ben's—lives. She needed it to be that, because life had been too hard for too long, and she wasn't sure she could keep slogging through, day by grueling day.

"So, you're still going to do it?" Lynn had asked, sounding a mix of incredulous and resigned.

Maggie had felt as if she were teetering on the edge of an abyss, about to freefall, windmilling her arms as she hurtled through empty space—to land where? "Yes," she'd stated firmly as she'd drained her glass. "We are."

And so here they were, driving to Starr's Fall, the moving truck approximately half an hour behind them. In the end, they'd taken only a handful of the furniture from the house in Greenwich—so much of it had been custom-made pieces, too big and brash for the humble apartment. Maggie had tried to rouse Ben's enthusiasm by promising to buy some new things, but, surprise, surprise, her son hadn't been all that interested in home decorating.

Still, Maggie herself felt a flicker of interest at the prospect. When they'd moved into that behemoth of a house back in Greenwich three years ago, she'd been given free rein, but it had all felt so overwhelming and enormous, and then Matt's mother-in-law had swept in, insisting that Maggie could never manage such a "serious responsibility" as decorating her own home, and so she'd gone with the interior decorator her mother-in-law had recommended, and she'd agreed with every single suggestion the bossy, stick-thin woman with talon-like nails had given.

Thankfully, those days were behind her.

That thought sent a flash of guilt like a blaze of lightning through her. How could she ever, *ever* be glad that her life had changed? Basically, be glad that Matt was *dead*, because one pretty much equaled the other. She was a horrible person for letting such a thought flit across her mind for so much as a second, no matter how challenging things had become in their marriage, and she vowed never to think that way again. Ever.

"Mom," Ben exclaimed in exasperation, "you almost missed the turn *again*."

"Sorry, sorry." Just like the last time, at Thanksgiving, Maggie was forced to put on the brakes before making a hard right. She let out a shaky breath and glanced at Ben with a smile. "I was distracted by thinking about everything we need to do."

"We don't need to do that much, do we?" Ben replied. "Just buy some games and tables and stuff. It'll be easy."

As if. Her son had no idea of the reams and reams of red tape that went into opening a business, especially one that offered food. The number of licenses, inspections, criterion, and guidelines she had to meet... She had a three-ring binder full of printouts of such stuff. She hadn't looked at any of it very closely yet, but she would. Soon.

"There's a little more to it than that," she replied lightly, "but we'll get there." Eventually. Maybe. No, they would. They *would*.

Starr's Fall was coming into view, and this time the Main Street looked like a snowy wonderland, the sidewalks heaped with the stuff, icicles dripping down from the eaves—apparently the snowplow hadn't been through the town yet, even though it was nearly noon and the snow had fallen last night. Well, it was off the beaten track, Maggie told herself. And the snow *was* pretty, even if it was already starting to melt.

"Okay." She pulled over in front of the store, the tires squelching through the slush, and parked the car. "Here we are." She let out a deep breath and turned to smile at Ben, and amazingly, wonderfully, he gave a small, shy smile back. It was enough to have her exclaiming, "Let's do this!" as she slapped the steering wheel for emphasis and Ben let out a groan and rolled his eyes. Way to ruin a moment, she thought wryly. Well, she'd been there before.

Maggie got out of the car, the air cold and crisp as she stretched her arms briefly above her head and surveyed their new abode. It was a lot smaller than the imposing McMansion they'd left behind, but it was quaint and cozy and she thought she'd like living on the Main Street, everything they needed just a stroll away.

She took the key out of her pocket and unlocked the front door, step-ping inside to the store. It looked just as it had six weeks ago, on Thanks-giving, only dustier and colder. She needed to figure out how to turn the heating on, and quick.

"The moving truck should be here soon," she called to Ben. He was standing in the doorway, his backpack slung over one shoulder. "Do you want to close the door?"

"Yeah..." He hesitated, sliding his backpack from his shoulder. "By the way, I made this."

"You made something?" Maggie turned around, smiling in surprised expectation. Her son was not a crafty person, so she was curious as well as heartened that he'd had the urge to make anything at all. He unzipped his backpack and took out a long, silvery sheet of paper. As he unfolded it, she saw it was a banner, complete with glittery writing.

Grand Opening Coming Soon! Your Turn Next Boardgame Café!

He'd even designed a little logo underneath, with a pawn, a die, and an elven figure that Maggie knew was from his beloved RainQuest.

"What do you think?" he asked, a wobble of uncertainty in his voice.

Maggie's heart melted, expanded, and twisted all at once. "I love it," she said firmly. "Let's put it up right now."

Ben's eyes widened. "Really?"

"Yes! Why not?" Of course, she could answer that very easily—because she had no idea when they'd actually get this place up and running, and the thought of all the work that lay ahead of her was truly daunting. She didn't want to make promises to the public that she couldn't keep, but neither was she about to rain on her son's parade. She didn't even want to *drizzle.* "Let's do it," she said again, with the same slightly manic excitement that had had him rolling his eyes before.

"Okay, Mom, chill. Anyway, we don't have any tape."

"I think there's some in the car." She'd packed a box of emergency supplies for when the movers came—scissors, tape, coffee mugs, kettle. "Hold on one sec," she said, and headed back outside.

A few minutes later, she was back with the promised tape, and she and Ben unrolled the banner to position it diagonally across the window.

"Maybe it's too much," he said, the self-doubt that had so often dogged him creeping back once more.

"It's not," Maggie insisted. "We want people to know what we're doing. Why not make a little bit of a splash?"

"I guess." But his brief moment of buoyancy had clearly gone flat, and Maggie knew that trying to jolly her son back into any sort of enthusiasm would backfire bigtime. She focused instead on simply getting the banner up, and by the time they'd done that, the moving truck was pulling up in front of the store. Their life here really was beginning.

\* \* \*

The next few hours were a blur of boxes, as Maggie told the movers where she wanted the furniture, made them endless cups of coffee, and discovered that the big armoire she'd brought from her bedroom did not fit up the second set of stairs.

"Just put it in the living room," she said, determined to be pragmatic. "We can keep books in it, I guess."

A headache was thrumming at her temples and her shoulders had been creeping up toward her ears all afternoon. She didn't *want* to be stressed, but she was. Every box or piece of furniture that the movers brought in made her realize yet again that this was really happening. She had moved, at the age of forty-one, to a place where she knew absolutely no one, to run a business she had absolutely no experience of. Her sister was right. This was insane.

Her mother had thought she was crazy as well. Widowed herself three years ago, she'd made herself indispensable to her community in Pennsylvania—baking for charity, delivering Meals on Wheels, volunteering at the local preschool. Just hearing about her mother's schedule exhausted her.

"You should stay in Greenwich, Maggie," she'd said when Maggie had first floated the idea of moving to Starr's Fall. "Where you know people. Get involved in things. Keeping busy helps, trust me."

Maggie had definitely *not* kept busy. She couldn't count the number of days she'd lain in bed till noon or binge-watched *Is It Cake?* until her eyeballs ached. She could tell a real cake from fifty paces, however, or so she liked to believe. As for the people she knew? A lot of them hadn't wanted to know her, after Matt's death, and her friends from college or high school had slumped into yearly Christmas cards and the occasional well-meant text.

Maggie knew that all of that was at least partly her fault. When Matt had got his mega promotion, she hadn't really gelled with the new group of hedge fund managers and their blonde, Botoxed wives that had become their social circle. To be fair, she hadn't really tried, and she should have. Blonde hair and Botox did not disqualify someone from being a kindred spirit. It just meant they were starting from a different place.

But because of Ben, she'd chosen to leave it—and them—all behind. Sometimes a fresh start was what you needed.

"No regrets," Maggie muttered under her breath, and Ben gave her a sharp look.

"What did you say?"

She tried for a sunny smile. "Just talking to myself. I think the movers are almost done. How about pizza for dinner?"

He gave a little shrug. "Okay."

"Great." Maggie went in search of her wallet to tip the movers and get her credit card out. She really hoped Starr's Fall had Door Dash or Uber Eats. Surely they weren't *that* far off the beaten track.

They were. After the movers had left, happy with their generous tip, she tried four different delivery services, only to be informed that they did not deliver to her zip code. Never mind. There had to be a pizza place in Starr's Fall, right?

"Did we get pizza when we had that vacation here?" she asked Ben, and he looked at her blankly.

"I don't know. I don't remember."

Of course he didn't remember. It had been two and a half years ago. In fact, Maggie reflected, both her and Ben's memories of those two vacations were probably very hazy indeed... and yet they'd based their whole life plan on returning to a place they barely remembered and had only been to for two weeks in total.

Why, again?

*No regrets.*

"Slice of Heaven is five minutes outside of town," Ben ventured, scrolling on his phone. "No delivery, but they take phone orders."

"Great." Maggie made the call, ordering their usual—a large cheese pizza with black olives and pineapple—and then turned to her son. "You want to come with me to pick it up?"

Ben's gaze slid sideways as he shook his head. "No, I'm good. I think I'll unpack some stuff in my room."

"Okay." Her heart gave a painful little twist at the thought of leaving him alone, which was kind of ridiculous, because he was fourteen years old, fifteen in April. But still... "I'll just be a few minutes."

"Yeah, okay."

"And you can always call me if you need to. Or text—"

"*Mom.*" Ben gave her a look that was half hurt, half exasperation. "I'll be fine."

"Okay." She nodded mechanically. After everything he'd been through, it was hard not to be overprotective. She was in a constant battle with herself not to swoop in and hover over him, protecting him from so much as a paper cut. Like Ben had said earlier, she needed to chill. "Okay," she said again, and headed outside.

Starr's Fall at five-thirty on a January evening was, Maggie discovered, both dark and freezing. The wrought-iron streetlamps lining the street were like something out of Narnia but only half of them were working, and the air was cold enough to freeze the inside of her nose, which was not a pleasant feeling.

She climbed into her station wagon, praying it would start in this cold, half-wishing she'd taken up Matt's offer of a Porsche SUV when he'd got his promotion. She'd refused, both out of pique and a deep-seated desire not to be *that* kind of person. When she'd tried to explain it to Matt, he'd been exasperated as well as a little hurt.

"What kind of person?" he'd demanded. "The kind of person who drives a Porsche?"

"Yes," she'd cried. "Exactly."

"But *I* drive a Porsche," he'd reminded her, to which Maggie had not been able to think of a suitable reply. Matt had been so proud of his sports convertible, bought with one of his bonuses. She hadn't had the heart to say she didn't like that car, either.

Okay, she really needed to stop thinking this way. "Only good memories," she muttered under her breath, a necessary reminder, and started the car.

Slice of Heaven was in a small, sad-looking strip mall on the far side of town that had exactly three storefronts, two of which were empty and clearly had been for a while. It was a depressing and salient reminder that Starr's Fall had hit on some hard times since they'd come here five years ago.

Back then, Maggie recalled seeing a few more cute boutiques and shops, as well as a Michelin-starred restaurant somewhere on the outskirts where she and Matt had eaten dinner. During her and Ben's brief visits over the last few months, she'd noticed quite a few empty stores, the for-rent or for-sale signs looking like they'd been out for a while. There had certainly been plenty to choose from when they'd made their purchase. And *this* was the place they'd decided to set up a new business? Her sister didn't even know the half of her insanity.

Still, she told herself as she headed into the pizza place, there were a few thriving businesses around. Laurie Ellis, who had so kindly introduced herself at Thanksgiving, clearly was managing to keep her pet store Max's Place going. And her boyfriend, Joshua, had the bookstore across the street, which looked inviting. Plus, on the way into town, they'd driven by a bakery, an ice cream parlor, and a diner. And now, as she headed toward the pizza place, she saw a "Now Open" sign plastered in the window, so she and Ben weren't the only ones starting a business here.

There was one customer waiting for his pizza in Slice of Heaven, his back to Maggie as he leaned against the counter. She'd just taken her place behind him in line when he turned around and she sucked in a startled breath, which caused her to choke, which was hugely embarrassing, because the only reason she'd been surprised at all was that the man in front of her was so ridiculously good-looking.

"Are you okay?" he asked in concern as he lifted a hand to pat her back, but then held back, no doubt wondering about the propriety of such an action.

"I'm fine," Maggie assured him, refusing to cough even though her eyes were watering with the desperate need to. "Fine. Just... swallowed the wrong way." The effort of speaking had her erupting into coughs she couldn't contain, so for a few seconds she choked and spluttered, feeling ridiculous. The man decided to pat her back, gently, his palm warm even through her coat. "Sorry," she wheezed, and then dragged another breath into her lungs, willing herself to stop hacking.

"It's okay. It happens." He smiled, flashing a full set of straight, white teeth, and Maggie stared at him, mesmerized. He was like a combination of all the gorgeous movie actors she'd swooned over through the years—dirty blond hair that was artfully disheveled, swept back from blue-green eyes that were so vivid they simply *had* to be contact lenses, except Maggie was pretty sure they weren't. A chiseled jaw glinting with golden stubble, and as for the rest of him... well, she could see the definition of his six-pack through his *sweater*. "Sorry," she murmured again, and took a step back for good measure, because besides looking good, he smelled nice too, like a pine forest. And, she told herself sternly, she was a widow and he looked to be about twenty years old, so *ew*.

"Zach?" A man emerged from the kitchen, holding a pizza box. "Extra spicy chorizo and pepperoni pizza?"

"That's me."

"Wow," Maggie said, and then could have cursed herself for being the nosiest, most awkward person imaginable.

The man—Zach—turned around, one golden eyebrow arched. "You have a problem with my pizza?" he asked, and to her mortification, his tone was flirtatious. Oh, heaven help her, to be the object of such pity, that a stunningly good-looking guy like him would flirt with her, the way you might toss a bone to an old, sad dog.

"Well, I certainly couldn't eat it," she replied, and to her further mortification, *she* sounded flirtatious. What on earth was wrong with her? She was a widow, for heaven's sake. She was a middle-aged, libido-less, desiccated *widow*. Flirting with a *kid* who looked young enough to almost be her son.

"No?" His mouth—and a very nice mouth it was—quirked into a smile. "Why not?"

"All that pepperoni? It would give me gas." Which was, Maggie realized as her cheeks turned scarlet, the verbal equivalent of farting in public. Which was basically what she'd just said she would be doing. So much for flirting; she was now being awkward and weird. Thank God Ben hadn't come with her. Although if he had, maybe she would not have acted like this. Clearly she could not be trusted in public on her own. After a year of watching and rewatching episodes of *Is It Cake?* by herself, she had no idea how to relate to other people in a vaguely normal way.

Zach, however, laughed, sounding genuinely amused. "That doesn't mean it isn't worth eating," he pointed out. "You just have to take the consequences."

Maggie only shook her head. Her whole face was hot, and she wanted nothing more than to escape to her car so she could privately melt into a puddle of pure mortification.

The guy behind the counter was looking bemused by their whole exchange. Hanging her head, Maggie stepped forward to receive her own order. "Large black olive and pineapple pizza," she whispered.

"Black olive and *pineapple*?" Zach exclaimed from behind her. "Okay, now I think we need to have a serious discussion about pizza topping choices."

"It's a weird one," she managed to admit in a voice that she hoped sounded somewhat normal. "My son picked it so nobody else would ever ask to share his pizza."

If she thought he might be fazed by the fact she had a son—although why would he? She had no idea, since obviously there was absolutely nothing going on here at *all*—he wasn't. "Sounds like a smart kid," he remarked.

"He is," she agreed firmly. She took the pizza box with a murmured thanks and then, without meeting Zach's eye, started to sidle from the store.

"Are you new here?" he called just as she'd reached the door.

Maggie hesitated. Part of her wanted to pretend she hadn't heard his question and sprint for her car. The more rational part realized you couldn't do that sort of thing when you lived in a small town, which she now did.

"Yes," she admitted reluctantly. "Just moved onto Main Street."

"Oh, right." Zach leaned against the counter, his pizza box balanced on one well-muscled arm, like he had all the time in the world. "Well," he said with a grin that made his eyes sparkle, "welcome to the neighborhood."

**3**

Zach watched the woman hurry to her car with a wry smile. She'd clearly been embarrassed by their little exchange, which both amused him and gave him a strange sense of something almost like affection for her. And she was new to Starr's Fall? Why had she moved?

"Isn't she a little old for you, bro?"

Zach turned around to face Jake, who had opened Slice of Heaven a couple of weeks ago, Starr's Fall's first pizzeria, and who was now smirking at him. They'd gone to high school together, nearly fifteen years ago now, and Jake, like everyone else in Starr's Fall, liked to rib him about being a player. "I was just being friendly," he replied, keeping his voice mild. He'd found the best way to deal with these kinds of comments was mostly to ignore them.

"Friendly. Sure." Jake rolled his eyes and Zach smiled, just a little tightly.

"Thanks for the pizza."

Jake leaned over the counter. "I know her name, if you're interested," he drawled.

"Doesn't that violate some kind of privacy law?" Zach returned lightly.

Jake shrugged. "Just sayin'. You know, if you get tired of Tinder."

"Okay, well, I'll keep that in mind." He wasn't even *on* Tinder. Not anymore, anyway. Jake gave him a mocking salute as Zach headed outside into the freezing night. The lore that had risen up around his dating exploits was really its own kind of town mythology, he reflected as he climbed into his truck. He couldn't so much as *talk* to a woman in all of northwestern Connecticut without everyone in Starr's Fall thinking he was about to date her.

Which, Zach acknowledged, was at least a little true, but he didn't need everyone reminding him of his many failed romances. He thought about them enough as it was.

With a sigh, he started his truck and headed back home. Once again, he wondered who the mystery woman was, and why she'd come to Starr's Fall. She'd mentioned a son, but was there a husband or boyfriend in the picture? Probably, he decided, and then he pushed the thought of the woman, whoever she was, out of his mind as he pulled into the gravel parking lot of Miller's Mercantile that he ran with his sister Jenna.

The store, with its old-fashioned front porch and vintage signs offering pickles for a nickel and jukebox songs for a dime, was darkened as Zach got out of the truck and walked around to the back, where he and Jenna lived in the house they'd grown up in. As he came into the cluttered kitchen, he saw Jenna was seated at the table, hunched in front of her laptop, squinting at a screen of invoices, a mug of soup forgotten at her elbow.

"I got pizza," Zach remarked as he tossed the box onto the counter, where several days' worth of mail was gathering dust. "Thought I'd support Jake's new venture."

"Extra spicy as usual?" Jenna asked. "No, thanks."

"Suit yourself." He flipped open the box and took a slice as Jenna clicked sporadically on the computer mousepad.

"What are you looking at?" he asked after he'd chewed and swallowed a bite of pizza.

"Some invoices." Jenna's tone was vague, a bit of repressive, as it so often was when Zach asked her about the store. He had to keep from gritting his teeth. To say his sister was sparing with any information about the managing of the store was to put it mildly.

They were *supposed* to be business partners, running it together since their parents had retired four years ago, splitting both the work and responsibility fifty-fifty, but at seven years older, Jenna had decided way back at the beginning that she was the boss and that, it seemed, was that. Zach could do the heavy lifting and the grunt work, but Jenna was the one who was in charge.

He could acknowledge that he had often let her shoulder the brunt of the decision making because it was simply too hard to fight against the stubbornly relentless tide of his sister's, and even the entire town's, prejudices. In addition to being some kind of womanizer, the residents of Starr's Fall, his sister included, seemed to think he was kind of lazy. Zach had learned long ago that when it came to small-town life, there wasn't much point in trying to change people's misconceptions. No matter what you did, they were going to have them anyway.

"What invoices?" he asked, making sure he sounded patient and not annoyed. He loved Jenna, and he knew she loved him. From the outside, everyone assumed they were super close, especially since their parents had moved to Florida and they'd taken on the store together.

And they *were* close... sort of. It was just that Jenna liked to be in charge. A lot.

"Just for some new stock," she answered in that same vague way.

"*Jenna.*" This time Zach couldn't sound patient. "What new stock? I thought we were meant to go over all stock decisions together." This was not the first time they'd had this kind of conversation. The last four years had been a stop and start of Jenna making decisions by herself, then Zach arguing with her about them, her agreeing not do it again, and then—guess what—doing it again. As time had gone on, Zach had started to push back less rather than more, but right now, for some reason he couldn't quite discern, he felt like a fight.

Jenna heaved a sigh as she swiveled around to face him, her heavy auburn braid lying over one shoulder. "I know we were, but... really, Zach? You need to know about every can of beans I order for the store?"

He gritted his teeth. Again. "You know that's not what I mean." They'd had this conversation too many times before. Unlike Jenna, he had no desire to micromanage, but he did want to be involved in the *direction* of the store, as she very well knew. But it seemed he was going to have to remind her yet another time.

She arched an eyebrow, her friendly, freckled face that everyone said was so approachable looking decidedly not. "Then what *do* you mean?"

"As I believe I've said quite a few times before, I'd just like to be informed about what's going on," Zach told her evenly. "We're supposed to be running this store together, remember? Making decisions together, deciding what direction we're going in... *together*."

"And you're supposed to be doing 50 percent of the work," Jenna reminded him, her tone just as dangerously even as his. "Which you're not. So."

"I would do more if you'd let me," Zach replied. He flung his half-eaten slice back into the box, his stomach churning too much to eat anymore. "Which I've *also* said before, many times. We keep having this conversation, and nothing ever changes."

"Maybe that's because *you* don't change," Jenna fired back. "You're more interested in dating the female population of—"

"Oh, for the love of—" Zach blew out a breath as he raked a hand through his hair. "Please do not bring my dating life into this. It hardly interferes with my work." And he hadn't gone on a date in over a month, since Kayla from Bridgewater had told him she was only interested in having fun. "But you always make these decisions and tell me after," he continued flatly. "And I *do* do 50 percent of the work, although not the managerial part, because that's apparently what only you can do. But then I don't see you doing the stuff I get left with—stocking shelves or unloading trucks or doing anything a sixteen-year-old on minimum wage could do, easily."

This time both her eyebrows rose as his sister sat back in her chair, her arms folded, the look on her face making Zach think she was merely humoring him by having this conversation. "So, what, you want to start taking an interest? Doing the hard graft?" She sounded so skeptical that Zach had to bite back a sharp retort.

He loved his sister. He really did. When they'd been little, he remembered running to Jenna when he'd fallen and scraped his knees; as a toddler, he'd climbed into her bed after having a nightmare. She was the one who had had the guts to tell him he was a jerk when he had been one in high school. In some ways, she'd been more of a parent to him than his own mom and dad, who admittedly had often seemed like their children came beneath both the store and their marriage in terms of priorities.

He and Jenna had history, a lot of history, but there were things she didn't know about and others she didn't understand. And sometimes, a *lot* of the time, she could be an annoying know-it-all, especially when it came to him. Jenna, like everyone else in this town, had frozen him in time as a seventeen-year-old baseball star who had, he could admit, liked to party and been more than a little full of himself. But he was thirty-one years old now, and those days were long, long behind him.

"I'm not opposed to some hard graft," he replied, doing his best to keep his voice measured. They'd had these discussions before, plenty of times, if not quite as plainly, and he wanted to get the words right. "In fact, I think I'm the one doing a lot of it. But in terms of the decision making... when Mom and Dad left the store to both of us," he stated slowly, "we agreed we'd both be involved."

Jenna sighed, the sound a decidedly reluctant acknowledgment. "I know, I mean, I get it, but Zach... come on." She rolled her eyes, inviting him into a joke he already knew he wasn't going to find funny. "Let's be real. You've always seemed more interested in your love life than making this store work." Those were not mutually exclusive, but Zach held his tongue. Jenna gave a little what-can-you-do shrug. "I always thought you were happy doing the manual labor kind of stuff. You didn't seem to complain, anyway."

"Maybe that's because I'm a good person," he retorted, and she gave another sigh.

"Do you really want to be involved in *all* these decisions?" She gestured to the laptop. "This isn't exactly earth-shattering stuff. I'm thinking about how many kinds of soup we should stock—chicken noodle, tomato, and beef barley. The beef barley is the one I'm not sure on." Her eyebrows inched higher. "Care to offer your opinion?"

She didn't *mean* to sound condescending, Zach knew, but the truth was, she did. Ever since they'd started on the store together, Jenna had been passive-aggressively possessive of it, grudgingly giving him any information about the managerial decisions—a fact that was especially annoying because Jenna had moved to San Francisco and then New York to make her way in the big wide world, while Zach had stayed in Starr's Fall and done all that *hard graft*. That seemed to count for nothing now, though, because Jenna was older, wiser, and as she occasionally liked to remind him, had a degree in marketing while he'd dropped out of college in the middle of freshman year, something that she knew hadn't been his own fault, but still, he'd never gone back.

"As a matter of fact, I think it's the chicken noodle you should be questioning," he told her. "Nobody eats that anymore. Canned chicken?" He shook his head. "That's so 1970s, and you can pretty much guarantee it isn't free range."

Jenna pursed her lips, looking decidedly skeptical. "Oh, really? Because chicken noodle has been consistently selling since we started stocking it."

"And how many cans do you stock?" Zach countered. "And for what return on the profit?" Jenna pressed her lips together and he decided to push a little. "By all means, keep selling grocery staples. That's important since there's no other grocery store in Starr's Fall. But if we're going to make a profit, or even break even, you know that we need some higher profit margins. Some luxury items, locally sourced, like candles or blankets—"

"We are not Litchfield," Jenna said, cutting him off, as she had whenever he'd tried to have this discussion before. "We will never be Litchfield. We are a simple store that serves a local community."

"Which is great," Zach agreed. "But we can also be a luxury destination for the discerning tourist." He'd been pushing having a section for tourists in the store, just a corner, with luxury, locally sourced items. Beeswax candles, paintings by local artists, high-end jams and chutneys. There was so much they could offer, if she'd just agree.

Jenna rolled her eyes, the only response it seemed she was going to give. She was determined not to change the store from what it had been in their parents' time—homegrown, lovable, its quaintness teetering on the edge of kitsch, all the while providing very basic staples for people who couldn't or didn't want to go to the Price Rite twenty minutes away in Torrington.

The trouble was, in this day and age, that wasn't cutting it. It certainly wasn't paying the bills. Zach might have dropped out of college, but even he could see when the numbers weren't adding up, and they hadn't been for over a year, ever since Instacart had extended its delivery service to the area.

"You know something has to change," he said quietly. Jenna, too, could crunch the numbers. Whatever sentimentality was making her hold on to the past—if that was even what it was—she would only be able to do it for so long.

"I'm not opposed to change," Jenna told him as she turned back to her laptop. "But it has to be the right kind of change. There's no point selling high-end items that cost the earth and only out-of-towners will buy."

"No point?" Zach repeated incredulously, even though he knew he'd already lost the argument. Jenna was back to tapping away at her laptop. "A few specially selected..." he began, and then stopped. She wasn't listening.

Zach grabbed the pizza box and headed upstairs to his bedroom. Living in the same room as he had during high school could feel like something of a depressing time warp, but he'd gotten used to it, and there was no point—as well as no money—to get his own place, at least not yet. Sometimes, when he was feeling a little down, Zach wondered what his future might hold. Here he was, thirty-one years old, without a degree, schlepping boxes for the failing family business. If he could have had a *vision* for the store, if Jenna would let him share some of the decision making, then maybe it would feel different. Purposeful. As it was, he felt like he was spinning in a hamster wheel with no real way to get off.

He *liked* Starr's Fall. He liked the store. He didn't want to move away in a huff; he had no more wild oats to sow, not that many people believed that. He just wished things were different.

With a sigh, Zach flipped open the pizza box and took out another slice. He thought, briefly, of the mystery woman who was now most likely eating black olive and pineapple pizza with her son, a prospect that made him both smile and wince at the utter grossness of that combo. Would he see her again? Probably, since Starr's Fall was a small place. The question was, he reflected, what would happen when he did.

* * *

Two days later, Zach was whistling as he walked down Main Street, a spring in his step because the sun was shining, there was snow on the hills, and the truth was, he just couldn't stay grumpy for long, even when his sister was being a pain. As it happened, he'd looked at the latest invoices and had seen that Jenna had halved the order of cans of chicken noodle soup. A small victory, it was true, but he was still counting it as a win. She'd listened to him, if just in this one very small matter.

He waved to Laurie Ellis, who was behind the counter at Max's Place— a cute store, even if Zach couldn't entirely understand the idea of a bakery for pets—and then glanced across at Reilly's Books. He and Joshua had been in the same grade at high school, but they hadn't been friends, mainly because Joshua had been kind of a nerd, and Zach had been kind of a jerk. He hoped Joshua was starting to change his mind now that their social circles were more of a Venn diagram than they ever had been before, thanks to Jenna and Laurie being friends. He suspected it would be a slow process, but things could always change.

Zach had been telling himself that ever since he'd come back to Starr's Fall in February of his freshman year. He was still hoping.

Three doors down from Max's Place, he skidded to a halt. A glittery banner had been put up in the window of a formerly empty storefront:

Grand Opening Coming Soon! Your Turn Next Boardgame Café!

Underneath was a little logo—a die, a pawn, and what definitely looked like Sylvana from RainQuest. Without even thinking about what he was doing, Zach went to the door, threw it open, and strode inside.

A woman was at the back of the empty store, unpacking boxes, her head bent, but she jerked up when the door crashed closed behind him.

"May I help..." Her voice trailed away as they stared at each other. It was Black-Olive-and-Pineapple-Pizza Woman, who had gotten so embarrassed by their funny little conversation. Zach found himself unabashedly grinning at the sight of her.

"You certainly can," he said.

**4**

What on earth was Mr. Extra Spicy doing in her café, especially when it wasn't even open yet, and Maggie was pretty positive he could not possibly be the gaming type? She stared at him gormlessly while he—Zach, because she hadn't forgotten his name—grinned. Once again, he'd sounded flirtatious when he'd spoken. Maybe it was a default setting, like when Buzz Lightyear switched to Spanish in *Toy Story 3*. Zach just couldn't help himself... But then again, maybe it was that way with all ridiculously good-looking guys. They flirted as naturally as they breathed. They probably didn't even realize they were doing it... or the effect they had on their all-too-willing victims.

"I can?" she answered, sounding dubious, when she'd remembered how to form words. "Help you, that is?"

"You're opening a boardgame café?" he demanded, and she nodded dumbly. "And that logo out there on the banner—is that Sylvana?"

*Syl-what*? "Umm..." Maggie stared at him blankly. "I..."

"Yes, it is." Ben's voice, coming from behind her, had her spinning around. Her son was standing in the doorway of the kitchen and stock-room, looking uncertain but also hopeful and even a little defiant. There was clearly a lot going on here, and she had no idea what any of it was. She turned back to Zach, who was giving a slow, approving kind of nod.

"You play RainQuest?" he asked Ben, and Ben nodded back. "What are your stats?"

Her son then reeled off what sounded to Maggie like a whole lot of gibberish—something about strength, endurance, shapeshifting, combat skills, potion making and a few others, followed by a bunch of numbers and a couple of caveats—"I bought an extra skill point from the guild" and "I chose healing over strength, I think it's a strat," none of which Maggie really understood.

"What are yours?" Ben asked Zach, and he reeled off a similar list of gibberish. They stared at each other for a moment in what looked like approving assessment, and then Ben asked, "What do you play as?"

"Halfling, usually, but sometimes an orc."

Her son snorted. "No way."

Zach rolled his eyes. "Tell me you are not an elf, or like, I don't know, a *selkie*."

"Djinn, usually," Ben replied with dignity.

Zach gave a slow, considering nod of acceptance. "Decent," he proclaimed, and Ben grinned.

To Maggie, they might as well have been speaking in a foreign language; they *were*, and yet it was one Ben was fluent in, and Zach apparently was, too. She simply could not get her head around that... but she couldn't remember the last time she'd seen her son so animated.

"What's your username?" Zach asked, and Ben wrinkled his nose, looking uncertain again.

"Alacenima."

Zach nodded, instantly understanding. "Elvish. Cool."

Ben's eyes widened with surprise. "Most people don't know that."

Zach's mouth quirked in a wry smile. "Then clearly they're not serious about gaming. Or Tolkien, I guess."

Her son laughed then, a sound that filled Maggie with joy, because she heard it so rarely. She still wasn't entirely sure what was going on, though. Was Mr. Extra Spicy actually a *gamer*? A serious one? That was her mind officially blown.

"Have you played the latest update?" Ben asked, and Zach frowned.

"You mean the Almedian waterfall extension? Yeah, I'll be honest with you, I was a little disappointed with the interactive map."

Ben's face lit up. "Me too!"

"I mean, you want more than a couple of clicks, right? And they clearly hadn't done enough with the woodland maze. Way too easy, and the treasure boxes were, like, seriously disappointing." Zach grinned, and Ben grinned back. Watching them share a moment of gaming solidarity almost made Maggie laugh. This was so very unexpected... and wonderful.

"So... you play RainQuest?" she asked Zach, which was not only a painfully obvious question, but it also had the effect of pouring cold water all over their conversation.

He turned, managing to look amused, knowing, gorgeous, and slightly embarrassed all at once. "Yeah." He nodded toward the banner in the window. "And you're opening a boardgame café?"

Maggie looked around the empty room, at the box of small business software she'd only just started to sort through. "Hopefully," she replied.

"Mom." Ben sounded both exasperated and a little hurt. "We *are*. That's why we moved here."

"Right." Maggie decided a formal introduction was needed, and she stuck out her hand. "I'm Maggie Parker, and this is my son Ben."

"And you both eat black olive and pineapple pizza," Zach added. "Zach Miller." He shook her hand, his palm warm and dry, his grip firm and sure. And she did *not* feel any tingles from his touch. That pleasurable awareness rippling along her skin was something else entirely. It had to be, because Zach Miller was at *least* ten years younger than her, and she wasn't looking for romance of any kind anyway.

Zach glanced at her, a smile lurking in his eyes, as if he could sense her reaction, which was a truly mortifying thought. Maggie slipped her hand from his and he turned back to Ben. "So, where did you move from?"

"Greenwich." Ben ducked his head, his bangs sliding into his face, as if just the memory of where they'd come from and what had happened there was enough to have him slipping back into his old ways, hiding behind his hair, trying to disappear.

"Cool." Zach nodded, jamming his hands into the pockets of his jeans as he rocked back on his heels. Maggie noticed the way the taut denim stretched across his powerful thighs and quickly jerked her mortified gaze away. "Do you play RQ in person," he asked Ben, "or just online?"

"Just online," Ben half-mumbled. Maggie knew what he was thinking —that everyone in high school had thought he was a major geek for being into the fantasy game—and had made sure he'd known it. The fact that Zach, of all people, was into it too was, in its own way, an unexpected blessing. She was grateful, but she still felt blindsided by the whole notion. Mr. Extra Spicy was not quite who she'd assumed he was.

"Me too," Zach replied. "Hard to find real-life gamers, but it would be awesome if you got a club or something going here. Do you play solo or in a team?"

"Solo, usually." Ben's expression became animated again. "I was in a team with a human and an elf for a while, but I was seriously carrying them. And the human was, like, a *total* bot."

Zach nodded knowingly. "Sometimes it's better on your own."

That was, Maggie thought, an achingly prescient remark, because Ben had been on his own friendship-wise for most of his life, and certainly since middle school.

Zach looked around the empty room. "So, looks like early days for this place," he remarked with a friendly smile. "When are you hoping to have that grand opening?" He nodded toward the banner plastered to the window.

"Well..." Maggie began, before Ben interjected firmly.

"February first."

Maggie gaped at him for a second. "Ben," she protested weakly, "that's only two weeks away."

"We can do it, Mom." His tone was truculent, but his eyes pleaded with her. Heaven knew, she wanted to agree with him. She wanted to make this happen for her son, but... there was so much to *do*, and she didn't know how to do pretty much any of it.

"We can try," she finally replied, knowing she sounded unconvinced, and Ben's pleading gaze turned to something like a glare. As much as Maggie wanted to wave a magic wand and make it all happen, she knew she had to be realistic... for both their sakes. March seemed much more likely.

"Well, if you need any help, let me know," Zach told her. "My sister and I manage Miller's General Store, so we know a thing or two about starting a business in this town."

"Oh..." Maggie had no idea if the offer was offhand or genuine, and so she couldn't think of how to respond.

"I mean it," Zach continued, an earnestness to his tone she hadn't expected. "It can be hard, knowing where to begin with this kind of stuff."

"Did you start the store from the ground up?" she asked curiously. She was trying to envision him as an entrepreneur; she realized, somewhat to her shame, that she hadn't been imagining him as anything more than eye candy.

"My parents did," he replied. "About forty years ago. Bought an old barn and turned it to a general store, offering an eclectic mix of the necessary and the unique." He sounded like he was quoting from the store's sign. "They retired four years ago, and by that time the store was pretty much just kind of sputtering along. It was an everything-and-nothing store, if you know what I mean. They made a living out of it, just, but we're trying to repurpose it for the twenty-first century."

Intrigued, Maggie asked, "So what does that look like?"

Zach's smile was wry as he gave a little shrug. "My sister and I disagree on that point somewhat, so we're still trying to figure it out. But we'll get there."

Did she detect the *tiniest* note of bitterness in his voice? "You grew up here, then," she surmised.

He nodded. "And pretty much never left."

It sounded like something between a confession and a warning. Clearly there were depths to Zach Miller she hadn't appreciated during their admittedly very brief first meeting. "We'll have to stop by sometime. It sounds like an intriguing place." She glanced at Ben, wanting to draw him back into the conversation. "Have you been by there, Ben? To the general store?" She knew he'd had a wander through town yesterday.

Ben shook his head. "Not yet."

"It's on the outskirts of town, about half a mile past the church," Zach told them. "You're welcome to stop by anytime. And I meant what I said about helping." He smiled at Ben. "As one gamer to another, I'd seriously love to see a place like this open in town."

"What's your username?" Ben asked abruptly.

Zach gave a grimacing sort of grin. "Zachanator." He held up one hand. "I know, I know. All I can say is, I was young when I made it, and it sounded cool. And once you build up your stats, you don't want to change, you know, and lose everything?"

A smile lurked about her son's mouth. "Yeah, I get it." He hesitated and then blurted uncertainly, "Maybe I'll look you up."

"Yeah, you should." Zach glanced at Maggie, a question in his eyes. "Assuming that's okay, of course..."

"You mean online?" she asked. "Um, okay." She wasn't entirely sure what the parenting protocol was meant to be here. Her rule had been that Ben could only play with people he knew, but it hadn't ever been an issue because he so rarely gamed with anyone else. And she supposed he did know Zach Miller... sort of.

"When do you play?" Ben asked, and Zach shrugged.

"Evenings, mostly, from seven onwards, but not every day."

"Okay." Ben nodded, smiling, seeming both relieved and excited. "Great."

"Well, I should go." Zach glanced at Maggie, and she thought she saw another question in his blue-green eyes, this one more personal, but she didn't know what it was or how she could possibly answer it. This whole conversation had bordered on the seriously surreal. "I guess I'll see you around?" he asked, and she heard the same kind of hesitancy in his voice that she'd heard in her son, and she didn't know what to make of it. Zach did not seem a hesitant kind of person.

"Yes." She nodded. "I'm sure we'll both see you around."

He nodded back, waved to Ben, and then he was heading back out into the street.

"Well," Maggie said once the door had closed behind him. "That was unexpected."

"RainQuest is a really popular game," Ben told her, somewhat reprovingly. "Lots of people play it."

"I know. I just didn't expect..." She wasn't sure how to finish that sentence. "Anyway," she remarked brightly, "nice to know there's some interest in the community."

"We can get this place going by February first," Ben told her. "We just have to work at it."

"Speaking of work..." She glanced at her watch. "You need to finish your chemistry."

"*Mom*." Ben rolled his eyes. "I want to work on this." He gestured to the boxes of boardgames stacked in the stockroom. Ben had been in charge of ordering them all; Maggie wouldn't have even known where to begin with all the different games that were available, but Ben seemed to know about every single one. So far the many boxes hadn't been opened, never mind organized.

"We made a deal, Ben," Maggie reminded him as gently as she could. "We'd do the boardgame café if you'd do your schoolwork."

"It's boring," he muttered. "And stupid."

"It's school," she replied, making sure to keep her tone light. "Sometimes it can be both of those things, but it's still important. Why don't you finish your chemistry and then you can get back to the games?"

"Fine." With ill grace, dragging his feet, Ben headed for the stairs, closing the door behind him with a borderline slam.

Maggie sighed as she turned back to the box of small business software. A wave of loneliness was sweeping through her, and she'd learned to just let it happen rather than attempt to resist its pull. Life was hard. Moving to a town where you knew no one was harder still, especially when grief was still your main emotion, along with a treacherous helping of guilt. She wanted to believe it would get better, she *did* believe it, she just wished she knew *when*. Or how.

She thought about calling Lynn, but she was afraid her sister would simply tell her to pack it in and head back to Greenwich, or even to Boston to be with her. Those weren't solutions, Maggie knew. She needed to give Starr's Fall a real chance, and to do that she needed to make an effort.

With determination, she picked up the software manual and started to open it. When Ben had first come up with the idea of opening a boardgame café—from his hospital bed back in May—they'd agreed he would be the gamer guy, organizing the games and the café space, while she would handle the financials and the food.

Fortunately, thanks to Matt's generous life insurance policy as well as the proceeds from the sale of their house, money was not an issue, and wouldn't be for some time. Maggie had a day-long barista course booked in Hartford in a few weeks' time, although she was reluctant to leave Ben alone for an entire day. He'd insisted he'd be fine, but...

Maggie didn't want a repeat of last spring. She didn't think she could survive it, and there was a very real and frightening risk that Ben wouldn't.

But she couldn't let herself think like that, not here in Starr's Fall, which was meant to be a new beginning for them both. Taking a deep breath, Maggie reached for her laptop and headed back to the desk in the stockroom that also served as an office. The least she could do was to start figuring out an accounting system for Your Turn Next.

Half an hour later her eyeballs were aching, and she'd waded through pages and pages of how to navigate the red tape of small business owner-ship. She desperately needed a coffee, and she should probably check that Ben was actually doing his schoolwork. With a sigh, Maggie pushed away from the desk, only to still when a woman's voice called out, "Hello...?"

"Hi, can I help you?" Maggie asked as she came into the front room. A woman stood in the doorway, balancing a bouquet of early daffodils and a plastic-wrapped plate, a little wiry-haired dog at her feet, his head tucked firmly between her ankles. It was Laurie Ellis, Maggie recalled, from Thanksgiving. "Hi," she said again. "Nice to see you."

"Welcome to Starr's Fall!" Laurie's smile was bright as she held the flowers out. "I brought you some housewarming flowers—"

"That's so kind." Maggie came forward to take the flowers, smiling down at their cheerful yellow heads. "They're lovely."

"And some chocolate chip cookies," Laurie continued, brandishing the plate. "How are you settling in?"

Considering the rush of loneliness she'd just experienced, Maggie wasn't sure how to answer. "Mixed," she finally admitted. She felt too tired to be anything but honest right then. "But it is early days, I know, so that's to be expected."

"Moving is hard," Laurie agreed sagely. "I only moved here myself in September, so it hasn't been that long for me, either."

"Really, only September?" Maggie experienced a pang of envy. That was four months longer than they'd had here. "You seem so settled already."

"The people of Starr's Fall were very welcoming," Laurie replied. "Wait until you meet them all—you'll have to join the Starr's Fall Business Association! And I came here to invite you and your son to dinner, actually, if you're free. Nothing fancy, just a few people over, so you can meet some of the locals."

"Oh... that's..." For a second, Maggie floundered. As much as she wanted to make friends, she'd been in a state of social hibernation for so long that the thought of having dinner with strangers, well-meaning as they most likely all were, was nothing short of terrifying. "Very nice," she finished a bit lamely. She couldn't say no, she already knew that. It had to be glaringly obvious that both she and Ben were free, and if she turned down the first invitation she'd received in Starr's Fall, chances were she might not get another one. This was all part of making an effort. It was just so hard to *do*.

"Tomorrow night?" Laurie asked, eyebrows raised in expectation.

*So soon?* Panic swirled in Maggie's stomach and crawled up her throat. "Umm..." There was absolutely no good reason why not. "Sure." She smiled weakly. "Thank you." Ben was not going to be pleased, she knew. His state of social hibernation had been even more pronounced than hers. Yet this was why they were here, wasn't it? Why they'd come to Starr's Fall in the first place. To start over. To make friends. To have a total life reset, if such a thing was possible.

"Great." Laurie beamed at her and then, after thrusting the plate of cookies at Maggie, who took it, she bent down and scooped up the little dog. "This is Max," she told her. "He can be a little shy at first, but then can't we all?" Her smile was so full of warmth and understanding that for a second, Maggie's eyes stung.

"Yes," she agreed as she scratched Max under his chin. "We can." Maybe they really should get a dog, she reflected. Or a cat. Or both, even. Why not? Matt had been allergic to cats and hadn't wanted the hassle of a dog, but she and Ben were free agents now. They could finally do what they wanted, with no one to sigh or scowl or make pointed remarks under his breath.

*Stop thinking like that.*

"Great." Maggie found she had to clear her throat. "Thank you so much for being so welcoming. It's really kind of you."

"No problem. Shall we say six-thirty? Tomorrow?"

Panic fluttered once more beneath Maggie's ribcage, but not quite as strongly as before. Maybe they could do this. It would no doubt be stressful and emotionally exhausting, but still... possible.

"Six-thirty tomorrow," she repeated as firmly as she could. "Wonderful. Can I bring anything?"

"Just yourselves," Laurie replied, and with one last sunny smile and a wave, she turned for the door. "See you then!"

"See you then," Maggie agreed. The door closed behind her, and she sagged where she stood. Now she had to break the news to Ben that they were going to have to be sociable. That conversation was going to go well... not.

With a sigh, she turned and headed upstairs. Their apartment, at least, was becoming cozy; their old family room sofa dominated the living room but there was still room for the painted armoire that hadn't fit up the stairs to her bedroom. It had been too shabby chic for their house in Greenwich, but was now filled with books and pottery that had been in boxes since her marriage. Was it wrong, Maggie wondered, to feel a sense of liberation at having her own things displayed around their little home? It wasn't as if Matt had *forbidden* her from having them in their old house. It had just felt a little like he had.

"Ben?" she called as she headed into the kitchen, where her son's desk was wedged under a window. After what they referred to as an accident, although it really hadn't been, she'd insisted his computer be in a public space rather than his bedroom. Too many bad things could happen behind closed doors. Too many bad things *had*.

Ben was hunched over the computer, clicking madly on the mouse.

"You're not doing schoolwork," she observed as she gazed at the screen that was full of the vivid green and purple graphics of RainQuest.

"I finished it," he replied. "It was easy."

"Already?" He shrugged in reply, and she suppressed a sigh. The online school she'd enrolled him in was supposed to be challenging, but surely there was something wrong with the educational system if he could finish a day's work in less than ninety minutes. Or was Ben really that smart? "What are you doing?" she asked.

"Checking Zach's stats. He's, like, *really* cracked."

His awed tone almost made her smile. Maggie leaned against the door-frame as she watched Ben continued to click. "What does cracked mean in this scenario?" she asked.

"He's really good," Ben explained. "His KD is insane..." Maggie had no idea what a KD was, never mind what qualified as insane, so she just nodded.

"We've been invited to dinner at our neighbor Laurie's place tomorrow night," she said in as casual a voice as she could manage. "Do you remember we met her back when we came at Thanksgiving? Laurie Ellis. She runs that little pet store, Max's Place."

"Huh... okay..." Ben mumbled, his gaze still on the screen. Then the penny dropped with a thud, and he swiveled to face her. "It's just you going, though, right?"

"No, Ben," Maggie replied gently. "I thought we should both go. We were both invited."

A look of trapped terror came over her son's face as he pulled the sleeves of his sweatshirt over his hands in what had become something of a nervous tic. "Mom..."

"You know what we agreed," she reminded him quietly.

Another proviso—that he would try to make friends in Starr's Fall, even if he was doing online school. Ben shook his head, more of a reflex than anything else. Maggie understood his fear. For months now it had just been the two of them, hiding away from the world. It was hard to come out of that. Hard to know even how to be.

"Like I'm going to make friends with some middle-aged mom?" he said with an attempt at a sneer.

"*I'm* the middle-aged mom," Maggie pointed out. "Laurie is only in her twenties, and as far as I know, she's not a mom. Besides, you can make friends with anyone, Ben." She stopped, not wanting to point out that his success rate at making friends with kids his own age was pretty poor.

Ben turned back to the screen and resumed clicking, this time with a morose sort of concentration.

Deciding not to press for an actual acceptance, Maggie walked to the fridge and opened it, surveying its paltry contents for something to make for dinner. She should do a proper grocery shop, she thought with a pang of guilt. Fill the fridge with all kinds of good things. She wanted to have the will as well as the energy to do that, to do *lots* of things like that—make soup and knit blankets and write flowery messages on handcrafted cards —but right now it all eluded her.

She thought about Laurie's kind housewarming gifts which she'd left downstairs. She glanced back at Ben, who was once more engrossed in the make-believe world of RainQuest, and she suspected that at the moment it felt like a safer place than Starr's Fall.

Changing locations, Maggie reflected, did not mean you actually changed *yourself*. Your feelings, your fears, your weaknesses... they all remained depressingly the same. Had she really thought she'd suddenly, magically become a sort of cheerfully capable and socially confident business-minded woman, simply by moving to Starr's Fall? Or that Ben would suddenly *not* be an antisocial, game-obsessed teenaged boy with scars on his wrists he still had to hide?

She closed the door with what would have been a slam if not for the soft sucking noise of the fridge's suction liner.

"Ben," she asked, "do you want a cookie?"

No reply.

Maggie headed downstairs for the plate of homemade chocolate chip cookies. Maybe she'd eat them all herself, and she'd binge-watch a few of her favorite episodes of *Is It Cake?* while she was at it. Some things, it seemed, really didn't change.

# 5

"So, no date tonight?" Laurie asked teasingly as she kissed Zach's cheek. He handed her the hand-tied bouquet of winter jasmine he'd bought in Litchfield and she murmured her thanks.

"Nope, no date," he replied breezily. "I'm taking a break."

"What he really means," Jenna informed Laurie as she unzipped her parka, "is that there are no more eligible women in the entire Litchfield area. *Or* Torrington."

Zach strolled over to the kitchen table, keeping his smile in place. These kinds of jokes never got old with the good citizens of Starr's Fall *or* his sister, he reflected sourly. It was amazing how easily some people were amused, Jenna included.

"I'm sure you'll find the right woman one of these days," Laurie remarked diplomatically as she put the jasmine in a little pottery jug. She slid him a smile full of warm-hearted affection. "Won't you, Zach?"

"Here's hoping," he replied in the same breezy tone.

"Well, he's certainly found a lot of *right now* women," Jenna remarked, her joking tone not without the faintest touch of acid.

Zach's smile slipped as he gritted his teeth. He and Jenna had been coolly polite with one another ever since their argument four days ago, and that wasn't how they usually operated, mainly because Zach always kept up a jokey, devil-may-care attitude to alleviate Jenna's control-freak tendencies. But having her make that kind of pointed remark when they were already not quite getting along felt like a bit much to take, especially when they were with company.

"Since you don't go on the dates with me," he remarked in what he hoped was a pleasant tone, "or ever discuss my dating life with me, I'm not sure how informed you are to make that assessment of my motivations."

Both Jenna and Laurie gave him the sort of startled look that made him feel like he'd just burped or farted. He knew he didn't normally push back like that, but lately he'd been getting pretty tired of the status quo. Maybe it was meeting someone new, and seeing how Maggie and Ben Parker were starting their lives over in Starr's Fall. Could he do that too, even if he'd never left?

"Just saying," he finished with an easy smile. Max had come to sniff around his sneakers and Zach scooped him up in one hand and deposited the little dog in his lap, grateful for the distraction.

"So how is our newcomer settling in?" Jenna asked Laurie. "It was nice of you to invite her to dinner. What's her name again?"

"Maggie Parker," Laurie replied, "and her son is Ben."

An awareness twanged through Zach as his hand stilled on Max's back. He'd just been thinking about Maggie, recalling seeing her yesterday, the way her deep blue eyes had widened as she'd nervously tucked a strand of dark hair behind her ear, that single streak of gray reminding him of a bird's wing. So Maggie and Ben were coming to dinner. When Jenna had relayed Laurie's invitation, she hadn't mentioned that salient fact.

"I asked Annie to come too," Laurie continued, "but she has to stay home with her mom." She gave an unhappy frown, and Jenna nodded in understanding. Annie Lyman ran Lyman Orchards and Zach knew her mother had advanced Parkinson's. He'd known the Lymans his whole life; it was a terrible and yet also inspiring thing to witness Barb Lyman's decline, managed with both humor and dignity, yet inevitable and tragic too, as she succumbed more and more to the ravages of the disease.

"What's their story?" Jenna asked as she took a pile of silverware from Laurie and started setting the table. "Maggie Parker's, I mean?"

Zach carefully deposited Max back on the floor and went to get the plates, trying to act as if he wasn't eager to hear every word Laurie was about to say.

"I really don't know," Laurie admitted. "Only that she and her son moved here on their own to start this boardgame café. But maybe she'll tell us something of it tonight." She paused, her head cocked in thought. "I get the sense," she finished slowly, "that she's been a little... battered... by life."

It was the same sense Zach had had not just of Maggie, but of Ben too. There had been a fragile and bruised quality to the pair of them that had made him feel weirdly—and nonsensically—protective of them both. Like they'd had a few too many hard knocks and might not survive another one unless they had someone to keep them upright. Or was he just being fanciful, wanting to swoop in as the protector, finish the fairy tale? He had a tendency to overthink these things. Overimagine, too.

"Haven't we all," Jenna replied on a sigh. Laurie gave her a commiserating look while Zach kept quiet. He knew that during a year-long internship in San Francisco more than ten years ago, back when he'd had his brief stint in college, Jenna had had some kind of heartbreak. She didn't talk about it, and he didn't ask, but he suspected it was what was behind some of her more barbed remarks about his dating life—not that knowing that made taking them any easier.

"Hello?" a voice called up the stairs, and then a few seconds later Joshua appeared at the top, giving Zach his customary cautious smile, almost as if he was afraid Zach might vault over the table, pull him into a headlock, and give him a wet willy in his ear. And in truth, he *might* have done just that when they'd both been fourteen, but not now. Not for a long time.

Zach raised his hand in a salutary fashion. "Hey," he said, and Joshua gave a nod back, along with a very small smile.

"Hey. What's up?"

"Not much."

It wasn't much conversation, but it was at least a start, Zach supposed. He watched as Joshua went to Laurie and kissed her hello, and then gave Jenna a quick, one-armed hug. Okay, he wasn't feeling like an outsider, he told himself, even though he knew he kind of was. But then, he'd felt like an outsider in Starr's Fall for a long time, which was kind of ironic considering he'd spent basically his whole life here, and he had no great desire to go anywhere else. Kind of a conundrum, really, to not entirely like where you were living, even if the place itself felt as if it had settled right into his bones. Truth was, he couldn't imagine living anywhere other than Starr's Fall. He just wanted it to feel better.

A sigh escaped him, and Jenna glanced over. "What?" she asked, her tone landing somewhere between teasing and nettled. "Bored already?"

"Nope," Zach replied as he finished laying the plates on the table. He purposefully ignored his sister as he turned to Laurie. "What else can I do?"

"Oh..." Laurie glanced between him and Jenna, clearly sensing the palpable tension. They obviously needed to clear the air about managing the store. Zach had been working on a new business plan for some high-end tourist items, and he was determined for Jenna to take it seriously.

"Um, do you want to fill a jug of water?" Laurie suggested. "Joshua, why don't you put some music on? I'll just check on the lasagna..."

She went to the oven while Joshua fiddled with his phone to connect it to the speaker. Zach reached for the blue pottery jug above the sink and started to fill it with water, all the while feeling his sister's assessing gaze on him.

"You okay?" she asked after a moment, her tone mild, maybe the tiniest bit apologetic.

"Yup." He turned off the sink and went to put the jug on the table. Now was not the time to have it out with Jenna, not that he'd even know what that would look like. As close as they were, or at least as people *thought* they were, they'd never really done heart-to-hearts. Jenna was too prickly and private, and he was... well, he was too wary. He didn't need his sister throwing yet more assumptions at him about who he was now, just because of who he'd once been.

Cello music floated from the speakers, the mellifluous sound seeming to ease the unspoken tension between him and Jenna. It was hard to stay grumpy when Yo-Yo Ma was playing Bach in a way that wrapped around your soul. Zach gave her a quick, semi-conciliatory smile, and she nodded back. It would, he suspected, take the place of a proper conversation.

"I think dinner's ready," Laurie said as she straightened from the oven. "Now we just need to wait for Maggie and Ben."

As if on cue, the doorbell rang.

"Jenna, can you get it?" Laurie asked. "I'm just going to drain the green beans." She turned back to the stove. "Joshua, do you want a beer? Zach?"

"Sure." Zach opened two bottles and handed one to Joshua as he listened to the murmurs and exclamations coming from downstairs. He felt a curiosity as well as an excitement flare to life inside him, and he realized just how much he was looking forward to seeing Maggie Parker again.

He took a long swallow of his beer just as they came up the stairs—Jenna first, following by Maggie clutching a bottle of wine like a life preserver, and then finally Ben, his shoulders slumped, his sneakered feet dragging along the floor like he was entering the ninth circle of hell, which, for him, maybe he was.

"Maggie!" Laurie exclaimed. "And Ben, too. I'm so glad you both came." She went forward as Maggie held out the bottle.

"I brought this," she said uncertainly, her gaze darting from person to person and then landing on Zach, her startled gaze widening as color flooded into her cheeks.

Oh, that was a *nice* reaction. Zach tipped his bottle back and took another swallow as Maggie's gaze darted away.

"Let me introduce you," Laurie continued, blithely unaware of any undercurrents. "This is my boyfriend Joshua, and my friend Jenna, and her brother Zach. They run the general store, which is so cute and old-fashioned. You should definitely have a look through it when you get the chance."

"I will," Maggie replied, her voice coming out slightly strangled. "Nice to meet you all." Her gaze moved around the kitchen once more, this time not resting on Zach, something he suspected was deliberate.

"Mom, we already know Zach," Ben told her, sounding exasperated, like she was just being slow, and Zach took another swallow of his beer to smother his laugh. Maggie's cheeks had flared pink again.

"You do?" Jenna asked, sounding both curious and a little miffed.

"I came into their café," Zach explained. "Yesterday."

"Why?" Now his sister sounded mystified.

"Because I wanted to know when it was opening," Zach replied mildly. He smiled at Ben as he cocked his beer bottle toward him. "February first, right?"

Ben grinned back. "Right!"

"Well, we'll see," Maggie murmured. She tucked a tendril of hair behind her ear, her composure seeming mostly restored. She looked understatedly elegant in a fitted gray cashmere V-neck sweater paired with wide-legged black pants and black leather ankle boots. Discreet diamonds winked at her ears. Zach wondered how old she was. Forty?

As she tucked her hair behind her ears again—clearly something of a nervous tic—he saw the glinting flash of a platinum wedding ring on her finger. Huh. He'd definitely been getting single mom vibes from her, but who could tell? Maybe her husband worked in the city and would be joining them on the weekend... a prospect that made him feel like kicking something.

"I'd never heard of a boardgame café before," Laurie told her as she took the wine and handed it to Joshua to open. "But that sounds like such a cool idea."

"Oh, well, it was Ben's idea, actually," Maggie said. She smiled at her son, her hands fluttering by her sides like she didn't know what to do with them. "I'm just along for the ride."

Laurie's smile was warm as she turned to Ben. "So, tell us, Ben, what exactly *is* a boardgame café?"

"It's, um, a café with boardgames." Ben flushed, looking as flustered as his mother. "I mean, you play them while you're having a coffee or hot chocolate or whatever. And there's someone in the store, staff, I mean, who knows how to play all the games and can help you with learning the rules and stuff."

"That sounds so cool," Laurie enthused. "Did you think of it yourself, or had you been to one before?"

"Oh, I've been to one," Ben said quickly. "There's one in New Haven, and I mean, in general, there are lots all over the country."

"And now one in Starr's Fall," Jenna chimed in with a smile. "Nice. We could use some more entertainment, along with a place to have decent coffee."

"Let's hope the coffee's decent," Maggie joked, a tremor to her voice. She really was nervous, Zach realized, with a twist of sympathy. What had happened—or not happened—in her life to make her so uncertain of herself in what was a pretty basic social situation?

And Ben too... He glanced at the teenager, noticing the way he hid his hands in his sweatshirt, ducked his head. They both seemed out of their element, in a way that made Zach feel both curious and sympathetic. How could two people who were so uncertain about themselves work up the courage to move to a new town, where they seemingly knew no one, and open a business?

Unless it wasn't courage, but desperation? And yet even that required its own sort of bravery.

Zach realized he'd missed the rest of the conversation, and everyone was staring at him. He raised his eyebrows in query as Jenna said dryly, "Earth to Zach. Did you hear Laurie's question?"

"Sorry, I was a million miles away." He gave his hostess an apologetic grin. "What were you asking me, Laurie?"

"Just if you liked boardgames," Laurie replied. "Since you went into the café. I've pretty much only ever played Monopoly, myself."

"Yeah, I like games." He glanced at Ben, who was frowning slightly, looking apprehensive and maybe even a little confused, no doubt by Zach's measured reply. The truth was, he didn't particularly want to explain about his gaming life; a lot of people, his sister most likely included, assumed a thirty-one-year-old guy with a gaming interest was, well, *weird*. And yet... what was he saying to Ben, by *not* mentioning it? Ben was obviously a diehard RQ fan. Zach had a sudden, strong sense that not mentioning his gaming would feel like some kind of betrayal.

"I play an online game," he stated, like an announcement. "RainQuest. Ben does, too." He nodded toward Ben. "I was asking about it because the café's logo had one of the characters from the game on it."

"An online game?" Jenna looked incredulous. "Wait, *what*?"

"It's fun," Zach replied, a slight warning note to his tone. The last thing he needed was Jenna sounding scathing about a game Ben clearly loved, never mind how he felt about it. He had a feeling the kid wouldn't be able to take that kind of implied criticism. "Right, Ben?" he asked, with a pointed look at his sister.

"Yeah, really fun." As Zach had expected, Ben sounded cautious, like he didn't want to admit too much to this crowd. Zach didn't blame him.

"RainQuest," Jenna mused, clearly getting the warning and moderating her tone. "Wow. Well, I've, um, never heard of it."

"It's a fantasy game," Joshua chimed in. He also sounded cautious, but he shot Zach a commiserating smile, which he returned with a grin. He should have figured Joshua played RQ. "I've played it a little."

"Really?" Ben looked heartened by this news. "What's your username?"

"Umm... MusicMan15." Joshua smiled, clearly embarrassed. "I mean, it's been a while..."

"Has it?" Zach raised his eyebrows. "You know we can check the last time you played?"

"Busted," Joshua conceded with a wry grin. "Fine, full disclosure, I played last week. You?"

"Last *night*," Zach replied, in the unlikely manner of a boast, and Joshua chuckled.

"You got me beat, man," he said. "*This* time."

Emboldened, Zach held out his fist for a bump, and sheepishly, Joshua lightly bumped it. Then Zach turned to Ben, who did the same with a shy awkwardness that tore at his heart. The kid clearly needed friends.

"All these secret players!" Laurie exclaimed. "RainQuest. That's such an interesting name. Ben, you'll have to tell me all about it." And with an ease that came from an innate warmth and friendliness, she began ushering everyone toward the table. "Maggie, you're on the left with Ben there," she instructed, "and Joshua and Jenna on the other side... Zach, you can go on the end, next to Maggie."

Laurie beamed at them all as she brought over the lasagna, its golden top bubbling with melted cheese. "I'm so glad you all came!"

Zach slid into his seat as Maggie sat down in hers and fumbled with her napkin. Her head was bent, and he had the feeling that she was deliberately choosing not to look at him. Interesting.

Laurie cut into the lasagna and started serving out portions as Joshua poured the wine and Jenna got a Coke for Ben.

"So tell us about yourself, Maggie," Jenna invited in a way that was both typically friendly and forthright. "What made you choose Starr's Fall as the place to open your boardgame café?"

Maggie's dark blue eyes widened as she froze, her napkin clenched in one hand. It was almost as if Jenna's friendly-sounding question had been akin to asking her to strip naked. Either she was a very private person, he reflected, or she had secrets to hide. Either way, it was intriguing. She was.

Zach lounged back in his seat, reaching for his wine as he waited for her answer.

# 6

This was a disaster. *She* was a disaster. It had been so long since she'd been to a social occasion that Maggie had completely forgotten how to behave like a normal, well-adjusted, *sane* person. She was sitting here like the proverbial deer in the headlights, frozen in terror simply because a perfectly nice, well-meaning woman had asked her why she'd moved to Starr's Fall. What was *wrong* with her?

It didn't help her struggling sense of composure that Zach was sitting next to her, looking amazing and smelling like a pine tree. He was wearing an unbuttoned plaid shirt layered over a forest-green t-shirt, with faded jeans tucked into well-used hiking boots, and the casual ensemble suited him perfectly. Since she'd arrived, he'd slid her several simmering sort of looks that made everything in her turn both hot and watery. Her physical reaction to him was both overwhelming and alarming, and she wasn't sure she could just chalk it up to the fact that he was gorgeous. She felt his presence on a visceral level... But no. She was being ridiculous. It was just that it had been so long since she'd had any male attention. So long since she'd felt that inward yearning for a look, a touch... Far longer, she knew, than since Matt's death.

*Stop, Maggie.* She really needed to say something *now*.

"Umm…" Her voice wobbled, which was seriously embarrassing. "That's a really good question, actually."

Jenna raised her eyebrows, seeming a bit bemused by Maggie's obvious nerves. She glanced at Ben, who was looking guarded. Maggie knew she could not put him on the spot by explaining everything, but she felt she had to say at least some of it. "My husband, Ben's dad, he died a little over a year ago." She rushed on, over the expected murmur of sympathies. "Ben and I were up for a change, and we really liked Starr's Fall," she stated as firmly as she could. "We went here on vacation a couple of times, and it just seemed like such a… great town. And we thought it would be a good place to start a boardgame café. So… we decided to move."

A short silence followed this fairly anodyne statement, full of generic ideas and no real information besides the fact that she was a widow, and now everyone was going to feel sorry for them both, which was something she knew neither she nor Ben had wanted.

"Well, I certainly understand about wanting a change," Laurie finally said and handed her a plate with a piece of lasagna.

"Thanks," Maggie mumbled and took it before looking down at her lap. She needed to get a grip, but the truth was she just wasn't sure how. Then she felt a touch against her ankle, gentle yet purposeful, sending sparks all the way up her leg, and she glimpsed Zach's work boot nudging her own under the table. Was he playing *footsie* with her?

She looked up and saw him smiling at her, his blue-green eyes full of warmth rather than the expected flirtatious amusement. No, not footsie, she realized, just a little nudge of solidarity. She smiled, or tried to, but she still felt like a jumble of rusted parts rather than anything sensible or even sentient. She really needed to remember how to operate in the land of the living, and quickly. And yes, her leg was still tingling from that little nudge of Zach's. Her reaction to this man was seriously unsettling.

A silence stretched on for a few uncomfortable seconds before Jenna asked Joshua something about the bookstore he ran, and whether he was getting in the latest thriller, and they bantered good-naturedly about the merits of him stocking it. Maggie and her awkwardness had been forgotten, which was a good thing, even if she felt semi-abandoned and was desperately wishing she was capable of handling this whole evening better.

"So," Zach asked her as the others continued their spirited debate, "that must have been some vacation, for you to up and move here."

She blinked at him, having to reorient herself because frankly he was simply too dazzling to look at. Who had hair that movie star shade of dirty blond, bright gold at the tips? Or eyes the color of the Caribbean? Or...

*Talk, Maggie.*

"Yes, it was," she told him with the same tone of manic brightness that she often used with Ben. "We first visited about five years ago and had a great time. Ben didn't want to leave, and I promised we'd come back, and so we did two years ago." For a second, she recalled Ben sitting by the lakeside, his head bent, his hands on his elbows. *Mom, can we stay here forever?* So much sadness in his voice, instead of the playful, little-boy wistfulness of before. She would have given him just about anything in that moment, and it turned out that she had.

"Where did you stay?" Zach asked, startling her out of her thoughts.

"Oh... we rented the same place each time. A little converted barn on the outskirts of town." It had been cozy and sweet, almost like living in a dollhouse, compared to the huge house Matt had just bought for them that had felt so echoing and empty. "I think it was called Maple something," she told Zach.

"Maple Leaf Farm," he answered with a nod, before swallowing. "I know it. That's a cute little place."

Maggie let out a slightly shaky laugh. "I guess you know everywhere around here."

"Pretty much." He raked a hand through his hair, sliding it back from his forehead, his direct gaze making Maggie feel like shivering. She hoped he didn't notice. She really needed to better control her reactions to him. "But I don't know many other places," he continued, "so I guess it's a tradeoff."

"Did you never move away," she asked, "even for a little bit?"

He shook his head. "Discounting six months for college, nope."

"Only six months?" she asked in surprise, before realizing how nosy an observation that was. Whatever happened to keep Zach from completing more of his college education was definitely *not* her business.

He seemed to think so too for he didn't elaborate, merely confirmed with a nod. "Yep. Only six months."

*And let the awkward silence ensue*, Maggie thought with an inward sigh. *Again.*

"How are the plans for the café coming?" Zach asked after a moment, and Maggie tried for a rueful smile, wanting to lighten the mood.

"Well, I've managed to spend several hours trying to understand the small business software I bought. I was never good at math so accounting definitely isn't my strong suit, but you know... here's hoping I learn some of it by osmosis. If I put the manual under my pillow, do you think it might transfer to my brain while I'm sleeping?"

He gave a lazy little chuckle. "If that were a thing, I would have definitely sailed through high school." His laughing expression—eyes glinting, mouth curved—dropped as he asked more seriously, "And what about Ben?" He glanced beyond her to her son, who was silently and steadily working through his dinner, his head bent over his plate, seeming determined not to engage with anyone. "Are you going to the high school in Torrington, Ben?" Zach called over.

Maggie tensed instinctively. Ben stilled, looking hunted. A silence stretched on while Maggie waited for her son to speak, before she finally filled in as lightly as she could. "No, not just now. He's doing school online for the moment. We'll see about next year."

Zach eyed them both consideringly, clearly finding the little exchange slightly weird, which it was. Ben did even worse in social situations than she did. These kind people must have wondered if they'd invited in a pair of complete losers, Maggie thought despondently. She had to find a way to rescue the evening, somehow.

"So, tell me," she said to the whole table, her voice ringing out with overloud, forced jollity, "what do you guys do here for fun? I mean, in Starr's Fall?" In case they thought she was making some kind of insinuation, she clarified hastily, "I mean, you know, as a leisure activity. Or hobby. Like, what is there to *do*..." She trailed off, realizing that her babbling had just made everything more awkward.

"Jeez, Mom," Ben muttered under his breath.

"Well, there's the hike up to Starr's Fall," Laurie ventured after a moment. "That's a really fun thing to do." She gave Joshua a loved-up, laughing glance which he returned; clearly there was some kind of heart-warming romantic story there.

"And the town has lots of things going on," Jenna chimed in. "Joshua's bookstore runs a book club, and I hope you're going to join the Starr's Fall Business Association?" She rolled her eyes good-naturedly. "Admittedly, that's not exactly *fun*, but..."

"It *is* fun," Laurie returned loyally.

"If you're into Pilates, Elaine Barton runs a class in the church base-ment," Jenna continued. "I'd say it's great, but I haven't ever been to it." She grimaced good-naturedly. "But I will one day, I promise."

"Okay." She used to do Pilates, what felt like a million years ago, before Matt's death. Maybe she'd do it again... if she could work up the nerve to walk into a room full of strangers. Maggie smiled at everyone, feeling slightly heartened by all the options. "Thanks. I look forward to getting involved."

"And of course," Zach chimed in, lounging back in his seat, "there will be even more events once you get the café going. You could have tourna-ments... classes..." He smiled at Ben. "Maybe even an RQ marathon."

"RQ?" Laurie asked, wrinkling her nose.

"RainQuest," Zach clarified with another smile aimed at Ben. "For those in the know."

"Of course." Laurie laughed, shaking her head. "RQ. Glad I know the lingo. Especially if you play." She glanced at Joshua, who ducked his head.

"Only once in a while..."

Zach cocked his finger and thumb at him. "I'm checking out your stats online next time I play, MusicMan."

Joshua laughed. "Go for it."

Jenna shook her head in wonder. "I had no idea my brother was such a geek," she remarked.

"Well, define geek," Zach replied easily. "I prefer to call myself a connoisseur." He smiled again at Ben, and Jenna blushed, realizing her mistake.

"Right..." she murmured, shooting Maggie an apologetic glance.

Maggie gave a small smile of acknowledgment back. Yes, gaming could be considered geeky, but it was what her son *did,* and in that moment she was so thankful that Zach had bailed him out, and in such gracious style. The swell of gratitude and even affection she felt toward him was a little alarming. It could so easily morph into some other strong emotion. One she had no intention of feeling for Zach Miller or anyone else. Not yet, and maybe not ever.

"More wine?" Joshua asked her with a smile, and he refilled her glass before she could respond. Had she already drunk a whole glass? Maggie couldn't even remember, but now that she considered it, her head did feel like it was spinning. She glanced at Zach, who, by some spidey sense, felt her gaze and turned his head to meet it, smiling lazily.

That man was so, so dangerous.

Maggie reached for her wine. She didn't need her head to spin any more than it already was, heaven knew, but it was something to do, and she craved the fortification.

The conversation had moved on, to a dissection of Starr's Fall's Christmas festivities, and some Winter Wonderland event that had gone better than expected, thanks to the Christmas tree lighting they'd been able to have for the first time in several years.

Maggie focused on her wine. Part of her longed to be part of this community, feel included and welcomed in as she was or at least could be, if she just let herself, because these people were so nice, but another part of her was already determinedly inching away. She couldn't do this. She couldn't bear to be part of something, anything, ever again. It hurt too much; it carried too much risk. And she didn't know how to, anyway.

*And you don't deserve to be.*

She wasn't able to silence that dark little whisper in time. She replaced her wine glass on the table a little too hard, and then she rose in one abrupt movement that had everyone startling and turning toward her.

"Maggie...?" Laurie asked in concern, her forehead furrowed.

"Sorry," Maggie blurted. She had no idea what excuse to make, but she knew she needed to get out of there, just for a few minutes. She needed a breather... from life. Did those even exist?

"Mom...?" Ben prompted questioningly. He looked both concerned and annoyed. "Are you okay?"

"Sorry..." she said again, her mind both blank and racing. "Umm..."

"Are you looking for the bathroom?" Zach asked in his easy way. "I can show you where it is."

Mechanically, Maggie nodded. "Yes... the bathroom. Thanks."

As the silence stretched on, so clearly uncomfortable, she followed Zach out of the kitchen and up a narrow set of stairs to the hallway above.

"Thanks..." she began, only to have him turn to face her, taking her by the elbow and drawing her close.

"Are you okay?" he asked quietly. No flirtatious amusement now, no lazy smile. Just a genuine concern that Maggie knew she couldn't handle.

"I..." She couldn't think what to say. What to *feel*. His hand was still on her elbow, and he was close enough that their shoulders were brushing, and she could breathe in the scent of his aftershave, all of it making her head spin in a way that had nothing to do with the wine. She closed her eyes, wanting to say she was fine, but somehow she couldn't find it in her to summon the words.

"Maggie..." His voice was low, sure, and *kind*. Gorgeous *and* nice. A lethal combination. It was too much to take all at once.

"I know I must seem like I'm crazy," she whispered, her eyes still closed because she couldn't bear to look at him while she made this confession. "It's just... Ben and I... we've had a hard time. Matt... my husband... dying was a large part of it, of course, but there have been other things..." She swallowed hard. She couldn't go into all that now. She didn't know Zach Miller well enough, even if right now she weirdly felt as if she did. "We're trying to come out of it," she told him, "and moving to Starr's Fall was part of that. But it's... complicated." She finally opened her eyes, her heart doing a somersault at the almost tender look on his face, which was very close to hers. So close that if she moved just a couple of inches, she could practically kiss him. Not that she should be thinking of kissing him, or kissing at all, right now, or *ever*...

But there was no doubt that this moment was morphing into something even more intimate than the confession she'd just given, and she already knew she couldn't handle it.

Maggie tried to take a step back, but Zach was still holding her elbow, his fingers warm, his touch gentle yet sure... and very comforting as well as undeniably exciting.

"Yeah... I kind of guessed all that already, to be honest," he told her as he smiled wryly. "I mean, the hard time and things being complicated. But are you okay right *now*? Tonight, here? How can I help you? What do you need?"

What did she *need*? Everything and nothing. Maggie swallowed hard. She'd have liked a hug, for starters, and maybe someone to tell her it was all going to be all right, in time. She'd love someone to reassure her that she was not messing up her son by pulling him out of school and moving to a place where he, already isolated and alone, knew no one. She'd have loved someone to hold her while she cried, not that she had any intention of doing that, but sometimes it all just felt so overwhelming. So hard. "What I really need," she said, the words coming from deep within her, "is a friend for my son."

Surprise flashed across Zach's face, but he didn't say anything, just nodded slowly. "I'm not asking for you to..." she tried to clarify, then stopped, because she *had* been asking, which was both presumptuous and weird. Did she really want Zach to be best buds with Ben? How could she even ask him that? He was a grown man, and Ben was fourteen. It was both weird and ridiculous, and yet... "It's just, you seem to *get* him," she explained painfully. "The gaming thing. RainQuest. You don't know how important that game is to him—"

"Again, I kind of guessed that already," Zach told her. He gave another smile, this one endearingly crooked. "Give me a little credit here, for at least a small amount of emotional intelligence."

Maggie let out a shaky laugh. "I don't even know what I'm asking," she admitted. "I mean, if you played the game online with him, that would be great, but obviously I'm not asking... expecting... you to be best friends with my teenaged son. He's just been lonely and..." She trailed off, grimacing as she shook her head. "Sorry. I'm a mess. Clearly." This time she succeeded in pulling away from him, mainly because she really needed some space. She couldn't think when he was so near and smelling so good.

"We're all a mess," Zach told her, and Maggie gave a huff of disbelieving laughter. Mr. Extra Spicy did not seem like a mess to her. He exuded laidback confidence, the kind that came from being supremely good-looking. Not that she knew what that felt like, but someone with Zach Miller's genes just *had* to have sailed through life.

Except, she had to admit, considering what she knew of him—never leaving Starr's Fall, dropping out of college, playing RainQuest and battling his sister to manage their family store... he didn't necessarily *seem* like he'd been sailing through life all that smoothly. Maybe no one was, no matter how they appeared from the outside.

"Right," she said, dabbing at her eyes as discreetly as she could. "Sorry for falling apart, or almost. And thank you for being so kind."

Zach looked like he wanted to say something more, but he kept himself from it, instead offering an easy smile, his eyes glinting in the dim light of the hallway. "No problem. Now, do you really need the bathroom?"

Maggie managed another laugh, this one not quite so shaky. "I might as well," she replied, and then slipped inside, breathing a quiet sigh of relief as she shut the door. Zach Miller was too nice—and definitely too good-looking—for her own sanity. Her arm was still tingling from where he'd touched her, for heaven's sake. And then there was the fact that he had to be at least ten years younger than her, and probably more. Why she responded to him the way she did was both shameful and ludicrous... She needed to be hyper-alert at all times.

She steeled herself to look at her reflection—reddened eyes, the lines from her nose to mouth looking starker than usual. The gray streak in her hair that had appeared after Matt's death glowed white. She looked *old.* Zach probably thought she was ancient.

Taking a steadying breath, Maggie did what she could to repair the damage—wetting a tissue and dabbing at her eyes, running her fingers through her hair to fluff it out a little. She still looked haggard, but oh well.

She washed her hands, turned away from her reflection, and steeled herself to head back downstairs. When she came into the kitchen, she was surprised to see Ben bent over the table, drawing on a piece of paper as everyone watched. The dishes had been cleared away and more wine poured. Zach looked up as she approached, sliding her a smile that felt like a secret they shared. She forced herself to look away without smiling back, although it was hard. Harder than she would have liked.

"What's going on here?" she asked in what she hoped was a normal tone.

"Ben is drawing us a map of the RainQuest world," Jenna explained. "It's fascinating. So intricate and interesting, with all the details." Her tone was warm; Maggie suspected she was doing her best to make up for her geek comment earlier, and she appreciated the effort.

These people were *nice*, she thought with a rush of gratitude, and they were trying. She needed to try too, as much as for Ben's sake as her own. She needed to make Starr's Fall work for them as a family as well as a business.

No more falling apart, she told herself sternly. No more social awkwardness or endless evenings of watching *Is It Cake?* on her own. From now on, she was going to give their new life in Starr's Fall 110 percent... whatever it took.

## 7

Maggie squared her shoulders as she stepped into the church, her Pilates mat rolled up under her arm. It had been two weeks since that dinner at Laurie's, and she'd been determinedly making progress, one fumbling step at a time. Attending Elaine Barton's Pilates class in the church basement was the next step in her Make-Starr's-Fall-Work, or really Make-Maggie-Normal program.

Over the last two weeks, the boardgame café had begun to take shape. She'd ordered some furniture for the front room to be delivered next week; she'd set up a bank account; she was going on the barista course in a couple of weeks. They hadn't been ready to open on February 1st as Ben had hoped for, but, as long as they'd passed the necessary inspections for food hygiene and fire safety, they could potentially open their doors by mid-March, with limited offerings of coffee and cake. It was both an exciting and scary thought.

Ben had done as he'd promised and continued with his schoolwork, spending his free time either organizing all the boardgames they'd bought or gaming, often with Zach Miller. Apparently, they'd formed some kind of team and Zach was, according to her son, "killing it." Sometimes she heard him talking on his headphones to Zach, which made her smile because it was the most social Ben had been in well over a year, although she could barely understand the gaming slang.

"Complete skill issue!" he'd chortled last night, his thumbs moving rapidly over his controller. "You are *so* bot farming. I'm the one who secured the dub, are you kidding me? Oh, man, the lag!"

She hadn't been able to hear any of Zach's replies through the headphones, of course, but she had been curious as to whether he spoke the same incomprehensible language.

Her sister was less approving of their friendship. "Ben is playing with a thirty-year-old stranger?" she'd exclaimed when Maggie had explained the situation on one of their phone calls. She sounded both censorious and scandalized. "Maggie—"

"He's not a stranger," Maggie had protested. "And I don't know that he's thirty, anyway. He might be younger." Which was a depressing thought. "He's a neighbor," she'd continued, "and he's very nice. He's just about the last person I'd expect to be into gaming, but I'm very glad he is, for Ben's sake. It's good for him."

Lynn had still been dubious. "How do you know this guy isn't, I don't know, *grooming* him in some way?" she'd demanded.

"Grooming him?" Maggie had repeated in disbelief. "Are you serious? I mean, I know you like to be cautious, Lynn, but... I'm pretty sure he's just being nice." She'd taken a deep breath as she'd briefly closed her eyes. "I need you to be happy for me, okay?" she'd told her sister quietly. "This is working, or starting to. I need you to accept that. And if things get hard, which I know they will, I need you *not* to ask me to move to Boston or back to Greenwich or wherever. We're staying here. We're going to make Starr's Fall work."

Lynn had been silent for a long moment. "Okay," she'd finally said. "I get it. But if I'm right..."

"You aren't," Maggie had told her, exasperated as well as amused. "Trust me."

Although really, Maggie reflected as she headed down the stairs toward the church basement, Zach Miller basically *was* a stranger. She hadn't seen him in two weeks; they'd last spoken in the hallway at Laurie's, when she'd almost lost it. Was he avoiding her, the awkward middle-aged woman who had become too emotional? She could hardly blame him, and yet she knew she was disappointed. Some part of her had been hoping to run into him.

She had seen Laurie several times, at least; they'd chatted in the street, and Maggie had stopped by Max's Place to drop off a thank you card for the flowers and cookies as well as the dinner invitation. When she'd let it slip that she and Ben did not have a pet, Laurie had urged her to adopt one from the Humane Society. Maggie had demurred; she was barely managing to keep her and Ben together. Even though Ben had asked for a cat and she'd dreamed of a dog, she didn't yet trust herself with another living creature quite yet. But maybe one day...

"Are you new?" An athletic-looking woman in matching lilac leggings and sports top, her wavy gray hair pulled back into a loose bun, came toward her. "I'm Elaine Barton. Welcome to Peaceful Pilates."

Peaceful Pilates sounded nice, Maggie thought. Well, the peaceful part, anyway. "Thanks, I'm Maggie Parker. I just moved to Starr's Fall."

"You're opening the boardgame café with your son, aren't you?" Elaine remarked as she shook her hand. She let out a throaty laugh. "Everyone knows everyone else's business here, I'm afraid, for better or for worse. Such an interesting idea—I'm a backgammon player, myself."

"We'll have backgammon," Maggie promised. She was pretty sure it was one of the dozens of games they'd purchased a few months ago, when they'd first come up with the idea of the café.

"Looking forward to it." Elaine gestured to the basement floor. "Roll out your mat and we'll begin. Have you met the others?" There were three other women already sitting on their mats. "This is Annie Lyman," Elaine said, pointing to a solid-looking woman dressed in gray sweats and an old t-shirt. She had curly salt-and-pepper hair and looked to be in her mid-forties. She gave Maggie a friendly wave.

"And this is Zoe Wilkinson," she continued, pointing to the woman next to Annie, who was different from her in every way. She was in her late twenties, tall and lithe, with a shock of bright pink hair and a nose ring. While Annie was happy to simply sit on her mat, Zoe was already sinuously stretched out in a cobra pose, her head tilted back as she smiled at Maggie.

"Nice to meet you."

"And you—"

"And Liz Cranbury," Elaine finished, pointing to a woman in her fifties wearing high-end sportswear and a friendly expression. She tucked a tendril of frosted blonde hair behind her ear as she gave Maggie a smile.

"Great to have you here."

"Thanks," Maggie said. She was feeling less nervous than she'd expected to, which was a good thing. She rolled out her mat next to Liz's and stepped onto it gingerly. It had been a long time since she'd done any Pilates, and Liz and Zoe both looked like experts, although Annie appeared as if she'd been brought here under duress.

"Her doctor recommended it," Liz explained in a stage whisper. "For stress."

"Oh dear..." Maggie glanced at Annie, who was, it had to be said, looking a little doleful. "That's too bad." She wondered what she was stressed about; judging by the way the chat flew around this town, she'd probably find out soon enough.

"All right, ladies," Elaine called, moving gracefully to the front of the class. "Let's start with a few cat and cows." She glanced at Maggie, eyebrows raised in query, and Maggie gave a little nod. She knew how to do a cat and cow.

She came onto her hands and knees on her mat, arching her spine down and then up, "broadening through her collarbones," as Elaine encouraged in a gently sonorous voice. As she continued to move, she felt something in her start to loosen. She'd forgotten how much she liked this, and not just that, but she'd forgotten how to be in her body. For too long she'd been existing entirely in her head, and what an anxious, unhappy place that could often be.

As Maggie went into her "first downward dog of the day," muscles she'd ignored for too long stretched and the tension that had bracketed her neck and shoulders for the better part of a year started to ease. She moved into a cobra, feeling almost as sinuous as Zoe next to her, who was looking extremely supple and so very young. As Maggie went into a plank, she felt every single one of her forty-one years.

She moved through the rest of the class, enjoying the stretches and exercises, feeling pleasantly tired and yet also energized by the end of it. And for forty-five whole minutes, she hadn't thought about anything much, which felt like a relief as well as a miracle.

"After class we always go get something to eat," Zoe informed her with a smile once they'd finished and were all rolling up their mats. "We move around town—The Rolling Pin, The Starr Light, even The Latest Scoop." She gave an abashed grin. "That's the ice cream parlor I manage."

"Oh, right..." Maggie had enjoyed the Pilates class, but did she really have the energy to socialize afterward? "I probably should—"

"It's The Starr Light today," Elaine informed them. "They have a two-for-one brunch special." Her tone invited no argument. "Rhonda does a fabulous eggs Benedict."

Everyone was slinging their bags over their shoulders, tucking their mats under their arms. It would be churlish in the extreme to refuse, Maggie felt, and it wasn't even that she wanted to, but...

"Coming, Maggie?" Elaine asked, a very slightly imperious note to her voice, even though she was smiling.

"Yes, coming," Maggie replied meekly as she fell in step with Annie, who was still looking morose.

Outside, the day was bright and clear, the village green sparkling with frost, the air cold enough to freeze in Maggie's lungs. It was early February, but spring still felt a long way off.

"How's Barb, Annie?" Liz asked as they walked along, her voice full of compassion.

Annie sighed. "She's definitely declining. I wish I could say otherwise... hell, I wish I could *pretend* otherwise, but I can't." She pressed her lips together. "The truth is, what with managing the farm, I'm afraid I might have to put her in a home. I can't trust her to be okay on her own, and the carer only comes for a couple of hours three times a week."

"Oh, Annie." Liz rested a hand on her shoulder. "I'm so sorry."

"Barb is Annie's mom," Zoe murmured to Maggie. "She has Parkinson's."

"I'm so sorry..." Maggie murmured back, although she knew it was really Annie she should be saying this to, and Zoe gave a sympathetic grimace. Maggie's dad had died of Alzheimer's several years ago, so she had some idea of what Annie was going through—the slow agony of watching a loved one slip away memory by precious memory and knowing there was absolutely nothing she could do about it. Matt's death just a little over a year later had made her feel even more alone.

But why was she going into this doom spiral of thoughts? "How long have you lived in Starr's Fall?" she asked Zoe.

"All my life," Zoe answered with a laugh. "Although I went to art school in Hartford for a few years, and then I moved to New York for all of six months when I was twenty-two. I wanted to become an important artist, do the whole Greenwich Village thing, but I couldn't take it. I might have run riot in high school, busting to get out of here, but I finally realized I'm a small-town girl at heart."

"That's a good realization to have," Maggie replied with a smile.

"And what about you? Where did you move from?"

"Greenwich, but I grew up outside Philadelphia. I guess I'm a suburban girl, but I'm trying to be small town."

Zoe laughed. "Small town is best," she agreed.

Maggie nodded and smiled back. She felt as if she'd cleared a hurdle— a semi-normal bit of chitchat! She'd even laughed and made Zoe laugh. These things were definitely getting easier.

The grilling, however, was yet to come.

As soon as they were seated in a deep vinyl booth in The Starr Light Diner, with mugs of coffee and huge laminated menus in front of them, Elaine leveled her with a smilingly pointed look. "So, Maggie, what brought you to Starr's Fall? We know about the boardgame café," she continued, cutting to the chase, "and someone—Laurie, I think— mentioned you went on vacation here once?" She wrinkled her nose while Maggie took a sip of coffee, steeling herself for whatever coherent response she could come up with. "But how did you get from that to moving here?" Elaine finished, eyebrows expectantly raised.

"Well..." Was there any reasonable answer? "We needed a change," she explained helplessly, knowing she needed to say more. And really, didn't she want to be honest, for once? She couldn't hide who she was or what she'd lived through forever. "My husband died just over a year ago," she blurted. "A car accident."

Elaine's expression of good-natured nosiness morphed into pure apology. "Oh, I'm so sorry..."

"I told you it was something like that," Liz stage-whispered. She made a face at Maggie. "Sorry. We are all *so* nosy."

"It's okay," Maggie said, and surprisingly, it *was*. She was amazed they hadn't heard what happened from either Jenna or Laurie, but maybe her new friends could be discreet, even in a small town like Starr's Fall. And also amazingly, after a year of dreading talking about Matt's death and all the ensuing fallout, she found that now, sitting with these smiling women, she might be able to manage it. Mostly, anyway, and that was in large part due to the fact that unlike everyone back in Greenwich, these kind people didn't know anything except what she told them. "It's just been hard for my son Ben and me," she continued carefully. "And our life back in Greenwich... There were too many memories there. So we decided we needed a clean break. A fresh start. And we remembered Starr's Fall as such a happy place, so..." She trailed off, letting them fill in the many blanks.

"Sometimes a fresh start is the best thing," Liz remarked sagely. "That's how I felt after my divorce. I didn't want to move, but I did start helping out at Midnight Fashion, and now I'm the manager."

"Betty Stein *finally* retired," Zoe interjected wryly.

"Have you been in there yet?" Liz asked, and Maggie shook her head. "Well, you should," Liz told her with a smile. "It was all a little dated before, but I think I'm bringing it up to speed."

"Oh, you definitely are," Elaine assured her with a wink. "Why, even I'd buy something there now."

"Say it isn't so, Elaine!" Zoe teased. "I thought you were strictly couture." They all laughed, subsiding into mutual smiles, and Maggie felt as if she had become part of something, as if she'd been accepted, with no more questions asked. It was a good feeling.

"All right," Elaine said after a moment as she briskly picked up her menu. "Eggs Benedicts all around, and I think mimosas as well."

It was ten o'clock in the morning, but Maggie knew better than to object.

"I'll agree to that," Annie said on a sigh. She'd barely spoken since they'd sat down, and Maggie's heart ached for her. She knew all too well what Annie was going through. She hoped at some point she'd get a chance to talk to her more privately about it, although she wasn't sure what wisdom she'd have to offer besides a commiseration that watching an aging parent's health fail basically sucked.

A waitress sashayed up to them, a pencil tucked behind one ear, her tired peroxide-blonde hair scraped back into a bun. "What can I get you ladies?" she asked, and Elaine ordered for them all.

"Mimosas," the waitress remarked with a wink. "That kind of day, is it? Alrighty. Good thing it's after 10 a.m. You know I can't violate the new liquor laws."

"Rhonda owns the place," Elaine explained to Maggie. "Since forever. I don't think anyone can imagine Starr's Fall without her."

"And she makes a mean mimosa," Zoe confided with a grin. "This isn't the first time we've had a liquid lunch, as it were."

"It's not liquid," Elaine admonished her. "Remember the eggs Benedicts."

Maggie smiled, just glad they'd moved on from her sad story. And, she had to admit, she was looking forward to her mean mimosa.

"Ooh, ooh," Liz hooted softly, her blue eyes rounding. "Look who just came in. Starr's Fall's resident hottie."

"Liz Cranbury, he's half your age," Elaine chided. "Now as for Zoe…"

Zoe shook her head firmly. "Not my type. I like more grungy guys."

"As if you'll find one of those in Starr's Fall," Elaine scoffed. All four women's gazes followed the man who had just entered the diner, and somehow, Maggie just knew who they were looking at before she discreetly turned around.

Zach Miller, chatting to Rhonda with that oh-so easy smile before he threw back his head and laughed.

"Have you met our scrumptious Mr. Miller?" Liz asked Maggie, her tone playful.

Maggie felt her cheeks heat, and she reached for her coffee. "Um, actually, yes, I have," she replied, striving to keep her tone casual. She had nothing to hide, after all. "He came into the boardgame café to ask when it was opening."

"Did he now?" Elaine remarked thoughtfully.

"Maggie might be a bit old for Zach," Zoe chimed in, before giving Maggie an apologetic smile. "Sorry."

"I really don't think—" Maggie began, before Liz leaned across the table and confided, "You might as well find out now, Zach's kind of a player."

Zoe nearly spat out her coffee. "Kind of?"

"Okay, he's been around," Liz acknowledged. "But how could he not be, when he looks the way he does? What woman wouldn't want to date him?"

"He's dated every eligible woman under forty in the entire county," Zoe declared. "If not the entire state. I should know, I went to high school with him. He was three years older than me, but even back then he was something of a legend, and I don't mean that in a good way." She grimaced, only partially apologetic. "Sorry, I know everyone thinks he's charming, and I guess he can be, but back then he was kind of a jerk."

"That was a long time ago," Annie put in quietly, her tone gently admonishing. "Zach's a good guy. I've known him since he was a little kid, and yes, he had his wild high school days, but hasn't everyone, in one way or another?"

Zoe sighed in reluctant acknowledgment. "Guilty, I guess, but Zach was one of those *in-crowd* guys. You know the type?" She glanced at Maggie. "The cocky jock who goes around flirting with all the girls and toeing up to all the guys? And *knows* how good-looking he is, and how it means he can get away with anything? I just don't think that has changed."

Yes, Maggie knew the type. She remembered those kinds of guys from high school, and then later on, when they all became the bankers and hedge fund managers who schmoozed with her husband. In fact, her husband had been one too, which had all been part of the problem...

Not that she wanted to think about that. Maggie managed a stiff smile as she nodded her acknowledgment. She knew she shouldn't be surprised, and yet she realized she was. The Zach Miller she'd come to know, however briefly, the guy who had asked her if she was okay and what she needed, who gladly gamed with her son... he didn't seem like that kind of jerk. But if he'd dated all the women in the entire county who were under forty...

Well, good thing she was forty-one, she supposed.

Their mimosas arrived, and Maggie reached for hers gladly. As she sipped the cocktail, she realized she felt disappointed, which was stupid, because it wasn't as if she and Zach had even been *friends*. She hadn't seen him in two weeks, after all. If anything, he was more Ben's friend than hers, and he was almost closer in age to her son anyway, which was both humiliating and humbling considering the complicated nature of her thoughts.

Unable to help herself, she glanced over at the booth Zach had slid into, a cup of black coffee in front of him as he frowned down at his phone, his tousled hair sliding into his eyes. Wendy brought him over a plate of fried eggs and hash browns, and he tilted his head up, raking a hand through his hair as he smiled his thanks.

Goodness, but he really was ridiculously good-looking. That tousled, gold-tipped hair, eyes that glinted from all the way across the room, the hint of stubble on his lean jaw. He was wearing another plaid shirt over a t-shirt, navy blue this time, and the usual faded, well-molded jeans. Eek. She needed to stop looking.

Maggie glanced back at the table and saw that every single one of her new friends had followed her gaze, and judging from the smugly knowing expressions on their faces, had guessed the exact nature of her thoughts.

"Don't worry, darling," Liz said as she leaned over and patted her hand. "We all do it."

"But he's never dated any of us," Elaine put in, and they all burst out laughing. This time Maggie couldn't find it in herself to join in.

## 8

"I have a proposition for you."

Zach propped his elbows on the counter of the boardgame café. It was a week since he'd seen Maggie in The Starr Light Diner. He'd waved to her from across the room, and enjoyed the way she had blushed... just as he was now enjoying the way her dark eyes widened and flared in awareness... That was, until her mouth pursed up like a prune and she folded her arms across her chest.

"Oh, really?" she remarked coolly. "And what would that be?"

She sounded like a schoolteacher. Zach slowly straightened, raking a hand through his hair. It didn't take a rocket scientist to realize she must have heard some of the rumors about him, probably when she'd been brunching with some of Starr's Fall coven of gossips.

"What do you think it is?" he remarked with the slightest edge to his voice. All right, it was true that they didn't know each other very well, but he'd felt the flicker of *something* back in Laurie's upstairs hallway, when he'd asked her if she was all right and she'd closed her eyes and practically swayed into him. It had been a small moment, but it had still been a moment. There had been chemistry, he was sure of it. He'd certainly felt it, anyway. But now Maggie was looking at him like she suspected him of being a serial killer... or maybe just a serial dater.

Which, he wondered sourly, was worse in her eyes?

"I don't know," Maggie replied pettishly. She took a deep breath and then added more levelly, "Maybe you could just tell me."

They stared at each other for a beat that felt both laden and tense. Zach hadn't meant for things to escalate so quickly; in fact, he'd come into the café full of optimism and excitement. Now he took a breath that matched Maggie's as he decided to dial it down.

"It was about the boardgame café," he told her. "But I thought maybe we could talk about it over a coffee, my treat at the diner?"

She hesitated and then replied, "There's no need to go all the way to the diner. You can come upstairs and have a coffee there if you have something to discuss." She still sounded stiffly formal. "Ben's just finishing his schoolwork."

Zach had no intention of dying on that particular hill. He didn't really care where they had coffee. "Okay," he said. "Great. Thanks."

She paused as if she was going to say something else, and then turned on her heel and walked to the stairs that ran alongside the store. Zach followed her, unable to keep from noticing how her jeans emphasized the long slimness of her legs. She wore a quarter-zip fleece on top and her hair was pulled back with a clip, so tendrils fell about her face, including that one streak that was entirely silver. He liked it; it gave her both a vulnerability and a strength, a fragile Cruella de Vil vibe, if such a thing were possible.

He was being fanciful, he knew, but that was what happened to him when he met a woman he liked. He went into full fairy-tale mode, not that he'd ever admit such a thing to anyone. He'd rather be seen as a serial dater than a hopeless romantic. Well, maybe.

"I haven't been up here before," he remarked as Maggie led him into the living room. It was a comfortable space, similar in layout to Laurie's place, but with a bit more flair. The living area was taken up with a big, squashy-looking leather sofa, and tucked into one corner was an antique armoire painted in bold yellow, holding rows of paperbacks as well as a few eclectic bits of pottery. A vase of dried flowers was on the windowsill, and a crocheted patchwork throw in every color of the rainbow—in fluorescent—was draped over a deep armchair of eggplant-colored velvet.

Considering how Maggie had only worn shades of gray or brown since he'd met her, the splashes of vivid color were a pleasant surprise.

She led him into the adjoining kitchen, where Ben was seated at an antique desk pushed up under the window, a desktop computer in front of him. Open shelves above the countertops showcased a mix of cups and plates, each one looking like it had been selected from a different set. Maggie clearly had a funky aesthetic or was colorblind, but he liked the randomness of the assortment. It suggested a quirkiness to her personality that he hadn't totally expected.

"Zach!" Ben exclaimed, his face lighting up as he turned to face them.

"Hey." Zach smiled. He'd been spending several hours nearly every night playing RQ with Ben, but he hadn't seen him in person in a couple of weeks, and he was struck again by how young and vulnerable he seemed —the way he hid behind the dirty blond bangs that slid into his face, how he hunched his shoulders and covered his hands with his sweatshirt. "I hope you're not on RQ," he remarked with mock severity, "when you're meant to be doing your schoolwork."

"No. English." Ben made a face. "But I'm almost done," he added hopefully.

"I can't play till later," Zach told him. He didn't usually play RainQuest every single night, and certainly not for as many hours as he had with Ben, but it seemed like the best way to be the kid's friend, as Maggie had asked him to be, although she'd tried to pretend she hadn't. She probably thought he was some kind of sad weirdo, he reflected, playing video games with a fourteen-year-old most nights. Maybe he *was* a sad weirdo, but he felt sorry for Ben, and they'd chatted online as they'd played. While Ben hadn't revealed much about his life, what he had had made Zach suspect the teenager was deeply lonely.

He glanced at Maggie, feeling suddenly dispirited; never mind Ben, *he* felt lonely. He'd thought they were becoming friends, but it was clear from her stiff movements and the way she wasn't speaking that her opinion of him had seriously dipped since he'd last seen her.

Ben must have sensed the tension because he rose from his desk, looking between them both, and said, "I think I'm gonna go for a walk."

Maggie whirled around. "A walk? But your English—"

Ben waved her objection aside. "I'm almost done, and you know, I should be doing gym too, right? Physical exercise." He went to the row of hooks by the stairs and pulled off a parka. "I'll be back in a little while."

And then he was gone, disappearing down the stairs while Maggie gaped after him, looking she'd lost her best friend. After a few seconds, she snapped her mouth shut and turned back to the kettle she'd been filling. "Would you like coffee," she asked with excruciating politeness, "or tea?"

"Coffee would be great," he replied with the same politeness. "Thank you."

Maggie spent a few minutes spooning coffee into a French press as Zach rocked back on his heels, wondering how to break a silence that was definitely starting to feel uncomfortable. He could hardly sell Maggie his proposition when she was like this, and yet he was reluctant to ask her what had put her in this mood. What she'd heard about him... but he could already imagine.

"So how are you settling in?" he finally asked. "I like your place up here. Lots of color."

She glanced around suspiciously, as if looking for confirmation of his assessment, which hadn't been a criticism, even if, judging by the way she'd bristled, she seemed to have taken it as such. "I like color," she replied defensively.

"I do too." Zach had a feeling every topic was going to be a conversation minefield. "Looks like you've made some progress with the café," he remarked. When he'd come downstairs, some leather sofas had been pushed against the walls, and a wooden counter installed along the back, by the kitchen area. It was a start.

"Yes, some," Maggie agreed. She turned around, her arms folded, as she waited for the kettle to boil. "I'm hoping we'll be able to open by the beginning of March, but we'll see. I haven't done any marketing yet, and frankly, I don't really know where to begin with all that."

"Maybe I could help," Zach suggested. "I've done a little marketing for the store. I know what newspapers to put ads in, anyway."

Maggie's gaze narrowed. "That's very kind of you, but—"

"That's actually the nature of my proposition," he cut across her, not wanting to have to listen to her rebuff. "I'm not trying to come across as pushy, but I'd love to help you with the café however I can."

She cocked her head, looking uncertain, maybe even a little suspicious. "You've already got a general store to manage. Ben and I went in there the other day. It's very nice—"

"My sister does most of the management," Zach cut across her for a second time. In the three weeks since he and Jenna had had that clash, his sister had doubled down on her decisions. She'd canceled the order they'd already agreed on for some local artisan products and had stocked even more soup. Chicken noodle, too. He hadn't even bothered to show her his business plan, and now he wasn't sure if he ever would. Jenna seemed determined to do things her way, no matter how much sense his business ideas might make.

Zach understood her reasoning, sort of; the store had to carry some staples. But he was starting to suspect that Jenna was just disagreeing with him because she needed to be in control, rather than what made the most business sense. In an age of online shopping and easy delivery—even to Starr's Fall—it just didn't make sense not to stock a few higher-quality products for the occasional tourist.

"I'm not sure I understand," Maggie said slowly. "Are you asking for a job?"

He was saved from replying by the shrill whistle of the kettle. Maggie turned around and busied herself with making the coffee while he tried not to feel stupid. No, he was not asking for a *job*. Jeez, did she really think he was that pathetic? That desperate, that he was asking her to employ him at minimum wage or something? He already *had* that kind of job... being more or less employed by his sister, even though on paper they were fifty-fifty equal owners.

"Milk or sugar?" she asked as she poured the coffee and then brought two mugs to the table.

"I take it black, thanks." He joined her at the table, sitting across from her. "And no, I'm not asking for a job, not as such. I just thought you might appreciate the help, and I'd really like to see this place succeed. Starr's Fall needs more unique attractions. I checked and the only other boardgame café in all of Connecticut is in New Haven, so this could be a real draw to the area."

"And you think it won't succeed without your help?" Maggie asked a bit sharply, her eyes flashing, and Zach drew back, surprised as well as a little exasperated.

"I didn't say that."

She tucked a silver strand of hair behind her ear. "All right, but you implied it, though, pretty much."

Why, he wondered, were they arguing? Was Maggie just looking for a fight? "I'm sorry if it seemed as if I did," he said after a moment. "Trust me, that was not my intention. I just know how overwhelming it can be to start a small business. Jenna and I took over from my parents, and that was hard enough." Especially as his parents had had a decidedly haphazard approach to the whole enterprise and had let it limp along for well over a decade. "You're starting from scratch," he continued. "If I were in your shoes, I'd be taking all the help I could get, but maybe that's just me."

Maggie lowered her gaze, her dark lashes fanning across her pale cheeks, as she took a sip of her coffee. "Sorry," she murmured. "I know I must sound a little snippy."

"Yeah, why is that?" Zach asked, keeping his tone conversational. "Is it you... or is it me?"

Her startled gaze flew to his, and then darted away again. "What is that supposed to mean?" she asked uncertainly.

"I don't know." He hoped honesty was the best policy here. "Just that the last time I saw you, at Laurie's, I felt like we got along. Now I feel like we don't."

"I barely know you..." Maggie protested as a flush rose to her cheeks.

"Yeah, I get that. But I think you know what I mean." His words seemed to settle between them. Maggie took another sip of coffee, clearly stalling. Was he stupid to push this, Zach wondered. She was right; they did barely know each other. And he knew he could get carried away in any kind of relationship with a woman, even one as tenuous as this. It was why his dating history was so poor... and prolific. He just never seemed to learn his lesson, that not everyone was looking for forever, and those who were weren't necessarily a great fit. He had yet to find a woman he'd wanted to go the distance with, or even, frankly, a short way... but he kept trying. Hence his reputation.

But despite all that, he reminded himself, Maggie had asked him to be her son's friend, and had seemed like she'd *needed* him, and like a chump he'd been grinding RQ for two or three hours a night, which was *not* his usual MO, and all for Ben's sake. For *Maggie's*.

So maybe he would push it.

"What have you heard about me?" he asked quietly.

"What—" she began to bluster, and now her cheeks were fiery. "I don't know what you're talking about—"

"Maggie. Come on. I saw you with those women at the diner. I'm guessing one or all of them were talking about me."

"This is ridiculous..." she murmured and started to rise from the table.

Without thinking about what he was doing, Zach caught her hand in his. She stilled, and he realized it had been a bit presumptuous to touch her like that... just as he felt the electric charge run up his arm and twang through his body, and he could tell from the way her breath hitched that Maggie had felt it, too. The chemistry between them was real... and strong.

Her hair had fallen out of its clip and was tousled about her shoulders, and with her face flushed and her lips slightly parted she looked beautiful... and sexy. For a second, the moment spun out, turned into something else. Unthinkingly, Zach ran his thumb along her palm and a shudder went through her before she jerked her hand out of his.

"Don't," she said in a taut voice, "toy with me, please."

"*Toy* with you?" he repeated. "So you have heard something. What did they say?"

"All right, fine, some of the women I did Pilates with mentioned that you're... something of a player," she confirmed with a stiff nod, not quite meeting his gaze. "*Not*," she continued quickly, "that that sort of thing has anything to do with me. Your dating profile is... I mean, I'm old enough to be your mother."

Zach let out a huff of laughter. "Only if you had children when you were about ten."

She lifted her chin. "How old are you?"

He met her gaze squarely. "Thirty-one."

"Well, I'm *forty*-one," she shot back, as if that proved something.

"So ten years' difference," he replied, unfazed. He'd figured she was around that, anyway, and he really didn't care. "Hardly a parental kind of age gap."

"Speak for yourself." Her voice trembled and she took a deep breath, clearly striving to keep her composure. "I'm only mentioning it at all because you asked and also because of Ben. I need to be careful who has influence in his life, and you've been playing online with him a lot recently, so naturally I'm concerned about the sort of things you might be saying to him..."

She trailed off, as if realizing the gross offense of what she was insinuating, while Zach struggled to keep his tone level.

"So you think while we're gaming, I'm bragging about all the notches on my bedpost or something?" he surmised in derision. "That's pretty rich, considering the reason I'm playing online with him at all is because you *asked* me to be his friend. Or did I misread that part? Somehow I don't think I did." He didn't wait for her to reply as he continued recklessly. "As for what you heard... you could have asked me outright. Yes, I've gone on a lot of dates. That doesn't make me a player. In fact, it's the opposite, if anyone in this town cared to ask about it or believe that people can change. I thought someone who was new here might reserve judgment, but clearly I was wrong." He was working up a full head of steam, his voice throbbing with emotion, and not just anger. If he had the self-control to stop and think for a second, Zach knew he'd reel it back in, but the truth was, he was just too worked up. Hell, he decided, he'd just keep going for it.

"As for Ben... he's a good kid," he told Maggie, "but he's clearly been through a *lot*, stuff neither of you have ever said to me, so I have no idea what any of it is, but it's clearly there and it's a thing and I've just been trying to be a friend to him, shooting the breeze while we're online. Sorry to have exerted some of my *influence*." He was tempted to storm out right there and then, but he didn't normally do drama, and Maggie's face had drained of color, which concerned him. She looked both shocked and mortified.

"Sorry to dump all that on you," he finished gruffly, "but I've kind of had it up to here with the jokes everyone makes about my dating life, especially when they don't know the first thing about it."

"It's none of my business..." she whispered, still looking mortified. "I shouldn't have said anything—"

"You're right to be concerned about Ben," Zach cut across her wearily. All the rage he'd felt seconds ago was now gone, leaving him feeling flat. "Especially since we've been spending so much time together online. If I were a parent, I'd have the same concerns. In fact, I'd be wondering what the heck a thirty-one-year-old guy is doing, playing RQ with my teenager. I don't normally play it that much," he continued with an attempt at wryness. "I do have a little more of a life than that." It was one thing for a fourteen-year-old boy to grind a game every evening, another for a grown man.

"Well, you do need time to go out on all those dates," Maggie replied with a small, weak attempt at a smile.

Zach let out a huff of tired laughter. "I've actually given up on dating," he told her. "Tinder let me down."

Her cheeks were pinkening again, no doubt at the mention of Tinder. "Oh? How so?"

"You don't swipe right for the love of your life," he explained with a shrug. "It took me a while to realize that."

"Is that what you're looking for?" she asked, sounding both surprised and a little too incredulous. "The love of your life?"

"Isn't everybody?" Zach returned lightly. He wasn't going to get into it more than that; he'd had quite enough of baring his soul for one afternoon. "Anyway. Maybe we should talk about the café."

Maggie stared at him for a moment, and then she surprised him by saying, "Maybe we should start over."

## 9

Clearly she still needed some catchup sessions on how to have a normal conversation. This one with Zach had gotten seriously out of control, and in ways that were still making Maggie's heart somersault and her mind race. He was looking at her bemusedly now, his hair sticking up where he'd raked his hand through it, in agitation at her admittedly spurious accusations. Maggie had thrown that line about influence over Ben at him mainly because she didn't want him thinking she was inquiring about his dating life on her own account. It had been stupid and thoughtless, and she was sorry for it now.

"Start over," Zach repeated neutrally, his eyes narrowing.

"With this conversation." She tried for a jokey tone, although in truth she felt like she was grasping at straws. "How about you come in again and tell me you have a proposition for me? And I respond like a normal, well-adjusted person, and then we take it from there?"

His mouth quirked up at the corner, which, she had to face it, was very sexy. Not that she should be thinking that way at *all*. "Sounds like a plan," he remarked. "So, should I go all the way downstairs, come in the door again? Is this a full retake?"

This was starting to feel a little ridiculous, but Maggie decided to roll with it. "Sure, why not? And I will, too. Let's have a complete re-do." She needed it... in all sorts of ways.

Feeling more than a little silly at perpetuating this charade, she followed Zach downstairs. He gamely went outside while she took her position behind the counter. She could practically hear an imaginary director calling, "Take two..."

Zach opened the door. He stood there for a moment, bracing one arm against the doorframe as he gave her a slow, sexy smile, which he definitely *hadn't* done before. His eyes glinted and the curve of his mouth was knowing and lingering, full of sensual promise. While Maggie watched, he started a slow swagger toward her, making her stomach flip and her knees go weak. Yowzers. When Zach Miller put on the charm, he was... irresistible. And that was more than a little alarming.

"Hey there," he said in a low, meaningful, bedroom type of voice. He was clearly rewriting the script, and she wasn't sure how she felt about that, but she did know her heart was starting to thud hard, and she felt tingly in all sorts of places. "I have a... *proposition* for you, Maggie Parker." He waggled his eyebrows suggestively, a smile still lurking about his mouth as he came to stand before her, his thumbs hooked through his belt loops, that sexy smile still curving his mouth.

It was all so clearly, deliberately over-the-top that suddenly Maggie had to bite her lip to keep from laughing as she folded her arms and attempted to stare him and his gorgeous bedroom eyes down. She was still affected, definitely, but she was also, surprisingly, having fun. "And when you say it like that," she told him with mock sternness, "is it any wonder I jumped to conclusions?"

He burst out laughing, and gratified by his reaction, she smiled. Were they flirting, she wondered, or were they just pretending to flirt? Did it even make a difference? Maybe it was just Zach's MO; it certainly wasn't hers... but she realized she was enjoying it. A lot.

"Okay, for real, now," he told her, dropping the languorous look and the innuendo-laced tone to gaze at her with an endearing earnestness. "The truth is, like I said, I'd love to help you set up the café. I absolutely believe you could do it by yourself, but, full disclosure, you'd actually be doing *me* a favor. My sister doesn't think I can manage so much as an ant farm, and I want to prove her wrong."

Maggie raised her eyebrows. "*That's* what this is about?"

He shrugged, unrepentant but also seeming slightly embarrassed. "In part, yes."

Maggie realized she admired him more for his honesty. And she felt reassured that his offer wasn't made out of pity... or some other, murkier motivation. "So what would this look like?" she asked. "You helping out here?"

"It can look however you want it to look," Zach told her. He glanced around the empty room. "I could start by moving those sofas if you wanted." He nodded toward the furniture stacked against the wall.

"That would be great, actually." Somewhat to her own surprise, Maggie found herself warming to the idea of Zach helping out around the café. She could certainly use another pair of hands, but beyond that, she could do with a friend. She'd asked Zach to be Ben's friend, more or less, but was she willing for him to be her own? Was *he*? "First, though," she said impulsively, knowing there was still more air to be cleared, "let's finish our coffee before it gets cold. And... based on what you said before, I think I should probably explain some things."

Zach's eyebrows rose briefly but then he nodded in acceptance. "Lead the way."

Upstairs, Maggie heated their mugs of coffee in the microwave, more to have something to do and to stall for time. She'd already decided she was going to fill Zach in on some of her and Ben's history, because she'd realized it wasn't fair to leave him in the dark when he was befriending her son. But how much did she really want to share? *Not much* was the obvious and overwhelming answer, but if he was going to be part of her life—and, more importantly, Ben's life—then she knew she needed to level with him, at least a little bit. Even if part of her would prefer stripping naked than sharing her painful past... and Ben's.

Well, not quite, she realized. It had been a long time since she'd been naked in front of anyone.

"So, I told you that my husband died," she stated quietly as she returned to the table with their reheated mugs and sat down across from him.

Zach's expression was somber but alert as he nodded. "Yes, and I know it was in a car accident. That much traveled through the Starr's Fall grapevine. I'm very sorry."

"It was hard," Maggie replied, her gaze downcast. "And obviously very sudden. He was driving home from the train station after a day working in the city—a trucker fell asleep at the wheel and veered into his lane."

"I'm so sorry," Zach said again quietly.

Maggie waved her hand, the gesture not quite dismissive, but almost. "That's not actually what I want to talk about. I mean, yes. It was hard. Very hard, of course. But... it could have been harder." Zach's eyebrows rose in surprise and belatedly Maggie realized how that sounded. But she couldn't explain any of that now, not that she would even know how, because she hadn't been meaning to talk about herself.

"I wanted to tell you about Ben," she stated quietly. "I don't want to violate his privacy, but as his mother, and with you being his—his friend, I think you need to understand just how vulnerable he's been, and why I seem so protective."

"Okay," Zach said after a moment.

Maggie hesitated. Was it her place to tell Zach about what Ben had been through? She knew Ben would never offer the information voluntarily, just as she knew how furious her son would be if he discovered she'd been spilling his secrets, especially when she was still very much reluctant to admit any of her own.

Zach must have sensed her confusion, because he reached out and rested his hand over hers, the feel of his palm on top of hers both reassuring and unsettlingly exciting. "Maggie," he said, "the last thing I want you to do is betray Ben's trust. If he wouldn't want me knowing, you don't have to tell me." He paused, squeezing her hand, which sent tremors of awareness through her. "But I think I could guess some of it, at least, already."

"Oh?" She sounded nettled when she didn't mean to, but how could he possibly know? What assumptions was he making, just because Ben was quiet and shy and liked to game? And even if those assumptions were right, should someone like Zach be making them?

*Someone like Zach.* Clearly, she was making some assumptions, too.

"I just mean," Zach said quietly, "that he's a quiet kid and I'm guessing what with you pulling him out of school, and him being happy to do his work online, he might have been bullied or something at his old school and that must have been pretty tough, for you guys to feel like a big move was needed. Plus the amount he games... well, usually you do that when your real life kind of sucks."

"Oh?" Now she really did sound defensive. "And you would know that how?"

Zach frowned, and belatedly Maggie realized how aggressive she'd sounded.

"Because that's why I started to game," he told her, removing his hand from hers. She found she missed it. "You know," he added, gentling his tone, "you're not the only one who's had a hard time. I mean, I know you've really been through the mill, and I haven't lost a life partner or anything remotely close to that, but, Maggie..." He hesitated and then finished, sounding as if he semi-regretted saying it even before he had. "You don't have the monopoly on struggle."

Maggie drew back, chastened and yet still feeling defensive. "I know that," she said, and Zach cocked an eyebrow, clearly trying to lighten the mood, at least a little.

"Look me in the eye and tell me you haven't assumed that I've had it easy my whole life."

Maggie could feel her cheeks heating. Okay, she *had* assumed exactly that. She just hadn't thought Zach had realized.

"You wouldn't be the first one," he told her, trying to sound light-hearted but not, Maggie thought, quite managing it. "Most everyone in Starr's Fall thinks I'm a lucky, lazy you-know-what. And they don't mind telling me as much."

"So why do they think that?" Maggie asked.

"Because I was, back in high school," Zach replied matter-of-factly. "I was on the baseball team, I had my pick of the girls, I thought I was all that and more. I was obnoxious, probably insufferable, and I'll be the first one to say so." He shrugged. "People change. But sometimes other people don't let you, though, or don't believe that you have."

"And is that the entire population of Starr's Fall?" Maggie asked, caught between sympathy and skepticism.

"Not everyone," Zach allowed, "but more people than I'd like."

"And all the dating?" She decided to be brave—or foolish—enough to ask. "What's that about? Everyone I've talked to thinks you're a... well, you're a player."

"I *was*," Zach emphasized, "in *high school*."

"But you still date a lot."

He straightened, his eyes flashing as Maggie realized how prudish she'd sounded. "I didn't realize that was a crime."

"It's not a crime, obviously," she said quickly. "But it is a... a *thing*, especially in a small town."

Zach looked like he wanted to make a sharp retort, but then he sighed and slumped back into his chair. "Yeah, I guess it is," he said quietly. "And maybe that's part of the struggle." He glanced at her, his eyes glinting with amusement. "Poor little baseball star, people think you're shallow. Boo hoo." He leaned forward, his elbows on the table, his voice dropping an octave, his tone turning intimate. "I know that was what you were thinking."

"It wasn't," Maggie protested, and then gave an embarrassed laugh. "All right, maybe a little. From the outside, you seem like you've lived a charmed life, Zach. But I don't want to be like everybody else."

"I don't want you to be like everybody else, either." He held her gaze for a long moment, the humor dropping from his eyes as they lit with a certain knowledge as well as a sudden heat that made Maggie's stomach flip. She tried to look away and found that she couldn't.

"Zach..." she began, feebly. She didn't know what she was going to say. This wasn't the joking leer of earlier, when they'd had their re-do. He looked utterly serious... and thrillingly intent. And she wasn't ready for him to be either.

He leaned forward a little more, so she breathed in his spicy, woodsy scent and her head started to swim. "What?" he asked quietly, a challenge.

Maggie shook her head. She was not going to spell it out for him.

"I like you, Maggie." Okay, apparently *he* was.

"You barely know me—"

"Yes, and what I know, I like." He made it sound so simple when Maggie already knew it was anything but. "Is that a problem?"

"Yes, it is," she burst out. "For a lot of reasons."

"Okay." Zach leaned back in his chair, seeming to enjoy this little exchange. "Name them."

"*Name* them?" Maggie spluttered. Her mind had, predictably and stupidly, gone blank. And even if it hadn't, she was pretty sure she didn't want to have this conversation.

"Yes." He folded his arms, the knowing smirk on his face not annoying so much as adorable, which in itself was annoying. "Name them."

"I... I don't *need* to name them," Maggie blustered. To this, Zach merely arched an eyebrow. "I mean, it's obvious," she continued, her tongue tumbling over the words. "You're so... and I'm not... and it's just..."

"Care to finish any of those sentences?"

"*Zach.*" Maggie leaned forward, her embarrassed outrage dropping away as she stared at him with more honesty—and vulnerability—than she'd meant to. "Please don't flirt with me. I know it's fun for you, but..." She shook her head, her throat thickening. "I'm just not in that place," she admitted wretchedly. "I'm too... raw. From everything."

Zach leaned forward too, taking her hand in his. Maggie knew she should probably pull away, but she liked the feeling of his strong fingers encircling hers, the warmth of his palm against hers, far too much. "Maggie, I'm not flirting," he said quietly. "I mean, yes, okay, maybe I am, but it's not without... I mean it. This. *Us.* This isn't... this isn't just *fun* for me, although, I have to say, it's that, too."

"What is it, then? This?" Maggie forced out of a throat that felt painfully tight.

"Like I said," Zach replied, his gaze steady on her, his hand still holding hers, "I like you. I'd like to get to know you. Go out on a date, if you feel you might be ready for that, but if not, then just hang out."

"Is that why you want to help with the boardgame café?" She wasn't sure if she meant it as a joke or not; she'd sounded a cross between uncertain and outraged.

"In part, yes." Zach grinned, giving an unrepentant shrug. "Is that a bad thing?"

Maggie stared down at their clasped hands. Her mind was whirling. She hadn't expected so much honesty from him... if that's what it was. "I don't... I don't even know," she admitted in a low voice.

"Look, if you're not ready for romance, that's fine," Zach told her. "I'm not in a rush. We can just be friends." He gave her hand a little squeeze and then released it as he sat back. "No pressure."

She looked up at him, taking in his tousled hair, the bright blue-green eyes, that *jaw*. He was so ridiculously good-looking, and she was... she was a mess. In more ways than one. "Why?" she blurted. "Why me?"

Zach's brows drew together in a frown. Even then he looked sexy. "I told you, I like you—"

"Yes, but *why*?"

"Do you really need to ask that question?" His tone was so gentle that it made Maggie's eyes sting. For the last year, she'd been beating herself up for being a bad mom, a bad wife, a bad *person*. She couldn't keep herself or her son together, and she hid from the world because it felt safer. Yes, she really did need to ask that question.

"Okay, for starters," he began, "because you're beautiful. But not to be shallow, you're also funny and clearly kind, and you did something most people don't do, which is take a huge leap out of your comfort zone, and more importantly, you did it for your son. Plus you can make fun of yourself, an essential quality in my mind, and you don't mind eating gross pizza, although clearly I still have to convince you of the merits of chorizo. But beyond that..." He shrugged. "I guess I don't know you well enough to reel off a laundry list of your amazing qualities. My point is, I'd like to."

Maggie shook her head slowly. She couldn't remember the last time someone had said so many nice things about her. She was blushing again, but in a good way. "I don't know what to say," she whispered.

"Say you'll go out on a date with me. A very low-pressured, no-expectations kind of date, just to see if you might like me back."

Oh, but that was tempting, and yet... she knew she wasn't ready. She shook her head again, with some regret. "That sounds... nice," she offered hesitantly, "but I don't think I'm ready for that just yet." What on earth would the good people of Starr's Fall say, Maggie wondered, if they knew she and Zach, the town's infamous player, had gone on a *date*? What would *Ben* say? They really shouldn't even be having this conversation.

"Okay," Zach replied equably, completely unfazed. "No date. Let's just get to know each other through me helping with the café and see how that goes."

Maggie stared at him. Could it really be that simple? That... *nice*?

"Okay," she agreed at last. "Although now that we've had this conversation, working together might feel weird."

Zach laughed. "We're not in high school, thank God," he told her. "I don't think it will be weird." He pushed himself up from the table. "How about I move those sofas for you now? Come downstairs and tell me where you'd like them to go."

"Okay."

It seemed it really *could* be that simple. That nice. They headed downstairs, and Maggie directed him, discreetly enjoying the sight of Zach's biceps rippling as he hefted the sofas. He'd shrugged off his button-down shirt, so he was dressed only in faded jeans and a fairly fitted t-shirt, and Maggie had to admit it was a *very* nice view.

Within fifteen minutes, he had the sofas scattered around the space, creating inviting little nooks and alcoves with the furniture. "You'll want to buy some smaller tables too, I think," he told her once he'd finished and they were both surveying the welcoming scene. "For two-player games. You could get high ones with bar stools, maybe, but you want to create spaces for different sized groups—the big families or parties, but also the couple or pair of friends who want the space and time to play a long game." He slid her a laughing glance. "You know something like Wingspan can take two or three hours to play, minimum?"

Maggie had never heard of Wingspan. "That's a boardgame?"

"Yeah, it's been popular recently. I've played it online, but I've heard it's better in real person."

"So you're into more games than just RainQuest," she surmised. Perhaps that fact shouldn't surprise her, yet somehow it did.

He shrugged, hooking his thumbs on the pockets of his jeans. "RQ is definitely my favorite, but I like all kinds of games. I've played mostly online, though, which is why I'm so psyched for this place." He smiled wryly, seeming slightly abashed, which Maggie realized made him even more appealing.

"I have to admit, I'm not much of a gamer myself," she confessed with a laugh. Even if Ben loved them. "I didn't grow up playing games, so maybe that makes a difference, but I've got only the basics—Monopoly, Scrabble, that kind of thing."

"I didn't grow up that way, either," Zach told her with a smile. "My parents were too busy with the store, and Jenna was very driven with her schoolwork, and I was too into baseball. I didn't start playing any games until I was eighteen."

"So what made you start?" Maggie realized she was truly curious; she wanted to get to know Zach better, just as he wanted to get to know her. As friends, of course, but still... it was nice.

He hunched his shoulders, digging his hands deeper into the pockets of his jeans. "Remember what I said about having only six months of college?"

She nodded. "Yes..."

"Well, I came home in February of my freshman year because there was something of a crisis at home. My mom got diagnosed with breast cancer, and my dad needed help with the store and stuff. It ended up being a lot more complicated than I expected, and it was kind of lonely, just me and the parents for such a long time. All my friends from high school had gone to UConn, pretty much, so..." He shrugged. "I ended up gaming. It was pretty much my whole social life, for the better part of a year, while my mom did her chemo."

So he could relate to Ben much more than she'd realized, Maggie acknowledged with a prickle of shame. She really should not have judged him the way she had. "And you never went back to college?" she asked.

"Nah. By the time my mom was better, and I could have gone back, everyone was midway through their second year, and it just felt... I don't know... pointless. Everyone had moved on, and I had too, in a different way."

Maggie supposed she could understand that, but it still felt as if he'd missed out, and she wondered if maybe he thought he had, too. Still, she was glad they'd had this conversation. It was a start of getting to know each other, and that felt like a good thing.

"I keep telling Ben I'll learn how to play RainQuest," she told him with a wry smile. "But the few times I've watched him, it's all seemed super complex, to put it mildly. I'm not sure I could ever get the hang of it."

"I bet you could," Zach replied, grinning. "You could join our team. What do you think your character would be?" He scratched his chin, his face screwed up in thought. "I'm feeling like it could be an aasimar," he told her. "Or maybe a shadar-kai."

Maggie gave a little laugh as she shook her head. "A what or a what?"

"An aasimar is a planetouched humanoid with celestial lineage," Zach explained. "And a shadar-kai is an elf who was blessed by the Raven Queen and transformed by the Shadowfell."

Maggie shook her head again, laughter bubbling up. "Sorry, you have completely lost me."

"They're species types from the original Dungeons & Dragons," Zach explained. "A lot of the new roleplaying games use D&D as their template." He gave her a slow, knowing smile that made her toes curl up and her stomach fizz. "Look them up online and tell me if you think I got it right."

"Okay..."

"Aasimar and shadar-kai," Zach confirmed. "I want to know what you think."

"Okay," she said again. She was both curious and bemused; he was acting like he'd made some kind of pronouncement on her personality, and she had no idea what any of it meant.

Just then the door burst open and Ben came in, faltering in his step as he saw the two of them standing together. "Hey, you got the sofas and stuff arranged," he remarked as he looked around. "Cool."

"Yes, we did. Well, Zach did." Maggie took an instinctive step away from him, needing that little bit of distance. "Looks pretty good, doesn't it?"

"Yeah." Ben nodded in approval as he looked around. "Yeah, it does." He turned back to Maggie. "Can we have pizza for dinner?"

"Oh, well, I suppose—"

"And can Zach stay?" He beamed at Zach. "I have this new plug-in I want to show him on RQ. It's *insane*."

"Ben," Maggie began in gentle reproof. "Zach probably has plans—"

"Actually, I don't." He raised his eyebrows, a glint of both humor and challenge in his eyes. "I can stay if you don't mind an extra for pizza." The teasing look on his face made her suspect she knew what he was thinking. *This kind of counts as a date, doesn't it?*

"Sure," she relented. She felt she could hardly say no without a good reason, and the truth was, she realized, she wanted him to stay.

Even if that almost certainly spelled trouble.

## 10

"So when is the café opening?" Laurie asked, her elbows propped on the counter. Maggie had, on impulse, popped into Max's Place to have a quick catchup with her friend and neighbor.

The last two weeks had been so busy she felt as if she was in constant motion. She, Ben, and Zach had been using every spare minute to get the café up and running—Maggie had worked on organizing the kitchen, Ben the games, and Zach had been the maintenance man. He'd suggested built-in shelves to line the walls for the games, and somewhat to Maggie's amazement, had even offered to build them himself.

"You're a man of hidden talents," she'd told him as he'd spent several days setting up a workshop in the café area, sanding and sawing and generally looking very sexy and capable.

"I am indeed," he'd replied with a rakish grin, his eyes glinting with humor. "I've picked up a good bit of woodworking through the store, and I actually found I liked it, more than I expected. It'll be great to have a bigger project."

Zach had been as good as his word and kept things very much friends-only, but Maggie still felt the undercurrents between them, like an electrical wire pulsing with every word either of them said. She watched him discreetly when he was working, and thought he probably noticed. Sometimes, with a thrill of wonder, she saw him doing the same thing, watching *her*. Their gaze often met, slid away, and met again. All of it made her tingle. She hadn't felt this much physical awareness of another person since she'd started dating Matt.

*Matt*. She found herself thinking of him less, missing him less, and that made her feel both relieved and guilty. Surely she should still be mourning her husband, *longing* for him every day, after just a little over a year? It was, she knew, what her mother-in-law expected, *demanded*, after telling Maggie at the funeral, in icy tones, that she was "at least partially responsible" for Matt's death.

"He'd been distracted by things between you," her mother-in-law had insisted. "If you'd been a better wife…"

Maggie had not dignified that with an answer, but it had hurt her deeply. She should have been a better wife, she knew. But something she was starting to understand more and more now that he was gone was… Matt should have been a better husband.

And yet those kinds of thoughts were receding the more time she spent with Zach. Matt had retreated to the background of her mind, her memory, as she focused on the present… as well as the future. Zach, she thought, was both a friend and a welcome distraction… and what an appealing distraction he was.

"Next week," she told Laurie now. "The first Saturday in March is the grand opening. I'm waiving the fee for booking tables for the day and offering a free coffee with every boardgame purchase." Buying the boardgames was one of the ways she hoped the café would eventually turn a profit, along with the coffee and baked goods she'd ordered from The Rolling Pin, as a way to encourage another local business.

Eventually she hoped to offer a full menu of snacks and treats, but at the moment she relied on the Harpers at The Rolling Pin; they'd been friendly and welcoming when she'd worked up the nerve to stop in their bakery, and had seemed thrilled with the prospect of supplying Your Turn Next.

"Wow." Laurie looked admiring. "It sounds like you have everything in hand."

"It doesn't feel that way to me," Maggie confessed. "And it's all taken a lot longer than Ben hoped, but at least it's coming together."

She was fortunate, Maggie knew, that at the moment, thanks to Matt's life insurance and the sale of the house in Greenwich, money was not an issue for them... but she supposed it would be eventually. In the meantime, she wanted to make sure she paid it forward and made Your Turn Next as charitable an enterprise as she could.

"Are you excited?" Laurie asked. "I know what it's like, working so hard and then the big day comes—it's both wonderful and pretty nerve-racking. It almost feels surreal."

"Yes, I can imagine that's exactly how it will feel." Maggie had definitely had a *lot* of nerves already. Most nights she lay in bed, staring at the ceiling as she thought about all she had to do and all the ways this venture could go so horribly wrong. "That's it, exactly," she told Laurie. "And there's still so much to do before the big opening. I still have to learn how to foam milk and master latte art in Hartford this week, for a start!" She gave a grimacing little laugh. She was nervous about leaving Ben to go all the way to Hartford, but she knew she had to get it done if they wanted to offer café service. The food inspection was next week, and she had to have her certification before then, just to be able to offer lattes and espressos.

"You'll be amazing at both," Laurie reassured her. "What's Ben doing for the day while you're in Hartford? He's welcome to come here, if he wants."

"Oh, ah... he's okay, actually," Maggie replied, hedging a little, and blushing too, before she felt compelled to admit, "He and Zach are hanging out. Zach will be working in the café, anyway, finishing the shelves. They've got a whole day planned, apparently, of doing guy stuff and probably playing some RainQuest."

"Do they?" Laurie's eyes gleamed with this insider knowledge. Zach's presence at the café hadn't, Maggie knew, gone at *all* unnoticed by the residents of Starr's Fall. It was hard for it not to be noticed, when he was right there in front of the window, sawing and hammering and working away most days. The shelves were really coming along nicely; Zach had been modest about his woodworking skills. He'd even whittled figures to decorate each joint of the shelves, including several characters from RainQuest that even Maggie had been able to recognize.

She hoped Ben's presence kept the gossip mill from churning *too* relentlessly about Zach's presence at the café, because she knew she wasn't ready for people to start speculating about a relationship between her and Zach. Not that they even would; in fact, in some ways, a greater worry was that such a prospect was so ludicrous it wouldn't even cross people's minds.

"So, is anything going on between you and Zach?" Laurie asked, putting paid to the idea that people *weren't* thinking about it, which filled Maggie with equal parts alarm and, damningly, pleasure. "Because, I have to say, he's certainly spending a lot of time at your place."

"He's just helping out at the café," Maggie replied quickly. "You know he's into games. And I get the idea that he's a little frustrated by what's happening at the general store." She hoped she wasn't being disloyal by sharing that with Laurie; although Zach didn't talk about it much, she could feel the frustration with his sister rolling off him in waves whenever the subject of the store came up. He'd usually quickly change the subject and Maggie let him, because heaven knew she wasn't one for confrontation, but she felt it from him all the same.

"He is?" Laurie exclaimed, frowning. "I didn't realize that. I've talked to Jenna about the store, but I have to say, I don't know Zach in the same way. He always seems so laid-back, everyone kind of assumes he just rolls with whatever. And I suppose you know about his reputation with the ladies."

"I know he's dated a lot," Maggie replied, unable to keep from sounding a little prim as she squirmed inwardly at the very mention of Zach's romantic life. "But Zach and I don't talk about that kind of stuff." At least, not since that day in the café when he'd mentioned that you didn't swipe right for the love of your life, a line that had stubbornly and inconveniently stuck in Maggie's head. "And I think he does roll with whatever," she added, realizing how true it was. Zach was practically the *definition* of laid-back... but that attitude, Maggie thought, took a certain kind of strength. "But even if he does," she finished slowly, "that doesn't mean things don't bother him."

Laurie's smile turned impish. "Sounds like you've gotten to know him pretty well there," she remarked.

"Not like that," Maggie said quickly, and then blushed. "I mean... we're just friends. Obviously."

Laurie raised her eyebrows, clearly enjoying their exchange. "Obviously?"

"I'm ten years older than him," Maggie explained a little stiffly. "It would be kind of ridiculous if something *were* going on." Even if she thought about just that more than she wanted to admit or was comfortable with herself.

"Not that ridiculous," Laurie protested, frowning. "I mean, Joshua is seven years older than me, and I don't even think about it. Age is just a number."

"Still..." Maggie protested. "It's different when it's the woman that's older."

"Now that's just sexist," Laurie replied, wagging her finger at Maggie. "There's no reason why a woman can't date a younger man. No reason at all."

*And be called a cougar?* Maggie thought, shuddering inwardly at the thought. She really hoped the good people of Starr's Fall weren't saying such things about her. "Well, nothing is going on," she replied firmly, "so the point is moot. And in any case, I'm not ready to date yet."

Laurie's laughing expression immediately dropped. "Of course not," she murmured. "I understand. I'm sorry. I shouldn't have teased you."

"No, no, it's fine." Talking about bereavement always felt like pouring cold water over a conversation, Maggie acknowledged with an inward sigh. "I mean, I might think about dating one day. It's just there's a lot to focus on right now."

"Of course. Although..." Laurie was back to looking playful. "Sometimes you don't choose to fall in love. It chooses you."

*Love!* Now that was something she wasn't remotely ready to think about, and yet maybe, she realized with a lurch, Zach was, with somebody. *You don't swipe right for the love of your life* suggested as much, surely. Admittedly, he'd said it in such an offhand way, but Maggie had still sensed a deeper emotion beneath the words. But if Mr. Extra Spicy was looking for

Miss Right... she surely could not be that woman. Not with her history, her emotional baggage, and yes, her age.

"I really don't think that's what's going on," she told Laurie, shaken by the nature of her own thoughts. "But I am very grateful for his help." She glanced around the cute little store; Laurie had set it up like a living room, with a cozy armchair, bookshelves to house the merchandise, and a coffee maker bubbling away. "I was thinking about finally taking your advice and adopting a cat from the Humane Society," she told Laurie. "I don't think we can manage a dog, and Ben has always wanted a cat, anyway. I wanted to ask you about it."

"Oh, wonderful! Cats are great pets. I've got some leaflets here, to take you through the process of adoption."

"Great." Adopting a cat was the next step in her and Ben's resettlement project, in terms of making Starr's Fall their home. Maggie wasn't quite ready for the responsibility of a dog, with walks and so forth, but she liked the idea of a purring cat curling up in a windowsill of the café, and she thought she could manage to feed and change its litter box, at least. Ben had promised to help.

"So you must be starting to feel settled," Laurie told her as she handed her the leaflet. "If you're thinking of getting a cat."

"We're getting there, certainly." She and Ben had been in Starr's Fall a month already, and it had flown by. Maggie had continued attending Pilates—with the often liquid lunch afterward—and she'd come to know Annie, Zoe, Liz, and Elaine a lot better and felt she could call them friends. She'd even gone over to Annie's for dinner and met her mother Barb, who was lovely but clearly declining in health as she struggled with the later stages of Parkinson's.

It had been heartbreaking to witness, but Maggie was glad she'd been able to have a conversation with Annie, commiserating about elderly parents and offering her support. She'd also stopped into The Rolling Pin on several occasions both to discuss including their business at the café and just for bagels. She'd enjoyed getting to know Lizzy and Michael Harper and their two children. She'd half-hoped that their fourteen-year-old daughter Bella might be a friend for Ben as she seemed to be interested in boardgames, but Ben had been adamant that he wasn't interested in having some kind of high school social life, and Maggie knew, after everything that had happened, she couldn't force it. It would come, she hoped, in time, with healing.

And then there was Zach. Zach, Maggie acknowledged, had been a much bigger part of her life than was either comfortable or wise... and yet, she'd come to depend on him. The other day he hadn't stopped by the café, and she'd felt down and out of sorts all afternoon, without realizing why until Ben had remarked upon his absence. He was easy company, often laughing and light, always willing to pitch in and do whatever was needed, whether it was schlepping boxes or talking RQ with Ben. He'd stayed for dinner more than once after that first pizza, when Ben had absolutely monopolized his time, which Maggie hadn't minded because she and Zach had had enough deep conversation already that day.

Two weeks on, they still hadn't talked about romance or lack thereof, which was *fine*, because she really was enjoying them just being friends. *And yet...* Zach's *I like you* had opened up a Pandora's box of unwieldy emotions and Maggie was struggling to put the lid back on it. Just as she'd told Laurie, she really wasn't ready for romance.

But maybe, Maggie acknowledged, she *wanted* to be... even if dating someone like Zach still didn't make sense, for all the same reasons she hadn't been able to articulate to him when he'd asked. They were still there—her age, her emotional baggage, Zach's history, Ben...

Way too much to think about. To deal with.

"It takes a while to feel settled," Laurie remarked sagely, drawing Maggie out of her uncomfortable thoughts. "To tell you the truth, I lived in Trenton for six years and I never felt settled there."

"That's how I was in Greenwich," Maggie replied, only semi-jokingly. "And I lived there for *twelve* years." She grimaced, acknowledging the semi-waste of those years... and yet they'd been the majority of her adult life, as well as her marriage. How depressing was that, to think of them as a waste? And they hadn't been, not entirely anyway...

"What didn't you like about Greenwich?" Laurie asked.

Maggie frowned, unsure how to articulate the complicated tangle of her thoughts on that subject. What *hadn't* she liked about her life? To outsiders, it had certainly seemed pretty charmed. Matt had thought it was, and with good reason, really—what had there been to complain about, after all? She'd had a big, beautiful house, a handsome, accomplished husband, a wonderful son, no worries about money, no need to work, a generous handful of supposedly like-minded friends...

And yet it was many of those so-called blessings that had made her start, guiltily, to resent her life behind the glowing, golden bars of what had felt, in time, like a gilded prison. And then there had been Matt... Matt, reveling in their new, blingy life, insisting she get on board in a thousand subtle and not-so-subtle ways that had made her feel farther from him than ever...

No. She didn't want to think like that. She couldn't let herself, because it opened the floodgates to too much guilt and regret. And she could hardly explain how her privileged life had felt like a prison to Laurie, whom she knew already from their conversations had had a difficult childhood in foster care and then the challenge of trying to make it on her own as an adult.

"It just felt empty," she finally said, feeling wretched for admitting that much. "Kind of... soulless." Which was a rather scathing indictment not just about her life, but her marriage. She looked away, wishing she hadn't said so much, or even anything at all.

"It's hard when life disappoints us," Laurie said after a moment, her tone quiet and a little sad. She had a look on her face that made Maggie think she was thinking of something in particular, maybe even something recent, rather than the sorrows of her childhood.

"Has life disappointed you recently?" she asked, and then worried the question was far too intrusive. She hardly wanted Laurie asking it back! "Sorry, that's not something I should ask," she added hurriedly.

"No, it's okay." Laurie hesitated, her gaze on the jar of dog treats she'd been restocking. "Yes," she finally answered. "Life has, actually. I... I moved to Starr's Fall to look for my birth mom. I mean, I wanted to open this place, of course, but the reason I chose Starr's Fall was because my biological mother put it on my birth certificate as where she was from. And I mean, I knew she'd probably moved on a long time ago, and I wasn't going to bump her into the street or anything, but... I was hoping for some *clues*, at least, and..." She grimaced good-naturedly. "In the back of my mind, let's be real, I was imagining some rose-tinted reunion, with hugs and tears and a selfie for social media." She laughed, or tried to, before subsiding into silence.

"And that didn't happen," Maggie guessed quietly, her heart aching for Laurie.

"Well, yes and no," Laurie admitted on a sigh. "I did find out who she was. And she *did* end up contacting me after I'd messaged her online, which thrilled me at first... but it was only to demand I never attempt to contact her again. She even offered me money to stay away from her forever. Talk about serious." Laurie tried for a smile, but Maggie could see from her pain-shadowed eyes and the tremble of her lips how much it still hurt. "So, to be honest, all that kind of sucked," she finished flatly.

"I'm so sorry." Maggie didn't know what else she could say. "That *totally* sucks," she said with feeling, and Laurie let out a huff of laughter.

"Yeah. Totally. But..." She hesitated, glancing uncertainly at Maggie before continuing. "I don't know exactly where you're coming from. I mean, losing your husband... it's got to be so hard. But maybe part of that being hard is that it's complicated?" She stopped, a question in her eyes before continuing. "Sorry if I'm way out of line, but if that is the case... well, I want to say I get it. Sort of, anyway. My relationship with my mother —or lack of it—might seem like an open-and-shut case, but it's never that simple, is it? The truth is, if she emailed me tomorrow, I'd go see her again, in a *second*. I'd try for that relationship, even if everyone was telling me it wasn't worth it, protect yourself, blah, blah, blah. Because when it comes down to it... she's my *mom*. And the important people in your life... well, sometimes it's all kind of tangled up, isn't it? As much as you love them, or *want* to love them... it can be hard." She trailed off, looking embarrassed. "Sorry. I was probably projecting a lot of emotional baggage onto you that you absolutely don't have. It's just... so many people see it as open-and-shut, you know? Even Joshua. Like, 'Your mom abandoned you? Well, good riddance.' And... that's not how I feel, even if sometimes I wish it was." She let out a trembling laugh as she brushed at her eyes. "Sorry. I've really offloaded onto you."

"No, don't be sorry. I don't mind." Maggie was grateful for Laurie's honesty, and unsettled by her perceptiveness at just how complicated everything had been.

She felt as if Laurie had looked right through her, straight into her soul, dark and guilt-ridden place that that was. Laurie had managed to articulate *exactly* how Maggie was feeling... the confusing mix of grief and guilt, the sweep of devastating loss and the faintest flicker of treacherous relief that she could hardly bear to think about. She hadn't said as much about any of it to anyone, and it was both gratifying and horrifying that Laurie, who barely knew her, had guessed. Was she that transparent? How awful... and yet how weirdly freeing.

"I..." she began, and then, shaking her head, found she couldn't continue.

"Sorry, I think I've probably said too much." Laurie bit her lip, apologetic. "I don't think sometimes—"

"No, no." Maggie took a deep breath. "You're right. It *was* complicated. And something that's been so hard to admit, even to myself, is that..." She paused, and then made herself continue. "Matt and I weren't doing all that well as a couple before he died. We weren't talking divorce or anything like that, and I don't think we ever would have, but... we'd gone in really different directions over the last few years, and that was something we were just both coming to realize when he died." She paused, picturing the way Matt looked at her, his eyes narrowed, his lips pursed, like she wasn't quite coming up to scratch. The suffocating sense of pressure she'd felt, to be what he wanted her to be, all the while kicking against it in passive-aggressive ways. It had been a miserable and even toxic combination.

"He'd got a big promotion a couple of years back," she explained to Laurie, "and he was all about the ambition, the house, the car, the country club, and I... I wasn't. I mean, I tried to be, for his sake, but I never really managed it." And his disappointment had felt like a weight she staggered under. When he'd died, she hadn't known how much longer she could have kept going, *not* being the kind of wife he wanted. But she wasn't ready to admit all that to Laurie right now.

"I think all relationships are complicated," Laurie told her with a wry smile, and then her eyes lit up as she nodded toward the door. "Speaking of..." she murmured before calling out gaily, "Henrietta! It's so nice to see you!"

An elderly woman, dressed immaculately in an admittedly slightly motheaten tweed skirt and jacket, a silk blouse knotted in a bow at her throat, was coming gingerly into the pet store with the help of a cane.

Laurie hurried to open the door for her. "Maggie, have you met Miss Henrietta Starr yet? Resident matriarch of Starr's Fall."

"No, I haven't had the pleasure yet." Maggie gave the older woman a friendly smile and was subjected to a beady stare back.

"You've moved here with your son?" she surmised. "I heard you were a widow."

Startled, Maggie nodded. "Yes. I was widowed a little over a year ago."

"Well, I'm sorry for your loss," Henrietta replied as she moved into the store and sat down in the armchair like a queen sitting upon her throne. "Having never been married, I cannot imagine what it feels like to be a widow." She sniffed. "But grief is grief, and I wouldn't wish it on anyone, even as it comes to all of us eventually." She gave a short sigh, having finished making this pronouncement. "How are you finding Starr's Fall?"

"Good, so far," Maggie replied cautiously. She had the feeling of needing to pass muster with the town's matriarch, and Henrietta Starr looked like she wasn't easily impressed. "But it's been an adjustment. Have you lived here all your life?"

"Save for two unfortunate years in New York City," Henrietta replied. Her gaze moved to Laurie, whom Maggie saw smile at her in sympathy. Clearly there was a story there that Laurie knew, but she wasn't about to ask now. "And this business of yours?" Henrietta barked, her beady gaze moving back to Maggie. "A boardgame café? I've never heard of such a thing." She gave another little sniff. "But I am partial to a game of Scrabble, as long as I'm playing someone who is actually competent at the game."

"We'll have Scrabble," Maggie promised her. "As for proficient players..." She smiled ruefully. "I'm sure we can find someone who is up to speed."

"We'll see." Henrietta sounded doubtful. She turned back to Laurie. "Now, onto important business," she declared. "Is there any coffee?"

Laughing, Laurie assured her there was and went to get a cup. As she left, Henrietta turned to Maggie once more.

"Don't worry, my dear," she said gently. "It will get better. Time doesn't heal all wounds, but it does make a difference." She gave her a kindly smile, her face crinkling even more into a mass of wrinkles, her blue eyes twinkling, and gratified and touched, Maggie smiled back. She'd been grateful for her conversation with Laurie, and she realized she was also grateful for meeting the imposing Henrietta Starr. She felt a lightness to her spirit, for having shared with Laurie something of the difficulties she'd had in her marriage. And while she hadn't shared every difficult and painful thing she'd experienced, she'd admitted something of the truth, and that was, surprisingly, a good feeling.

Even better was the feeling, the belief, that she'd made a true friend... maybe even two.

## 11

After six weeks in Starr's Fall, a day in Hartford felt like going to the big city. Maggie had left Ben that morning with heartfelt promises from him to do his schoolwork; Zach was coming over after breakfast to crack the whip and also work on finishing the bookshelves. The café was set to open in just eight days, which felt absolutely crazy. Maggie didn't think they were remotely ready, but Zach had argued that their supposedly "grand opening" could still be something of a soft launch, with limited kitchen offerings, and assured her that she didn't need to have absolutely every last duck in order to open her doors. Sometimes, he'd said, it was better just to begin. There was, Maggie had decided, wisdom in that. She hoped.

In fact, there had been a lot of beginnings in her life lately—the café, her friendship with Zach, Pilates, making an appointment at the Humane Society to get a cat. It all helped her to feel settled, just as Laurie had asked if she was, but the truth was no matter how many strides she took, Maggie still felt jumpy inside. Telling Laurie about her complicated feelings toward Matt's death had been both a relief and a terror, and a week on she still found she couldn't quite look her new friend in the eye; she wasn't used to or comfortable with having been so vulnerable or having admitted so much.

And now, with all that behind her, she was heading to Hartford for her eight-hour-long course in how to be a barista. It would be the longest Maggie had been away from Ben since he'd got out of the hospital, nearly a year ago. A shudder went through her as she remembered that dark, dark time—the endless days in the halogen glare of a hospital room, the persistent beep of the monitor as she'd sat by his bedside while he'd pretended to sleep, followed by her own sleepless and gritty-eyed nights of despair, and then, when he'd been discharged, the sudden clutches of panic when she wasn't sure where Ben was in the house, or what new terrible thing might have happened.

Heaven help them both, Maggie thought as she gripped the steering wheel so tightly that her knuckles ached, but she could *not* go back there again... and neither could Ben. She really hoped Zach was up to the challenge of watching her son today. She hadn't sold it to him as babysitting, for Ben's sake, but now she wondered if she should have been a little more forthcoming about her son's history. But wasn't that Ben's to tell?

It was so hard, as a parent, to know what the right thing to do was, Maggie reflected despondently. If she *knew* the right thing, she'd do it, absolutely. But a thousand questions and doubts plagued her daily— should she let Ben game or force him to find different interests? Should she tell people how he could still be considered at risk or let him start over with a clean slate, just as she was trying to do? Should she be protective because it might save his life, or let him make his own mistakes, knowing that was part of growing up?

And now she didn't even have Matt to back her up and offer a different perspective—not, she reflected, that he'd done that all that often, especially in the last few years. He'd become so busy with work, and in her darkest heart of hearts Maggie had sometimes felt that Matt had found Ben something of a disappointing mystery. He'd never said as much, but even so, Maggie had felt his confusion and even disapproval that Ben wasn't the kind of kid who played football and flirted with girls and cared about the stock market, the way he had hoped for. The way he himself had been. His mother had been even more vocal in her disappointment, which was partly why Maggie didn't mind not pursuing that particular relationship.

But could she really blame either of them, when she too had had a secret, shameful version of a dream child too—a son who had friends, and hobbies, and could look people in the eye when he spoke to them? A son who hadn't been bullied, sometimes relentlessly, since middle school, and who didn't cause her to lie awake wondering if she'd done something wrong, if she was doing it at that moment.

As parents, they had to let go of their dream children—she knew that, absolutely—but sometimes it could feel so very hard. Moving to Starr's Fall had been about letting Ben be who he needed to be, rather than the person she or anyone else thought he should be, but that didn't mean letting it happen was easy.

Zach, however, was making it easier...

Not that she let herself think that way too often. Still, over the last few weeks she had become unsettlingly used to having Zach around. More nights than not, he stayed for dinner, and while he and Ben spent a good amount of time playing RainQuest, Zach still made sure to chat to her, too. He asked her about the business, but also about her life, and he'd shared some of his. She'd admitted she was coming to enjoy the business side of things, and he confessed how much he liked woodworking. He'd even made Ben a little carving of a djinn, his profile on the game, which Ben kept by the computer.

"I hope," Zach had told her in a low, laughing voice when she'd walked him downstairs to the door last night, "that you don't think I game this much in real life."

She'd raised her eyebrows, lips pursed. "Is this not real life?"

He'd cocked his head, his blue-green gaze sweeping lazily over her. "Maybe it is," he replied slowly, in a way that made awareness and yearning flare through her. If only, she'd thought suddenly and fiercely, this was real life. Her and Zach...

But she couldn't let herself think like that, and so she'd kept it more about Ben. "You've been a good friend to Ben," she told him, "and for that I'm very, very thankful. I hope you know that."

"I do." He'd hesitated then, and Maggie had tensed, both afraid and hopeful that he was going to say something else. Something about her. About *them*. "I hope you feel," he'd finally said, carefully, "that I'm a good friend to you, as well."

It had been enough to make her stomach flip and everything inside her tingle. Part of her had longed to take a step toward him, tilt her head up to his, see his eyes flare with the awareness that was zinging through her... But she knew she didn't possess the courage to do that, and then a sudden suspicion had gripped her that maybe he was friend-zoning her, and considering the scenarios that had been playing through her mind, the thought was fairly horrifying.

"I... do," she'd finally stammered, and he'd laughed softly.

"Why do you look terrified?" He'd reached up and brushed a tendril of hair away from her face, letting his fingers skim her cheek. Maggie had had to bite her lip to keep from shuddering in response as the tips of his fingers brushed her cheekbone. That didn't feel like a friend-zone kind of thing, did it? "When did you get that silver streak in your hair?" he'd asked softly.

"A... a few months ago." When Ben had been admitted to the hospital; it had happened almost overnight. But she wasn't thinking about that now, not when his fingers were still lingering on her cheek, and she had a frighteningly strong impulse to step closer to him, into the shelter of his arms.

"I like it," he told her as he let his hand fall away from her face. "It's unique."

Maggie had opened her mouth to say it made her look old, thought better of it, and so had just smiled and shaken her head. Zach had stepped back as he'd given her a little wave. "Bye, Maggie. See you tomorrow."

Stupidly, she'd felt almost crushingly disappointed. What had she been expecting—some heartfelt declaration? A *kiss*?

Well... basically, yes.

And the fact that it hadn't happened had to be a good thing, Maggie told herself as she turned off the highway and headed for Cup of Joe, the coffee shop in downtown Hartford that offered barista courses. She felt a flutter of nerves as she thought about walking into a place where she knew no one and trying to learn. She'd been doing a lot of that lately, and it was getting a little easier, but it still felt hard.

Taking a deep breath, Maggie checked her phone—no messages from

Ben or Zach, which hopefully was a good thing—and then got out of
the car.

\* \* \*

"Going to see Maggie Parker again?"

Jenna swiveled around in her chair in front of her laptop as she raised
her eyebrows expectantly.

Zach shrugged on his jacket and then reached for his travel mug of
coffee. It was eight o'clock on a dark, frigid morning in late February, when
everything was gray sky and slush and no sign of spring. He wasn't in the
mood for another one of Jenna's piqued innuendoes.

"Ben Parker, actually," he told her. "Maggie is in Hartford, doing some
kind of barista course."

Jenna folded her arms. "You've been spending a lot of time over there."

Zach knew this was the perfect opportunity to say something pointed
about how that was because Maggie actually appreciated his opinion and
expertise, unlike his own flesh and blood, but he wasn't in the mood to
annoy his sister or have her annoy him. He felt too optimistic for that.

"Yep," he said instead, and started hunting for his truck keys.

"Yep?" Jenna repeated. "That's all you have to say?"

"Yep," Zach said again, even though he knew it would annoy her.
Maybe *because* it would.

Jenna sighed and slumped back in her seat, staring at her computer
screen for a few seconds. "And it isn't because of me?" she asked finally.

Now that was unexpected. Jenna was usually so wound up and defensive that Zach didn't even bother with the it's-actually-you vibe, and truth
be told, it was probably also him. "If you're asking if I'm disappointed
about how you've handled the decision making," he told her, making sure
to keep his voice mild, "then yeah. It is partly that. I have ideas. I would
like to see them implemented."

He paused, feeling a sudden twist of sympathy for his sister. He was so
frustrated with her so often that it felt weird and a little uncomfortable to
attempt to view things from her perspective and acknowledge how hard
she was working with very little reward. "I know I probably seem like I

don't really care about much," he said carefully, "because I guess it's something of a defense mechanism with me. But why are you so resistant, Jenna? Because I think even you can admit that we're not creating a time capsule here. Technology has forced businesses to move fast, to adapt or go bust. The store could be so much more than it is."

Jenna didn't answer for a long moment. Her gaze was still fixed on the computer screen, her body slumped in the chair, her long auburn hair falling down her back in its usual single braid.

"Yeah," she finally admitted on a long, world-weary sigh. "I know."

It didn't seem like much, and yet it was so much more than she'd ever admitted to him before.

"And?" Zach pressed after a moment, when it didn't seem as if his sister was going to say anything else. "If you agree with what I'm saying..."

"I just don't want to become something we're not," Jenna explained, a spark of fire entering her eyes. "I'm not going to start wearing fancy country gear and stocking two-hundred-dollar candles and acting like they're a bargain."

"That's not what I—"

"We're not Litchfield people," she cut across him, her tone fierce, too fierce for what they were talking about. "This isn't a Litchfield store."

"You know," Zach half-joked, "it's not like Litchfield is *that* nice."

She let out a huff of laughter that held no real humor in it. "You know what I mean."

*Did* he? Yes, Zach supposed, Litchfield was more upmarket than Starr's Fall, but what did Jenna have against a little class? Unless there was something else going on, which, judging by the ferocity of tone, the strength of her resistance, it seemed like there probably was. He glanced at the clock above the stove, wishing he had more time to hash this—whatever *this* was—out with his sister, but he'd promised Maggie he'd be with Ben by eight, and it was already five minutes past. He didn't want to be any later; she'd been worried already about leaving Ben alone even for a short time.

"I've got to go," he told Jenna. "But we'll talk about this later, okay?"

She shrugged as she straightened and then turned back to her laptop and started clicking on the mouse again. "Yeah, okay."

Suppressing a sigh, Zach scooped up his truck keys and headed out the door.

The sky was just starting to lighten to gray as he pulled up in front of Your Turn Next. The café was really starting to take shape, he reflected, which was a good thing, considering it was meant to open next week and there was still a ton of stuff to do. Maggie had ordered a sign, based on Ben's logo, but it hadn't been delivered yet. Once it was up, Zach thought, maybe it would start to feel more real.

As it was, today's job was to finish the built-in bookshelves, something he really was enjoying. Maybe he'd ask Ben to help him; he didn't want him upstairs on his own all day, staring at a computer for hours on end. In truth, Zach thought Ben would benefit from going to the local high school. It was obvious to him that he was lonely, and playing RainQuest night after night was not the same thing as a social life. He hadn't said anything about it to either Ben or Maggie, though, because it didn't feel like his place, and Maggie, he'd already sensed, could be pretty touchy when it came to her son.

Zach let himself into the café, breathing in the scents of cut wood and fresh paint. It really was looking good—his soon-to-be-finished book-shelves lined both walls from floor to ceiling, and in the corner by the window, a leather loveseat and armchair made an L-shape around a coffee table. A three-seater took up the main part of the café floor, with a long, low table in front, and then two armchairs with a little table in between on the other side.

Maggie had taken his advice about the smaller tables, and there were three high tables for two with barstools in the back, by the kitchen area. The chalkboard menu was also up, above the counter, with a glass display case beneath, for the baked goods they were hoping to offer eventually, sourced from The Rolling Pin, although Maggie hoped to offer some of their own food items as soon as they got the proper food certification. Once the shelves were finished and the boardgames were in, it was going to look really good, Zach thought with a flush of pride that he tried to temper. He'd been part of this, yes, but it was Maggie's project, Maggie and Ben's. Maybe he needed to remember that a little more.

He headed upstairs, knocking once on the door before he poked his head in. "Hello? Ben?"

There was no response, and Zach felt a tiny flicker of fear. It was only eight fifteen, but he'd told Maggie he would be here sooner. What if something happened on his watch because he hadn't shown up on time?

"Ben?" he called again and stepped into the living area. A small gust of relief escaped him when he saw the teenager in front of the desktop in the kitchen. "Hey," he called, and Ben stiffened, then quickly clicked off whatever he'd been looking at.

Uh-oh. Zach had been a teenaged boy once. Quickly clicking off anything was usually a sign someone was up to no good.

"That didn't look like schoolwork," he remarked lightly as he came into the kitchen. "Have you had breakfast?"

Ben shook his head, his gaze on the floor, his hands lost in the ragged sleeves of his sweatshirt. He still hadn't said so much as a word, Zach realized as he came to stand in front of him.

"Is everything okay?" he asked gently. Still no response. "Ben?"

"Yeah. Fine," he mumbled, his voice so low Zach struggled to hear him.

It clearly *wasn't* fine, but Zach wasn't sure what to do to get him to open up. He decided for laidback honesty, and cocking his head toward the computer, he asked, "Something going down on RQ?"

"No," Ben replied, his chin tucked toward his chest.

Zach had already figured it wasn't that. "Something else, then? Because, man, you're looking like your dog died and I know you don't have a dog, so... nothing happened to your future cat, did it?"

"We haven't even picked out one yet," Ben replied. He folded his arms, hugging them around his middle.

"Okay, then." Zach paused, trying to figure out what to say next. "I feel like this has something to do with what you saw on the computer," he said at last. "Am I right?" Ben shrugged. "Because whatever is out there online, it doesn't need to affect you. Cyberspace isn't a great place to occupy your head, you know?"

Ben glanced up at that, his mouth twisting. "Dude, nobody calls it cyberspace anymore."

"My bad. I'm getting old. Seriously, though." Zach stooped so he could look Ben in the eye. "Tell me honestly," he said quietly. "What's up?"

Ben glanced at him before quickly looking down again as he picked the ragged cuff of his sweatshirt. "Just stupid stuff," he finally muttered.

"Well, I figured that out already," Zach replied as he straightened. "Because if it's online, it *has* to be stupid. But stupid stuff can still bother you." He thought of all the careless little jokes and remarks that just about everyone in Starr's Fall made about him. They'd all been pretty stupid, but they'd still hurt. "Trust me," he told Ben, "I know how that goes."

"You do?" Ben glanced up again, brushing his bangs from his eyes. "Like, how?"

Zach shrugged. "People in a small town, or any small community, can think they know who you are, what kind of person you are, and then they keep trying to fit you in that box no matter how much you want to break out of it, and that's if you were even in it in the first place, the way they thought you were." Which all sounded pretty vague. "Basically," he told Ben, "people in Starr's Fall can't always get on board with people being different. So, to quote a famous song, haters gonna hate. You can't let it worry you." He paused, before adding, because he felt Ben needed to hear it, "But it can still hurt."

"Yeah." Ben was entirely focused on a loose thread on the cuff of his sweatshirt, his head lowered as he tugged on it. "These kids in my old high school," he said in a low voice. "They're still harshing on me and I don't even go there anymore. How stupid is that?"

"Very stupid," Zach replied swiftly. "And incredibly immature. And you know what else? Boring. I mean, are they such saddos that they can't think of anything better to do? Haven't they moved on in life? Jeez." He shook his head.

"Yeah." Ben didn't sound convinced, and Zach didn't blame him. He already hated these bullies, and he didn't even know what they'd done. "It's just stupid stuff," Ben said after a moment, trying for an offhand tone and not quite pulling it off. "On this online group chat for my grade. I'm still on the chat even though I left after Christmas."

"Maybe you should get off the chat," Zach suggested. "Doesn't sound like it's adding anything great to your life."

"No..." Ben looked up, a bleakness in his eyes that tore at Zach's heart. "I just wanted to know if they were saying anything about me because sometimes it's worse not knowing, you know? Like what you imagine. And for a long time they weren't saying anything about me, and then someone went and made a stupid *meme*."

"A meme about you?" Zach asked quietly.

Ben nodded miserably. "It's not even funny. It's just my class photo with a photoshopped gaming controller in my hand and this line underneath about the definition of a geek. Like, that's so *basic*."

Zach almost smiled at that. Ben sounded so scathing. "Well, let's be real," he said. "These people sound pretty basic to me."

Zach was rewarded with a very small smile. "Yeah," Ben said, with feeling. "They totally are."

"You could just as easily do a meme of *their* photo, with the word basic underneath," he joked. "Not that I'm advising that, of course. My motto is ignore, ignore, ignore. But... it's good to remember what people are like, and how unimportant their opinions can be."

"Yeah," Ben said after a moment. He didn't sound entirely convinced, but maybe a little more than before. A silence settled on them, and Zach let it rest for a few moments and then he straightened. "Look, why don't you help me with the bookshelves? I really want to get them finished off before your mom comes home. Let's work on them this morning and then go get a burger at The Starr Light. Then, if you want, you can finish your schoolwork this afternoon."

The corner of Ben's mouth quirked up. "If I want? Is that, like, negotiable?"

"Well." Zach smiled easily. "It can be."

## 12

Maggie had had the most amazing day. Admittedly, she'd been hyperventilating with nerves when she'd walked into Cup of Joe, and that had only gotten worse when she'd seen the other attendees—they were all about two decades younger than her, and impossibly hip and cool. She'd felt middle-aged and boring before she'd even walked in the door.

And yet... once the course had started, and she'd learned how to make espresso and foam milk and do latte art, she'd started to both relax and energize. It had been so long since she'd stretched her brain in any significant way, and the creative element reminded her that she used to love art, about a million years ago.

Her first job out of college had been an elementary school art teacher, part-time and poorly paid, but she'd loved it. She'd had to stop when school budget cuts had eliminated the position, and she'd ended up drifting into soulless marketing work for a big corporation, which was how she'd met Matt. But she'd always looked back fondly on those two years getting messy with paint and glue. She was glad to re-spark that part of herself, and so unexpectedly.

By seven o'clock that evening, when she was pulling into Starr's Fall, she was still buzzing from the day, although the creep of anxiety about her son had taken the edge off her excitement, if only slightly. She hadn't left him for this long—fourteen hours—since before Matt's death. She'd had a brief text from Zach telling her all was well, and typically nothing from Ben, but she felt that flicker of fear all the same. She wondered if it would ever go away. Some things, she supposed, scarred you for life, and that's just how it was. You had to learn to live with the scars, not try to erase them.

As she stepped out of the car, the cold air felt like a slap in the face. It was almost March, but the only sign of spring was a few chilled-looking crocuses next to the sidewalk, their bright heads huddled together as if that would keep them warm.

The café was dark, but Maggie could see lights on upstairs, and her heart lightened. She realized just how much she was looking forward to seeing Ben—and Zach. As she came up the stairs to the apartment above, she heard voices—Ben and Zach, talking animatedly about something, using a lot of slang she didn't understand.

"*Bruh*," her son said, with the emphasis of complete conviction. "That one is *such* a bullet sponge. But I was totally cheesing and it became, like, *the* most epic boss rush."

"Awesome," came Zach's reply, a lazy murmur that made Maggie want to shiver. He had a very nice voice.

"Hey, I'm home," she sang out as she opened the door, sounding like something out of an episode of *Leave it to Beaver*. "How was your day, guys?"

"How was yours?" Zach countered with a smile. He was standing by the sink, a dishrag draped over one shoulder. Ben was at the table, spreading tomato sauce over a pizza base. The scene was so unexpectedly homey that for a second Maggie just wanted to stand there and savor it—the warm lighting, the music, some kind of mellow jazz, on the speakers, her son looking happy and Zach seeming relaxed and comfortable.

"My day was great," Maggie said. "I now know how to make a heart in the foam of your latte. Or a fern, if you'd prefer."

"You had to spend eight hours learning that?" Ben demanded as he started sprinkling cheese.

"And a few other things besides," Maggie replied lightly. "I am proud to say I am no longer afraid of that big, shiny espresso machine downstairs."

"Good thing," Zach answered with a chuckle, "but to be fair that thing does look like a beast."

"Yeah." She smiled back at him, enjoying the warmth in his expression as his gaze rested on her, the way it made her tingle. "So tell me about your day."

Zach glanced at Ben, waiting for him to speak. "It was pretty chill," her son said at last. "We finished the bookshelves, and I got all my work done."

"That's great." She turned to Zach. "Sounds like a good day."

"Yeah." Zach nodded. "Pretty chill."

They both smiled at her, and Maggie smiled back. Even with everything seeming so relaxed, it was hard to let go of that hard clench of anxiety in her stomach that remained from having left Ben for an entire day. She glanced between him and Zach, as if testing the truth of their replies. Had it really been a chill day? She felt something unspoken in the air, but maybe it was just bro bonding.

Another beat passed and Maggie had to conclude that she was, as she so often was, being paranoid.

"So," she remarked as she nodded toward the pizza base Ben had been liberally spreading with sauce and sprinkling with cheese. "You're making pizzas?"

"Yep," Zach confirmed. "I'm trying to get Ben to move out of his comfort zone of pineapple and black olive, because frankly that's just so gross. We've got pepperoni, chorizo, as well as some peppers and broccoli to cover all our food groups."

"Good luck with that," Maggie answered on a laugh. "Ben has always been a creature of habit."

"You know I actually like pineapple and black olive," Ben told them. "Well," he amended, "I've learned to like it."

"And that is not something I'm going to do," Zach replied as he started slicing a stick of chorizo.

"Maybe you should go out of your comfort zone of extra spicy," Maggie challenged.

Zach slid her a laughing look. "The question is, why would I do that?"

"Just to show you can?" Maggie replied, trying not to let the teasing glint in his blue-green eyes affect her as much as it was and pleasurably failing.

"I'm perfectly confident in my capabilities in that area," Zach assured her as he scattered the sliced chorizo over his pizza. "But *your* pizza is a blank slate—please don't tell me you secretly like pineapple and black olive too because I won't believe you."

"I'll take the broccoli and pepper, then. I actually like vegetables, and I have the sense they won't get eaten otherwise."

"You are probably right there." Zach grinned at her, and Maggie laughed before catching Ben watching the two of them with an alert and eager sort of look on his face that made her mentally screech the brakes. Did her son *want* her and Zach to get together? She'd assumed that even the faintest whiff of romance would horrify Ben, but what if it was the opposite?

What if Ben got his hopes up that Zach might be in their lives forever, when, she had to face it, he most probably wouldn't be? Zach would marry the love of his life that he did or did not find on Tinder, have a bunch of beautiful blond kids, and convert a barn into a gorgeous house where he'd brew his own beer and set up his own carpentry and craft store. Or something like that.

He was so *young*, she realized afresh, with his whole life ahead of him. Of course he was going to do those things, or any number of other things. Maybe he was in a bit of a tricky transition stage at the moment, what with the store and his sister and the way he seemed to both love and resent Starr's Fall... but he'd figure it out. And when he did, he'd move on from their bedraggled little family. Understandably.

She took a deep breath and let it out slowly as those realizations trickled through her. She'd been getting way too close to him, when she knew any romance that might have blossomed eventually couldn't possibly last. And she could deal with that, she hoped, because she was an adult... but she could not—and would not—mess with her son's emotions any more than they had been already.

"Sure, I'll make a pizza," she said briskly, and Zach gave her a thoughtful frown—somehow he seemed attuned to her moods and how they just abruptly changed—before handing her a baking tray with a pizza base on it.

"Here you go."

"Thanks."

He rested his hip against the counter, watching her as she focused absolutely all of her attention on spreading the sauce, sprinkling the cheese. She sensed he wanted to say something, but he kept himself from it and she was glad as she finished making the pizza.

Once Zach had put them all in the oven and they'd both tidied all the ingredients away, he gave her a slow, considering look, the kind that made Maggie think he was going to say whatever he'd wanted to before after all.

"We've got ten minutes until they're done," he told her. "Why don't you show off your new skills and make me an espresso?"

"What, now?" Maggie looked at him, startled.

"No time like the present."

"Yes, but…"

"Don't make excuses, Mom," Ben chimed in, sounding excited. "Go show off your mad skillz."

"Oh, please." She shook her head, laughing, but then under Ben and Zach's challenging gazes, she gave a little shrug and said, "Fine. It might take a few minutes to fire up the machine, but… okay. One espresso coming up."

"I want to see how it's done," Zach told her as he started following her to the stairs.

"Ben?" Maggie called back. "You coming?"

Her son shook his head. "I'm good. I don't even like coffee." He settled into the seat in front of the computer, while Maggie hesitated. She really hoped Ben was not trying to give her and Zach some sort of *alone time*.

"I'll let you know how this goes," she muttered under her breath as she headed downstairs. She could feel the heat of Zach's body as he followed behind her, and a not-unpleasant prickle of awareness ran through her. She really reacted to this man, but maybe any red-blooded woman did.

Downstairs, the café was shrouded in darkness and Maggie flipped on the lights before heading over to the shelves to inspect the finished product.

"Wow," she said, heartfelt. "Zach, these look amazing." He'd finished the carvings on each joint and they were both intricate and whimsical, adding a classy yet fun vibe to the whole place.

Zach came to stand behind her. "Thanks," he said. "I really enjoyed working on them. I've always liked woodworking, but I didn't realize how much until I started a bigger project."

"And the wood is beautiful, too." She ran her hand over the burnished oak, the light catching the gleam of gold in its grain.

"Reclaimed from some old wardrobes we had in the barn. My parents collected antiques, but not the valuable kind. They've just been gathering dust for years. Decades, even, so I thought I might as well put them to use."

"Very good use," she replied, and turned around, drawing her breath in sharply as she realized how close he was. Close enough that when she stumbled a little, he put his hands on her shoulders to steady her.

"Easy there." His voice was a lazy murmur, his breath tickling her hair. Maggie's heart rate soared as she breathed in his woody scent and, by some superhuman effort, managed to take a step back.

"Sorry," she mumbled as she headed back to the kitchen. She shook her head as if to clear it, determined to get back on track. "I think you might have higher expectations of my abilities than is reasonable," she called over her shoulder as she turned on the espresso machine and it began to hum as it preheated. "Considering I have literally one day of training."

"I have faith in you," Zach replied as he came to stand in the doorway of the kitchen area, watching her start up the machine. Maggie felt both self-conscious and proud as she familiarized herself with the gleaming beast of Zach's description. Espresso machines were intimidating at the best of times, especially industrialized-sized ones made for a coffee shop, and her hyper-awareness of Zach wasn't helping her nerves, by any means.

"First I have to grind the beans," she told him as she opened a bag of fresh coffee beans and poured some into the built-in grinder. Zach had taken a few steps into the kitchen and she was very conscious of him standing so close that his shoulder was nearly brushing hers. "Thank you for looking after Ben today," she continued, raising her voice over the sound of the grinder. "I really appreciate it."

"It was fun." Zach hesitated, and she had the sense that he was about to say something else. She slid him a sideways glance, curious and a little apprehensive, but he just smiled. Maggie flipped the switch on the grinder, and the kitchen was plunged into a sudden, expectant silence.

"Well, I still appreciate it," she said, a little too loudly, as she poured the ground coffee into the portafilter and tamped it down. She turned to face him, something in her jolting at the sleepy yet intent look on his face, lids half-lowered, lips slowly curving. He took a step toward her, and her heart felt as if it had flung itself against her chest. "We—we'll need to wait a few minutes for the water to heat up," she said, sounding even louder. A blush was already rising to her cheeks which made her feel like some giggly teenager, and yet Zach had looked... he'd looked as if he'd almost been about to kiss her. Surely not. And yet... she knew how much she would like it if he did.

"Mmm—maybe you should check on the pizzas," Maggie stuttered.

"Okay..." Zach gave her a bemused look, as if he suspected she was suggesting such a thing simply because she was unsettled by his closeness, as well as by the fact that they were alone, and that would indeed be the truth. Maggie gave him what she hoped was a breezy smile as he headed upstairs, and her breath came out in a relieved gust.

What was going on with her? With *them*? Not that there even *was* a them... although when he'd been standing so close to her, it had almost felt like there was. Was she wildly delusional, thinking for so much as a nanosecond that he was going to kiss her? He might have said he liked her, and asked her out on a date, and touched her cheek... but it still felt so hard to believe that he was doing anything but amusing himself. Biding his time till something better came along, maybe.

She needed, Maggie thought, to give herself a hard mental shake. She'd already decided she wasn't ready for romance, and certainly not with a thirty-one-year-old semi-reformed player, and she wasn't interested in anything casual, so...

*You don't swipe right for the love of your life.*

Maggie closed her eyes. If Zach Miller was really looking for the love of his life, it surely wasn't her. It couldn't be. She couldn't let it be, because she wasn't ready and he was too young and then there was Ben...

So many reasons to be sensible about this.

"Pizzas are just about done. I turned the oven down."

Maggie let out a little sound of surprise as Zach strolled into the kitchen. He raised his eyebrows as he came closer. "Are you okay? You seem very jumpy."

"I'm fine," Maggie said quickly. "Just nervous about making that espresso, that's all."

"Somehow I don't think that's it." Zach's voice came out in a low, lazy murmur that twined around Maggie's senses. She focused on the espresso machine—inserting the portafilter and slipping an espresso shot glass underneath. She pushed the button to brew it while Zach took a step closer. And then another one.

"Don't," she said quietly. It was all she could think to say, because every sense and nerve was twanging on high alert.

Zach stilled. "Don't what?"

Maggie let out a shaky laugh as she felt a blush rise to her cheeks. "I don't even know. Show me those bedroom eyes. Stand so close to me that I can *smell* you—"

Zach laughed softly. "That's kind of worrying. Do I really smell?"

"You smell *good*," Maggie admitted hopelessly. "*Too good*." She couldn't believe she'd said so much, and yet right then honesty felt like the only way to preserve her sanity... and keep Zach at a distance.

Which was what she wanted, right?

"So you are tempted," Zach murmured, and Maggie let out a long, shaky sigh.

"Every woman in Starr's Fall is tempted, as far as I can see."

"Don't," Zach quietly, "make this about anyone else. This is about you and me."

*You and me.* Was there such a thing?

"The espresso is ready." She reached for the espresso glass and thrust it at Zach. He caught her hand in his, taking the shot glass from her nerveless fingers and setting it down on the counter while he still kept hold of her hand. When she dared to look up at him, she saw that same sleepy and intent look on his face. His lips were parted, his lids at half-mast, his eyes glinting. He was so darned good-looking, and he really was, Maggie thought with a thrill of wonder, going to kiss her.

And then he did.

He dipped his head slowly, taking his time, giving her every opportunity to pull away which she probably should have, yet somehow she couldn't. And when she didn't, he brushed his lips across hers just once, then twice, like a *hello*, and then a *how are you*.

And Maggie answered by parting her lips, letting her head fall back. Saying with her body what was cartwheeling through her mind. *I was pretty good, but I just got a whole lot better.*

Zach deepened the kiss. Maggie's head spun. At some point, her arms came around his shoulders, palms sliding over his biceps as a sigh escaped her and he laughed softly—and then kissed her again. Their hips bumped. Heat flared. And they were still kissing.

It felt so good—like coming home and zooming up to outer space all at once. She felt safe, but she also felt wildly excited, and the heady mix of both emotions sent everything in her swirling with both need and joy. Her hands roamed down his back as he pulled her closer. They were *still* kissing.

"Mom…" Ben's voice floated down the stairs. Maggie sprang away from Zach like a scalded cat, wiping her mouth while he looked at her bemusedly, his face flushed, his hair ruffled. "I think the pizzas are ready," Ben called.

"Coming." Maggie's voice sounded strangled. She couldn't even look at Zach, not until she'd gone over what had just happened and made some sense of it. Figured out why he'd kissed her, what it meant, and just how much she'd embarrassed herself.

"Maggie…" Zach began, but she couldn't listen.

"The pizzas," she gasped out, and ran up the stairs.

## 13

Maggie lay in bed and stared up at the sun-dappled ceiling as a rather silly smile spread across her face. She was thinking about that kiss. Again.

She stretched, pointing her toes and flinging her arms over her head. The doubts and worries and over-analysis could all come later—and certainly would—but for now, she just wanted to enjoy recalling the magical feeling of kissing someone who made her head spin.

She wouldn't think about the fact that Zach was so much younger than her, or that it might be Ben's heart that was broken if things went wrong, never mind her own, or the churning guilt she felt that after only sixteen months of mourning, she was kissing another man.

She wouldn't think of any of that, except, too bad, she was.

Maggie sighed as she lowered her arms and blinked hard. For just a few minutes she wanted to revel in last night. Admittedly, she had not handled herself as maturely as she might have wished, practically sprinting away from Zach after he'd kissed her, but she'd redeemed herself later when she'd managed to act mostly natural for the rest of the evening, although she'd felt anything but. She'd kept reliving that kiss and remembering just how good it had made her feel, and she'd realized she just wanted to focus on that. It had been so long since she'd felt wanted. Since she'd been *touched*. And even if it was just a kiss and didn't go anywhere—

which it probably wouldn't—she'd realized she was glad it had happened. And meanwhile, all evening, Zach kept sliding her curious looks, like he was trying to figure out her thought process.

He'd stayed until ten, playing RQ with Ben while Maggie did some paperwork for the café, and then she had walked him down to the front door to say goodbye while Ben got ready for bed.

As she'd woven her way through the sofas in the dark, moonlight slanting through the front window, she'd felt a sense of expectation coil through her. She'd opened the front door, turned to smile at him.

"Well..." she'd begun, and then laughed because she had no idea how to finish that sentence.

"Well," Zach had repeated. He'd propped his shoulder against the doorframe as he'd narrowed his eyes at her, smiling wryly. "I can't figure out if you're trying to pretend we didn't kiss, or if you've decided you're good with it."

"I can't either," Maggie had admitted, because really, what else could she have said? Her mind had been pinging all over the place, and yet she'd felt happy. Happier than she had in a long, long time.

Zach had cocked his head, his gaze sweeping slowly over. "If you had to say right now, which is it...?" he asked quietly, his gaze now steady on her, a hint of vulnerability in his eyes that had made her ache.

Still Maggie had hesitated. Could she really answer that honestly? Did she even know what she felt? The cautious thing would have been to say she wasn't sure, and it was just a kiss and they should sleep on it... separately, *obviously*.

But then some reckless, defiant spark of desire had made her lift her chin. Meet his gaze directly and say with more firmness than she'd thought she'd felt, "I'm good with it."

For a second Zach had looked startled, and Maggie had known he'd been expecting her to back away as she always did, get in a tizzy and start to stammer excuses. But she was tired of being that way. Of living a half-life because she'd forgotten how to live a full one, or if she was worthy of it after everything that had happened with her husband, her son. Even if the thought of anything happening between them still filled her with terror.

"I'm really glad to hear that," Zach had murmured, and then he'd leaned in and kissed her again, just a brush of her lips, but it was still enough to set her whole body to tingling. He'd given her one last grin before heading out into the night.

Maggie had practically floated back to her bedroom. She'd thought briefly of calling Lynn and telling her what had happened, but she'd been afraid her sister would only offer warnings and disapproval, and so she hadn't. The handful of friendships she'd left behind in Greenwich had fizzled since Matt's death, and the few college friends she still kept in touch with weren't so up to date with her life that they'd know who she was talking about. They didn't even know she'd moved to Starr's Fall. As for her new friends in the town... she definitely wasn't ready to share that she'd kissed Mr. Extra Spicy.

It would have been easy to fall into the funk of feeling lonely, but for once Maggie held herself from it. This was a secret she could keep to herself for now, she thought, although who knew who might have seen them kissing in the doorway of the café like teenagers. The gossip might be around all of Starr's Fall by breakfast, but for once she wasn't going to let herself care. She just wanted to enjoy the moment... even if it didn't lead anywhere.

"Mom."

Startled, Maggie pushed her hair out of her face to see Ben standing in the doorway, his face white with anxiety, his lip bitten to shreds, his shoulders hunched, and his hands lost in his sleeves. She scrambled up to a seated position.

"Ben, what is it?"

"Something's happened," he said miserably. "I... I've been stupid." He gulped. "I'm sorry, Mom."

"Okay." Maggie forced herself to sound calm even though her heart was pounding, and a dozen worst-case scenarios were flashing through her mind in lightning streaks of panic. What could have possibly happened between ten o'clock last night and eight-thirty this morning? "Let's go into the kitchen and you can tell me what it is," she said, and amazingly, she still sounded calm. She reached for her old cardigan and pulled it on, pushed her feet into her fleecy slippers. Ben sniffed, a telling sound, and followed her out to the kitchen.

On autopilot, Maggie filled the kettle and put it on top of the stove. She took a deep breath and turned around. "Tell me what happened, Ben."

Ben shook his head, his gaze downcast, his voice coming out in ragged gulps. "I didn't... I didn't mean anything by it. I was just so *mad*... and it was meant to be a joke..."

"What was?" Maggie did her best to keep her voice level, but it rose anyway, and she had to take another breath. "Ben, what *was*?" she asked again, more reasonably.

"It was... a meme. A stupid meme."

"A *meme*?" She needed to back up a few steps. "Can you please start from the beginning?"

The story came out in fits and starts, between gulps and sniffs, all of it news to Maggie. She'd had no idea he was still on the school chat at high school, something which boggled her mind because he'd been so miserable there. Then the geek meme that had gone out yesterday, while Zach had been here, and Ben's riposte made later that afternoon, a meme with photos of the main architects of his bullying, with the word *basic* underneath. But her brilliant son hadn't just sent it on the group chat as the others had done; no, he'd somehow managed to hack the school system and send it as an urgent announcement to every student and staff member, while she, Zach, and Ben had all been eating pizza and enjoying each other's company. And as of this morning the school was involved, and potentially the police due to the hacking, and it was a huge mess, much bigger than the original crime.

"Ben, *why*?" Maggie asked helplessly, knowing it was a pointless question and yet unable to keep herself from it.

"I just... I just wanted to *do* something. They get away with so much—"

"But that's in the past," Maggie cut across him, caught between a desperate sadness and an exasperation that could, if she let it, tip over into rage. How could Ben have been so foolish as to revisit all those old hurts, pick at them till they bled? "We came to Starr's Fall for a new start—"

"I *know*," he moaned, grabbing and pulling at his hair. "I'm sorry, Mom. I'm really sorry. Am I in big trouble? Will I go to jail? Someone said hacking the email system is, like, a major crime—"

"No, you will not go to jail." Although you did hear about people being imprisoned for something they'd posted on social media, Maggie reflected with an inward shudder. Still, she had spoken extensively with the principal and student counselor back when the bullying had been at its peak. They had been compassionate... to a point. She would have to call on the remnant of that compassion now, and hope that the most Ben was facing was a stern talking-to.

"I'll call the principal this morning," she said wearily. "After I've had coffee. But we've got to agree, Ben, that you are not going to go back there, not mentally, and not online, either. I want you off that group chat, and any other social media of the school. You wanted to leave, so leave. In every way." She managed a small smile as she tousled his hair. "Okay?"

Ben nodded, sniffing. "Okay."

"It's going to be all right," Maggie told him gently. "I promise." The kettle began to shrill, and she took it off the stove to make coffee. "I'm just surprised you'd do something like this," she remarked honestly. "You managed to avoid hitting back at them all year, and then one *meme*..."

"Well," her son replied, scuffing his foot along the floor, "it was Zach's idea."

Maggie stilled, then set the kettle down very carefully. "*What?*"

"He told me to make a meme and send it around the whole school, with the basic thing. He thought it would be funny." Ben lurched forward, alarmed. "But don't be mad at him for it—"

"I'm not mad at him," Maggie said quietly. No, she wasn't mad, she was furious. *Zach* had been encouraging her son to bully bullies? To do something stupid with potentially long-lasting effects because it was *funny*, and that was without considering all the mental health dangers that revisiting that painful episode in his life was likely to cause, some of which she knew he'd already guessed?

"You *are* mad at him," Ben stated, sounding miserable. "I shouldn't have said anything. He didn't—"

"I wish he hadn't made that suggestion," Maggie replied evenly. "But that's not your problem, Ben. Now why don't you shower and get dressed, and then you can get started on your work? I'll make a few calls." And once she'd sorted out the school, she was definitely paying a visit to Zach Miller.

* * *

Maggie's fury did not abate as she waded into the mess of the meme, calling various school officials, people she had hoped never to deal with again. They'd been understanding when Ben had been in the hospital, but Maggie had never been able to shake the suspicion that some of the staff believed Ben's problems were at least partly of his own making, simply because he wasn't the usual swaggering, lacrosse-playing jock that the school pandered to. Reassuring them that Ben would not hack the email system again was only part of the apologetic explaining she had to do. There was the mental health of his bullies to consider, of course, who had apparently played a harmless prank, only to be humiliated by Ben in a far worse fashion, something that made Maggie choke with frustrated rage.

"I understand Ben's been through some challenging times," the school counselor told Maggie rather sternly, "but that was a year ago and we won't let any student play the victim card forever."

"I'm pretty sure," Maggie remarked coolly, "that as the school's counselor, 'playing the victim card' should not be in your vocabulary. But in any case, Ben has learned his lesson, and this is the only time he has ever hit out against the students you know made his life a misery for an entire year—"

"Yes, I do realize that, Mrs. Parker," the counselor hastily assured her. "I'm only saying this because I had hoped that *everyone* in this unfortunate situation had moved on."

Mainly because two of Ben's bullies were stars of the school's lacrosse team, and the school had been *very* reluctant to discipline them in any noticeable fashion. Maggie felt the start of a headache at her temples. She had really, really wanted to have moved on from this, too.

"I promise you, it won't happen again," she said stiffly. "Ben is now fully off the grade's group chat and going forward we intend to have absolutely nothing to do with the high school." She could not keep a note of savagery from entering her voice. *Because in the end you did so little for us*, she wanted to say but managed to stop herself.

"Well, considering the circumstances," the counselor replied stiffly, "that's probably wise. But I do wish Ben the best for the future."

"Thank you," Maggie managed, her voice sounding strangled, before saying goodbye and hurling her cellphone onto the sofa in a futile fit of rage.

By the time she got off the phone, her fury at Zach for instigating the whole palaver was even hotter than it had been when Ben had first told her about it. *How* could Zach have been so thoughtless, so reckless, so *immature*, as to suggest such a stupid thing?

The answer, when it came, made her feel only worse. Because clearly he *was* thoughtless, reckless, and immature. A thirty-one-year-old hanging around and gaming with a fourteen-year-old boy? Maybe she should have heeded her sister Lynn's concerns. And Maggie had been right about worrying about Zach's influence over her son. As for that kiss... well, it was resigned to the trash heap of history, one of the stupidest things she'd ever done, and never to be thought of again. Just the memory of it made Maggie's face heat, and not in a good way. *She* had been thoughtless, reckless, immature, in welcoming that kiss. In telling Zach she was good with it. What on earth had she been thinking of?

Well, it ended here and now.

"Where are you going?" Ben asked when Maggie emerged from her bedroom, dressed and clearly on a mission.

"I just have a couple of errands to run. I'll be back shortly."

"Mom..." Ben sounded worried. "You're not—"

"It's fine, Ben." She moderated her tone as she gave him a smile. "I just have a few things to do. Why don't you get started on your homework, okay? I'll be back in a few minutes." She squeezed his shoulder, doing his best to reassure him. "Don't worry. The school's fine."

Outside, the sky was a pale, fragile blue, the air damp and cold but holding the barest hint of spring. Maggie was about to climb into her car when she heard a voice, filled with relish, call from down the street.

"*Well.* Someone looked like they had a nice evening last night."

Maggie closed her eyes, the car keys clutched in her hand, biting into her palm. Then she opened her eyes and turned to smile at Liz Cranbury, who was coming toward her, her Pilates mat rolled up under one arm. "I was out walking Frou-frou and I happened to see you and Zach," she explained unrepentantly. "I have to say I'm impressed. But don't worry. I won't breathe a word." Her eyes danced with delighted curiosity as she leaned forward. "But you have to promise to tell me all about it. How on earth did you snag Starr's Fall's most eligible bachelor? Not to mention its most notorious one?"

Notorious, indeed. "It wasn't a big deal," Maggie said rather tightly. "Trust me."

Liz's face softened into sympathy. "You've got to guard your heart with that one," she agreed with a nod. "From what I've heard, anyway. And men can be such jerks. I've got an ex-husband to prove it."

Maggie nodded mechanically, doing her best to sound normal. "I'm sorry."

Liz reached out and grasped her arm. "Just be careful, Maggie, okay? I know you must be vulnerable, just the way I was after my divorce. Grief can make you feel lonely, and it can also make you do stupid things." She made a face. "I bought three pairs of Louboutin shoes which I definitely could not afford. I had to sell them all on eBay."

Maggie forced a smile as everything in her ached. *Too late*, she thought, and then told herself not to be ridiculous. She wasn't hurt. And she wasn't going to let herself be, *or* Ben. "Don't worry, I'm not in danger of buying any shoes, or doing something stupid." At least, not something stupider than she'd already done, which had certainly been enough. "What you saw was a one-time event."

Liz nodded and released her arm. "That's probably just as well. Are you coming to Pilates?"

"Not today."

She had more pressing matters to attend to, like finding Zach and telling him she never wanted to see him again.

# 14

"You got back late last night," Jenna remarked as Zach strolled into the kitchen the morning after his and Maggie's kiss. She was sitting by her laptop as usual, sipping coffee and looking tired.

"Yep." He couldn't keep a satisfied smile from spreading across his face, and his sister, of course, noticed.

"Oh, boy." She shook her head. "Who is it this time, Zach?"

He didn't pretend to misunderstand, although her weary tone annoyed him. "None of your business."

"Oh, really?" She let out a huff of laughter. "You're usually a *little* more forthcoming than that."

He shrugged and reached for the coffee. He wasn't about to talk about Maggie, at least not until they'd spoken to each other and clarified the nature of what had happened last night. Then he'd shout it from the rooftops... assuming Maggie was on the same page he was, and he was pretty hopeful that she was.

Jenna took another sip of her coffee as she eyed him over the rim of her mug. "Don't you get tired of trying?" she asked, and this time there wasn't the spikiness she usually heard in her voice when she talked about his dating life, just a jaded resignation that bordered on sorrow.

He regarded her uncertainly, surprised by her tone. He'd never heard his sister sound like this before, like she was struggling against a tide of despair. "What do you mean?" he asked.

Jenna sighed and looked away. "Aren't you tired of trying to have what Mom and Dad have?" she asked bleakly. Zach simply stared at her. Why on earth were they talking about their *parents*? "What they have is unique," Jenna continued, "and frankly pretty unhealthy. I mean, it's more than a little co-dependent, don't you think? The way they've always been so wrapped up in each other? They have no emotional space in their lives for anyone but each other. Not even their own kids."

Now he heard true bitterness in her voice, and he marveled at it. They'd never talked about their parents like this before; like everyone else in Starr's Fall, he'd assumed his parents were a great couple, because clearly they *were*, even if they hadn't been the most hands-on mother and father. Slowly Zach lowered himself into the chair opposite Jenna's as he cradled his coffee mug between his hands. "Did you feel... neglected growing up?" he asked curiously.

Jenna gave him a belligerent look. "Didn't you?"

Zach considered this. *Had* he? He'd taken his parents' relationship at face value—intense, loving, and yes, maybe a little overwhelming. But he'd seen it as something to aspire to rather than feel left out of. Everyone in Starr's Fall marveled at the Millers, what a great couple they were, what perfect partners, running their store together, starting it from scratch, working so hard, never a cross word between them.

"I mean, don't you remember how it was?" Jenna pressed. "Really? Mom and Dad never went to any of your baseball games, but even with the store they still had time to take a two-week vacation to Hawaii by themselves for their anniversary."

"It was their twentieth," Zach protested. "And we were teenagers."

"You were twelve. I was eighteen." Jenna gave a twitchy kind of shrug. "I don't begrudge them the trip, but still—why didn't they come to your games? Why didn't they care about what we were doing? Do you remember when I gave that assembly my senior year, on the importance of small businesses?" He did, only vaguely, but he nodded because it was clear his sister was on a roll. "It was a big deal to me," she stated, "and they didn't even show up."

All right, yes, Zach remembered his parents not showing up to a lot of things, but it hadn't bothered him that much... had it? "They always had the store..." he protested, because that had always been their reason.

"Until they didn't," Jenna cut across him, "like when they went to Hawaii for that trip, or when they decided to retire to Florida four years ago without even asking if we'd like to take the store over, just assuming we would."

"But we did," Zach reminded her. "And they knew that was what we wanted. I mean, it was what you wanted, wasn't it, Jenna?" He certainly hoped so, considering how much control she exhibited over it.

"Yes..." she admitted, "but maybe for the wrong reasons. I don't know." She shrugged unhappily. "It just feels all kinds of seriously messed up, but maybe that's just me."

Zach was silent, trying to view their childhood through this new, unwelcome filter, and yes, he supposed he could see where Jenna was coming from, sort of. His parents had certainly been wrapped up in each other, with Jenna and him both treated more or less as afterthoughts; they'd always valued date nights but not so much family meals. They spent hours talking to each other but seemed distracted or disinterested whenever he and Jenna had anything to say.

The store had been their baby, their golden child, and Zach and Jenna had always been expected to help out while not being allowed any input, which was probably where Jenna got her control freakery from. Zach had been shocked when they'd handed the whole place over to them so abruptly; he certainly had not anticipated them moving to Florida the way they had. Truth be told, just about everyone in Starr's Fall had been a little shocked when the Millers had just *left*.

But maybe that was because once again they'd only been thinking about what they wanted. It felt weird, as well as wrong, to think about his parents like that. But the more he thought about it, the more he wondered if what Jenna was saying made sense... which was kind of uncomfortable to consider, because it never had even crossed his mind before, and what did that say about him?

"I know they knew we were willing to take over the store," Jenna told him, "but it was never about what we wanted. Only what they did."

Zach was silent again, absorbing this, accepting it. Certainly, he reflected, when his dad had called him up in the middle of freshman year and asked—commanded, really—that he come home and take care of the store while he supported their mother through cancer treatment, he had not been thinking about what Zach might have wanted or even needed. But truth be told, Zach had felt honored to be asked, had wanted to be needed by his parents. Was that part of it all? Because, he realized, even then he'd felt separate from them; they'd been in their own bubble through all the chemo treatments, essentially shutting him out of the whole difficult experience, which was how he'd turned to online gaming, for some social connection. He hadn't really thought about all that before, just accepted that was how it was with his parents. How it always had been. But as he'd told Maggie, it had been a long, lonely year.

"I don't know," he said slowly. "I mean, yeah, they did their own thing—"

"Zach," Jenna cut across him, sounding impatient, "it's been four years since they moved to Florida and we've only seen them twice. Don't you think that's weird?"

"We're in our thirties, Jenna. It's not like we're kids anymore—"

"But neither of us is married," she pressed, "with other families to go to at Christmas or Thanksgiving. They don't visit. They don't invite us there either. Why shouldn't we see them more?" She didn't wait for him to answer. "It's because they don't really care. They never did, not that much. Do you know, Mom let it slip once that I was an accident? I'm guessing you were, too, especially considering there are six years between us."

"*Whoa.*" Zach held up his hand. "Way too much information."

"Well, it's the truth," Jenna stated belligerently. Her eyes flashed with both anger and hurt; it was obvious this had been eating her up for a while. And maybe it would have been eating him up, too, if he'd thought about it. He'd told Maggie once to credit him with some emotional astuteness, but now he wondered if he actually had any.

"They just were never into being parents," Jenna stated flatly. "I mean, they fed and clothed us, and they weren't *cruel* or anything. When it came down to it, they just weren't all that interested." Zach couldn't keep from wincing a little as Jenna plowed on. "And fine, I get that, I can accept it, because that's just how some people are." She took a deep breath as she gazed at him squarely, her expression bleak. "But I realized a while ago that I was basically trying to replicate in my own life what they had with each other, and that trying to do that was toxic. For most of my adult life I've been looking for an ideal that shouldn't exist. Mom and Dad aren't the gold standard, Zach. *No one* should be that wrapped up in another person, and when you've held that up as something to aspire to... well." She sighed unhappily. "You're bound to be disappointed in your relationships, like I was. It took me a long time to realize that, and the reality is I'm still working it out... but I'd rather be single than have what Mom and Dad had."

Zach simply stared at her. They'd *never* talked like this before, and all these revelations were kind of blowing his mind. Making him wonder about himself in a way he didn't want to have to. "And you think that's what I've been doing?" he asked. "Trying to find what Mom and Dad had together, by dating so many different women?" It sounded kind of pathetic.

Jenna raised her eyebrows. "What do you think? I mean, I know I've treated you like some kind of womanizer, and that's my emotional baggage. I had... a bad experience with someone like that."

"In San Francisco," Zach surmised.

She nodded, her face tightening with remembrance. "It's been a long time, and I need to get over it, and I think I mostly have, but... I've started to see things differently with you, and I wonder, Zach... all these dates you go on? Are you looking for this great romance like Mom and Dad had? Because trust me, you're going to be disappointed. People are just people, pretty flawed, and that fairy-tale romance? It doesn't exist, and even if it did, it won't satisfy you."

Zach looked away. He'd woken up this morning thinking about Maggie, feeling so happy and hopeful about that kiss and their potential relationship, but now...? Now he felt like he had to reassemble all the scattered pieces of his history and figure out who he was and why he did the things he did, which sounded like a lot of work, and maybe none of it was worth it, because could people even change?

"Jenna, you might not be looking for some romantic ideal, but... aren't you trying to replicate what Mom and Dad had with the store? Is that why you're not willing to change anything?"

Jenna's brows snapped together. "Don't psychoanalyze me," she barked, and Zach almost laughed.

"What have you just been doing with me?" he demanded as good-naturedly as he could.

"Fine. Let's just stop this conversation." Clearly she didn't want the spotlight turned on her, and Zach understood that. Still, it gave him a lot to think about.

"I get where you're coming from," he told her. "But just because Mom and Dad might have been a little too intense in their marriage doesn't mean we can't be healthier about our own relationships and work lives." Hopefully.

"I know, but you've got to be *aware*," Jenna replied. "Are you?"

Zach decided not to parrot the question back at her, although he had a feeling Jenna wasn't as aware as she seemed to think she was. But was he? Zach felt an uncomfortable prickle of dawning realization that in every relationship he'd ever been in, no matter how short-lived, he'd been the one doing the heavy lifting. Determined to make it work, and not just work, but be the answer to everything, and it never was.

As for him and Maggie... in the last six weeks, he'd basically dropped everything in his life to help her with the café. To be a friend to her son. To do whatever he could to make her life easier and better—and make her see how she needed him. Which, frankly, maybe was also a little messed up. To be fair, he'd enjoyed it all and she'd been appreciative, but... maybe it wasn't a healthy way to go about things. Maybe their relationship—if they even had one—wasn't meant to be so one-sided.

"Just think about it," Jenna said, and Zach nodded. He certainly would, but right now his head hurt with all the info his sister had just dumped on him, and he needed to do something that didn't involve his brain.

"I'm going to go out to the barn," he told Jenna. "We had a delivery yesterday that needs to be shifted."

"Okay." Jenna's expression softened. "And thanks, Zach. I know I've been a control freak about the store, and you're right, that's part of my issues. I'm... I'm trying to be better."

He smiled, appreciating her saying as much, even if her trying wasn't all that obvious yet. Maybe it would be soon. "Thanks."

"How's it going with the boardgame café?"

"Yeah, pretty good." He wasn't about to say more than that until he'd seen Maggie again and they'd had some sort of discussion about what their kiss had meant. Although... considering everything Jenna had just told him, Zach didn't know what it should mean, or even what he wanted it to mean, anymore. He felt like everything he'd thought about himself and what he wanted out of life had been upended.

"You think a place like that will take off in Starr's Fall?" Jenna asked, sounding skeptical.

"I hope so."

She nodded slowly. "It would be good to have some more business in town, anyway. Is Maggie settling in? And Ben?" The questions sounded so innocent that Zach knew his sister didn't suspect anything between him and Maggie. Maybe the age gap really was a thing for some people. "Yeah, I think so."

"Good." She nodded and then turned back to her laptop, and Zach headed outside into the kind of dark, dank, frigid morning that only February could bring. Spring was on the way, but it didn't feel like that right now.

His mind felt too full of everything Jenna had said and he had thought, and he was relieved to empty it out as he started hauling boxes. He didn't want to think, wasn't ready to second-guess every decision he'd ever made, wondering why he'd been searching for the love of his life for so long and never had come close to finding her. Did his parents really have something to do with that? Was he stuck in his past?

And, while he was thinking about it all, what about why he'd always wanted to stay in Starr's Fall? Jenna had branched out for a little bit, and most of his high school friends no longer lived here. Admittedly, a lot of them had only moved as far as Torrington or Litchfield, but *still*. Why hadn't he ever thought about moving on? Doing or being something different? Was there something *wrong* with him?

He pushed the pestering questions away as he grabbed a heavy box of hardware supplies, his arms aching with the effort, some part of him glad for the distraction of pain. He didn't like thinking this way, like everything he'd ever done was because of some stupid childhood trauma. Besides, everyone had *some* kind of trauma in their past, right? It wasn't like he was different, and no matter what Jenna said, his parents hadn't been *that* bad. And wasn't everyone looking for love, in one way or another? That was the human condition.

In the distance, he heard the sound of a car coming up the drive and then parking. It was too early for customers, only a little after nine when the store opened at ten; it was probably someone for Jenna. Annie Lyman sometimes stopped by pretty early. He reached for another box.

A few minutes later, he heard the sound of footsteps crunching on gravel as someone walked up to the barn. He straightened, one hand going to the small of his back, as he turned around. A ripple of surprised pleasure went through him at the sight of Maggie standing in the doorway, dressed in a black turtleneck sweater, puffer vest, and jeans, the weak wintry sunlight filtering from behind her and giving her dark hair, pulled up in a messy bun, a golden halo. He drank in the sight of her as he smiled his greeting.

"Hey," he said softly. He'd been planning on heading over to the café later today, but he was glad she'd made the effort to see him. Really glad, even if his thoughts still all felt jumbled up from his conversation with Jenna.

"Zach," Maggie said, and her voice sounded hard, unlike anything he'd heard from her before. "I need to talk to you."

\* \* \*

Maggie had been doing her best to control her temper as she'd driven over to Miller's General Store, but just the sight of Zach looking gorgeous, giving her that lazy, knowing smile, was enough to send her blood back to boiling. He was so sure of himself, so arrogant, and so reckless. *How* could he have told Ben to do such a thing?

"Okay," he said, and now he sounded cautious, the smile sliding from his lips as he regarded her warily, his hands resting on his lean hips.

Maggie clenched her hands into fists at her sides and then forced herself to flatten them out. She wanted to sound reasonable, but she was just too angry and afraid to moderate her tone or her temper. "How could you have been so... so *stupid*, with Ben?" she burst out.

Zach stilled, his eyes narrowing as he cocked his head. "Care to elaborate?" he asked in that mild way that Maggie had once liked but now just seemed like craven thoughtlessness. Did he even care about Ben? About her? Or had it all—the gaming, the helping out, the *kiss*—just been a way to amuse himself?

"The meme," she practically spat. "Suggesting he make a meme and send it to the whole school? *Hack* into the school's computer system? You didn't think that might come back to bite him? That maybe telling an impressionable fourteen-year-old to do something *illegal* is not the best idea?" Once she started, she found she couldn't stop, the words spilling over, filled with both hurt and rage. "You didn't stop to consider that telling Ben to hit back at his bullies might not be the best advice, especially in today's climate where it seemed as if the police might knock on your door if you so much as like something on social media? That not only is doing such a thing immature, irresponsible, and unwise, but it could actually *hurt* him?" She shook her head, filled with bitterness. "You've acted so understanding with Ben, but you're still that high school jock inside, aren't you? You have no idea what it's like to be bullied, what Ben went through, what he's still recovering from. He was *hospitalized,* you know," she continued shrilly. "Those kids made his life such a misery that he... that he cut his own wrists." Maybe she shouldn't have admitted that, but right now she needed Zach to know.

Something flared in his eyes and his mouth tightened. "I didn't know that."

"I didn't tell you, because it felt like something Ben should share."

"You didn't think that maybe I should know, since I was spending so much time with him online?" His voice was mild, but Maggie heard latent anger underneath it. She knew he had a point, but she was too angry to acknowledge it.

"You knew he was vulnerable," she argued, her voice turning ragged as she tried to hold back her tears. "And yes, maybe I should have told you all that before, but Ben didn't want people to know. But even so, you *knew* he was vulnerable. You told me so yourself. Why would you do this to him?" she cried. "Or were you just not thinking?" She shook her head, unable to stop the torrent of words, of feelings. "Maybe you really are that thoughtless. And maybe it's my fault, for thinking someone like you was mature enough to—to be a *friend* to my son—"

"Someone like me?" Zach interjected quietly. He arched an eyebrow, looking nothing more than curious. "What exactly do you mean by that?"

"You know what I mean," Maggie cried. "All the signs were there, and I just ignored them. Everyone in town *warned* me what kind of man you are, and I chose not to believe them—"

"Oh?" he interjected again, and now he almost sounded amused. "And what kind of man am I, Maggie?"

"You're just a player, aren't you?" she exclaimed on something like a gasp. "You played with my emotions, and you played with my son's. I can forgive the first, because I'm old enough, *way* old enough, to have known better, but I can't when it comes to Ben."

Zach was silent, his expression impossible to read, although to Maggie's eyes he didn't look remotely apologetic or remorseful. A growl of frustration escaped her. "Aren't you going to *say* something?"

He shrugged, seemingly indifferent. "Why should I? You've made your mind up already."

Maggie stared at him. "Are you saying I'm wrong?"

"Would it matter if I did?" Zach countered. "You didn't *ask* me anything, Maggie. You just barged in here with all your assumptions and accusations and didn't even let me speak."

"The school was going to call the *police*—"

"Is Ben okay?" Zach asked quietly, and Maggie blinked, discombobulated by the sudden shift in his tone, the apparent evidence of his concern.

"Yes," she replied, drawing a steadying breath. "I mean, he will be. I made some calls, and the whole thing is hopefully going to be dropped. But Ben was freaking out, and he's so fragile, and it all could have been really, really bad for him—"

"Yes, it could have," Zach agreed. He turned back to haul another box, and Maggie gaped at him.

"That's it?" she demanded. "No explanations? You're not even going to apologize?"

"I'm sorry Ben got in trouble," Zach replied evenly. "That must have been very difficult for him."

He made it sound as if the whole episode had absolutely nothing to do with him. Maggie shook her head slowly. "I can't *believe* you—"

"No," Zach cut her off, his voice hard as he swung around to face her. "You can't." He stared at her for a suspended second, his blue-green eyes sparking with what looked alarmingly like anger.

Maggie stared back, a sliver of doubt slithering its way into her certainties. Had she gotten him so wrong? Had she stormed in here and jumped to way too many conclusions like he'd implied? But Ben had *said*... and Zach hadn't.

"Why won't you tell me what happened?" she asked, her voice wobbling.

"I don't recall you asking me to," Zach replied coolly, and then he turned away, effectively dismissing her.

Maggie stared at him for another long moment as he returned to shifting boxes, his taut back to her. She wanted to say something, but she didn't know what. She almost felt as if she should apologize, but *he* was in the wrong.

Wasn't he?

And even if he wasn't, she realized slowly, surely it was better this way? That kiss had clearly been a mistake. She knew now absolutely that neither she nor Ben was ready to have someone new in their lives. Someone like Zach.

But if she'd misjudged him...

"Zach..." Maggie began. She could tell he'd heard her by how his shoulders tensed, but he didn't respond. Didn't even look at her. Maggie waited another few seconds, but Zach didn't break his stride as he worked, stacking heavy boxes on top of each other. Frustration filled her, along with something like fear. What if she'd gotten this—him—completely wrong?

No. Even if she had, it was better this way.

Without a word, Maggie turned and left the barn.

## 15

"Penny is a *complete* doll. She'll curl up on your lap the second you sit down and purr to her heart's content. If that's the kind of kitty you want, she is the one, for sure."

*Was* it the kind of cat she wanted? Truth be told, Maggie had no idea what she wanted anymore, cat or otherwise. She and Ben were at the Humane Society because despite the awful argument with Zach last week, she was determined to forge ahead in every other aspect of her life, including getting a cat, maybe even little Penny right here.

"She's so cute," Ben said, reaching out his hand so Penny could sniff his fingers. She was a gray tabby, four years old, past the cute kitten stage but with the sweetest heart-shaped face and big hazel eyes. As Ben tentatively scratched her head, she gave a soft, rumbling purr. Ben laughed and Maggie smiled.

"She really is a sweetie," she remarked.

Julie, the woman who had been showing them the shelter's various cats, gave a sage nod. "She is indeed. Poor girl's been left on her own too long, though. She needs her forever home, and the adoption paperwork only takes a few minutes to fill out."

Maggie hesitated. Was she ready for this? The café was set to open this Saturday, and it still felt as if there were a million things to do. She'd been working flat out getting everything ready—arranging inspections, bringing in supplies, practicing her lattes. Zoe Wilkinson and Liz Cranbury had helped to put posters all over town, and Ben had taken over the digital marketing, setting up a website and social media accounts and posting everywhere either of them could think of.

They'd put ads in all the nearby Connecticut newspapers as well, that Ben had designed. That had been going to be Zach's job, but since Maggie had stormed out of the barn over a week ago, she hadn't seen him once, not even for so much as a second. He hadn't been playing online with Ben, either, much to her son's dismay.

"Did you say something to him?" Ben had accused, looking morose, when Zach failed to appear online the evening of their argument.

"Zach is pretty busy with his own stuff right now," Maggie had replied, wanting neither to lie nor admit the truth. "I'm sure he'll be back online soon."

But he wasn't, and Maggie knew that was her fault. No doubt Zach was staying away from Ben because she'd basically told him he was a bad influence on her son. Whether he was or not, she still wasn't sure, and that uncertainty was tormenting her when she let herself think about it, which was far too often.

"Mom?" Ben prompted as he stroked Penny's back. "Can we get her?"

Maggie hesitated. Was this really the right time to get a cat? But when would be? *Forge ahead*, she reminded herself. *Make a life for yourself, for Ben.* "Why don't we have a look at the adoption papers," she suggested to Julie, "and talk about the process."

Forty-five minutes later, they were walking out of the shelter with a cat. Ben held the pet carrier the shelter had kindly provided, Penny curled up inside, while Maggie carried the litter tray, fresh litter, and a week's worth of food. She had already texted Joshua, asking if he stocked an "everything you need to know about cats" book in his store, and he'd assured her he did. She still wasn't sure if she'd made a giant mistake or not, but she was tired of second-guessing herself on so many things.

"Welcome to the family, Penny," Maggie told the cat as she unlocked the car.

* * *

Back at the café, Penny sniffed around cautiously, her tail swishing, before settling herself in a corner of one of the leather sofas, her head tucked on her paws as she looked around, warily alert but also seeming interested. Maggie couldn't help but smile at the sight of her; the presence of a cat definitely added a coziness to the store that she'd wanted, and she hoped Penny would warm to them in time.

She glanced around the space, taking pride in how great it looked—the comfy couches, the games neatly stacked and labeled in the newly built shelves—she couldn't look at the intricate wood carvings without feeling a pang of something like grief—and a few abstract prints and paintings of the area that she and Ben had bought from various places on the walls. In the back by the kitchen counter, there was the chalkboard menu offering baked goods from The Rolling Pin in her neatest script, along with a few illustrations of cake and coffee that she'd enjoyed drawing. Yet even as that sense of pride gave her a warm glow of satisfaction inside, she felt an ache of regret and sadness for the absence of Zach. He'd worked so hard on everything to do with the café, and she couldn't help but feel that what they'd achieved there was as much up to him as it was her or Ben, if not more. He should have been there.

Would he show up to the grand opening in just three days' time? She hoped so, but at this point she had serious doubts. He'd absented himself from their lives so completely... as she'd basically demanded that he do. She could hardly blame him for not being here, and yet she knew she missed him.

"Do you think Zach is going to come to the opening?" Ben asked, almost as if he'd been reading her thoughts, or maybe just missing him as much as Maggie was.

"I don't know," she replied honestly. "I hope so."

Ben frowned as he slumped into one of the leather sofas, next to Penny, who stilled but didn't move away. Progress already. "Why hasn't he come around all week?" he asked mournfully. "And he's not been playing RQ, either. I messaged him online and he said he was busy with the store, but..." He shook his head, his bangs sliding into his face. "I feel like it's something else."

"I told you he was busy," Maggie reminded him gently as she smiled at her son. He really needed a haircut, she couldn't help but notice. His bangs were far too long, and a trim would give her son less to hide behind, which might be a good thing. They both needed, she knew, to take steps back to a normal life—school, friends, activities. It all felt very far off, especially without Zach in the picture, cheering them on, making them laugh. He really had been good company... for both of them.

"I know you miss him," Maggie continued, "but if he's busy, he's busy, I'm afraid. He'll come back when he's able." Maybe. She wasn't ready to admit to Ben her part in Zach's absence. Whether that made her a coward or a responsible parent she couldn't decide, but she and Ben needed to figure out a way to move on... together.

"But the grand opening?" Ben persisted. "After all the work he's done? He *has* to be here, Mom."

"We'll see," she murmured. It was all she could think of to say. She walked over to scratch Penny under her chin, grateful when the cat gave an approving purr in response. "Meanwhile we have this little lady to keep us company."

As cute as she was, though, Maggie thought, a cat was no substitute for a human... especially one like Zach.

\* \* \*

Maggie spent the rest of the afternoon doing the boring admin work for the café, which involved squinting at her laptop screen and filling out a lot of forms, while Ben did his schoolwork, Penny curled up on his lap like she'd known him all her life. Out of the corner of her eye, Maggie saw Ben absently pet the cat in his lap and she smiled. Getting Penny had clearly been a good decision.

Outside, spring was finally starting to bud—the sky was a pale blue with lemony sunshine bathing Main Street in brightness and warmth, and the tiniest, tightly furled buds on the cherry trees in front of their building had just begun to form. Maggie had checked her phone, and the weather was set to soar to a balmy fifty-two degrees. Well, you took what you could get in New England.

After several hours of sitting cramped in front of the computer, she decided she needed a break. She checked on Ben, saw he was deep into his math homework, Penny having disappeared to another part of the house, and dropping a quick kiss on his forehead—something he let her do if she was fast enough about it—Maggie told him she was going for a quick walk to "clear the cobwebs."

"Cobwebs, Mom?" Ben looked up from the screen, shaking his head. "You sound so old."

"Well, not literal ones," she replied with a smile. "I'm not quite that decrepit yet."

She slipped on her parka and a pair of ankle boots and headed downstairs, stepping out onto Main Street, which was empty. Foot traffic for the café was, she supposed, going to be pretty light. Was she crazy to have continued with this whole endeavor? Maybe, but she didn't want to think negatively. Not anymore, even if it felt sometimes like that was all she was doing.

Maggie took a deep breath, let the cool air fill up her lungs. Although the sun was warm, the breeze was brisk; spring hadn't quite sprung yet, although it was on the horizon. Maggie smiled to see a red-breasted robin flit from cherry tree to cherry tree. She set out up toward the village green, waving at Rhonda in The Starr Light Diner, Lizzy in The Rolling Pin and Zoe in The Latest Scoop, feeling heartened when each woman smiled and waved back. She kept going, up to the village green and around it, glad to see that the messageboards by the church, community hall, and library all sported Your Turn Next posters. Ben had done a very good job with the graphics, she reflected with motherly pride; he'd made the pawn, die, and elven figure 3D, with beams of light streaking out from each one. The writing had a retro vibe, which Maggie thought suited the feel of the café. She hoped others did, too.

It wasn't until she was on the road out of town that she realized where she was walking to. Miller's General Store. Had this whole clear-the-cobwebs idea really just been an excuse to accidentally-on-purpose run into Zach? What would she even say to him if she did?

Annoyed with herself, she turned around and started striding back into town. Her phone buzzed in her pocket, and she slipped it out to see it was her sister Lynn. She'd been avoiding talking to her for the last week because of this whole blowup with Zach, but maybe it was time to admit what had happened. Maggie swiped to take the call.

"Hey," she said, doing her best to inject some enthusiasm into her voice. Her sister wasn't fooled.

"What's wrong?" she demanded. "What's happened?"

"Oh, Lynn..." Maggie sighed. "Nothing all that much. I've been running myself ragged trying to get ready for the grand opening on Saturday."

"Yes, I'm planning on being there, you know, and with bells on."

"Are you really?" Her sister had made similar noises in the last few weeks, but Maggie had semi-discounted them, because it was a two-hour drive and Lynn was usually so busy with work.

"Yes, of course I am!" she exclaimed. "This is a big deal. And," Lynn added, her tone softening, "I took to heart what you said to me earlier. You want this to work, Mags. Well, so do I."

"Thanks." Maggie sniffed and then let out a shaky laugh. "Sorry, I've been kind of emotional lately."

"So what's been going on? Because I can tell something is eating you up. I *know* you."

"I know you do." Maggie decided to be at least semi-honest. "You remember Zach?"

"The thirty-one-year-old gorgeous gamer? *Yes.*"

Maggie smiled at that, even as her heart ached at the thought of him. "Well, things kind of... blew up there," she told her sister.

"I'm assuming not in a good way." Lynn sounded briskly matter of fact, which made Maggie feel a tiny bit better. Maybe it didn't have to be all drama and discord, the way it was in her head. Maybe there was a way through this.

"No, not in a good way," she agreed. "We were getting along so well, and he did so much for the café, and for Ben too. But then something happened, and it made me question everything." As succinctly as she could, Maggie explained about Memegate, forcing herself to include the salient detail that she and Zach had kissed the night before.

"Hmm..." Lynn said after she'd lapsed into a dejected silence. "That sounds... well, to quote Cicero, like a tempest in a ladle. Or as the Brits say, a storm in a teacup. But I appreciate it felt like a big deal at the time, especially for Ben."

This was not the response Maggie had been expecting from her sister, especially not after her ominous comments when she'd first told her about Zach. "Yes, Ben is okay now," she admitted. "Although it certainly shook him up a lot, and the last thing I needed was him going back down that rabbit hole of high school bullying." She had to suppress a shudder at the very thought. "But... do you think I overreacted?" It was what she had been thinking herself, but if her sister, who was the Queen of Caution, agreed...

"I can't say because I wasn't there," Lynn replied. "But from hearing it now, after it's all over... maybe?" She let out a short sigh. "I guess the real question you need to ask is, Mags, was Zach a good influence in Ben's life? I know I had my reservations at first, but the more you told me about him, the more he sounded like a pretty quality guy. So maybe you need to judge him by his actions, and not by the one thing Ben told you. I mean, Ben is fourteen. Are you sure that's what Zach even suggested to him? It sounds, as the kids like to say, a little 'sus.'"

"It's what Ben took away from their conversation," Maggie argued. "And Zach knows he's impressionable. Vulnerable—"

"And every adult knows you cannot be responsible for how a teenager takes your words. You've said yourself many times that you say one thing and Ben hears another."

Maggie closed her eyes. The creeping suspicion she'd had over the last week that she might have made a gigantic mistake was now becoming a tsunami of doubt... and yet what could she do? "Even if you're right," she said in a squeezed-out voice, "it doesn't make that much difference. I'm not ready for a relationship, and that's where Zach seemed to want to be headed, based on some things he said." Although maybe he'd completely changed his mind by now. She wouldn't blame him.

"And he did kiss you," Lynn pointed out. "How was that?"

*Incredible.* Maggie swallowed hard. "It was... okay."

Her sister let out a hoot of laughter. "Maggie Parker, you cannot fool me. I bet it was amazing."

"I thought you didn't like Zach," Maggie protested.

"Am I not allowed to revise my opinion based on new information?"

"Yes, but..." Maggie sighed. "Even if I was wrong about him," she said slowly, "it's only been a year since Matt died—"

"Nearly a year and a half," Lynn corrected her. "And let's be honest, Maggie. You and Matt weren't seeing eye to eye for a while before the accident. Years, I'd say, ever since he got that massive promotion and started insisting on country club memberships and driving a Porsche and all the rest of it. I'm not saying that means you don't grieve him, of course, I know you do, but..." She paused before finishing quietly. "I hope I'm not hurting you by saying that to me it looked like you hadn't had a healthy or happy marriage in some time."

Maggie's knuckles ached as she gripped her phone. She'd never admitted any of that to her sister before. How had she guessed? Had it been that obvious? Had she let little things slip? "Still..." was all she could manage to reply, stumbling over the single word.

"If you're not ready for a relationship, then you're not ready," Lynn stated in the same matter-of-fact voice she'd used before. "And that's *fine*. But don't let fear talk you into doing—or not doing—something. And I think you owe it to Zach to get to the bottom of what happened about that stupid meme. Don't leave it all unsaid and then try to fill in the blanks yourself, with what you've been catastrophizing."

Maggie managed a weak laugh. Her sister really did know her well.

"Now, I've got to head back to work," Lynn told her, "but I'll see you Saturday, okay? Bright and early. And I'm bringing a cake, a big one, so make sure you have plenty of forks!"

"Thank you," Maggie whispered. She really was incredibly grateful for her sister's briskly no-nonsense approach to life. She'd needed something of a stern talking-to, and she'd gotten one.

But what was she going to do about Zach?

## 16

As she ended the phone call with her sister, Maggie realized she was standing in front of Midnight Fashion, the ladies' clothing boutique that Liz Cranbury managed, under the beady eye of the original proprietor, Betty Stein. She'd been meaning to go inside, but she hadn't had a chance yet. Now, as she glanced admiringly at the mannequins in the window with their color-coordinated outfits, she decided she might venture in. A little retail therapy would boost her mood, and maybe she could buy something new to wear to the grand opening.

"Maggie!" Liz exclaimed as she stepped inside the store with a tinkle of bells. "I'm so glad you've made it in. Betty's visiting her grandson today, so I've got the place to myself. And look who's here." She nodded toward Annie, who was standing in front of the full-length mirror in a clinging navy-blue dress, looking glum.

"Oh..." Maggie smiled uncertainly, glad to see Annie, even if her expression was decidedly grim.

"She's buying something new," Liz explained in a stage whisper, "because she's going on a *date*."

"It's not a date," Annie barked. "It's just a friendly get-together, as I told you and every other darned person in this town."

Maggie smothered a smile. This sounded very interesting. "Oh?" she asked as she raised her eyebrows in inquiry. "Who is this friendly get-together with, Annie?"

"Mike the Mechanic," Liz answered for her. Annie was still staring dispiritedly at her reflection. "Do you know him?" Maggie shook her head. She hadn't had any need for a mechanic yet, thankfully, but maybe she'd meet him in relation to Annie.

"I look like I am trying to make a silk purse out of a sow's ear," Annie stated matter-of-factly as she plucked at the dress's stretchy material. "And I have not succeeded."

Maggie glanced at Annie's outfit—a navy dress made of a soft jersey that clung to her ample figure perhaps a little too closely, revealing every bulge and ripple. It wouldn't be flattering on anyone who didn't have a stick-thin figure, at least not without some army-grade control-top under-wear to smooth everything out. But beyond that, Maggie could see that Annie wasn't happy in the dress, that it wasn't *her*, and she realized she knew what that felt like.

How many times had Matt encouraged her to wear eye-wateringly expensive designers, when she would have been content as well as more comfortable in her slightly offbeat colorful clothes, the kind of things she'd worn before they'd become rich, or really, if she was honest, before they'd got married? Lynn's comment about the country club membership and the Porsche had hit home.

He had changed since getting that promotion, something she'd acknowledged herself many times, but what she hadn't fully realized was that despite her resistance, *she'd* changed, too. She'd let herself be changed, gone along with the interior designer and the swanky clothes and the new friends who helped his career, while putting her own preferences aside... so much so that she'd become afraid to voice an opinion, had tensed every time Matt had cast an appraising eye over her, or the dinner she'd made, anything. She'd felt like she was living on some kind of probation, never quite sure she measured up. It hadn't always been that way between them, she acknowledged, but the seed had been there, which had taken root with Matt's promotion.

If she'd been stronger, Maggie reflected, and if their *marriage* had been stronger, she would have explained how she felt to Matt and chosen her own furniture, her own clothes... just as Annie should.

"Tell me about this get-together," she encouraged. "Is it formal? Semi-formal? Smart casual?"

Annie plucked at the dress again, impatient. "What do those even mean?" she cried. "I don't know. How should I? I don't go on dates."

"Don't you mean 'get-togethers'?" Maggie teased, and Annie gave her a rueful smile, their gazes meeting in the mirror.

"I'm too old to go on dates or—"

"Not too old for get-togethers," Maggie insisted with a smile. "So, what do you think the dress code is?"

"He's taking her to the Litchfield Inn," Liz informed her in a hushed voice. "Which is only the nicest restaurant in all of northwestern Connecticut! Men have to wear jackets and there is a no-jeans policy. And I have it on good authority that Mike is wearing a *suit*."

"I can't believe he even owns one," Annie muttered. "And he won't have shaved that ridiculous beard and he'll still have grease under his finger-nails, so..."

"Wow, well, that sounds exciting," Maggie interjected cheerfully. She was dying to know more about this unexpected romance between Annie and Mike, but she decided to get the details another time. "What about something with a little more flow?" she suggested to Annie. "Maybe a pantsuit?"

"I know just the thing!" Liz hurried over to a rack and pulled out a simple but elegant pantsuit in deep red. It had a deep vee neckline but was otherwise perfectly modest, the cut of the pants loose and flowing.

"I've never worn a pantsuit," Annie remarked dubiously. "I really don't do anything like this."

"So you've said," Liz replied with a good-natured groan. "Just try it on," she coaxed. "I think Maggie is right. I think you're more of a pantsuit girl."

With a sigh, Annie took the hanger and disappeared into the dressing room. Liz took the opportunity to sidle closer to Maggie.

"So," she remarked in the same stage whisper she'd used before, "I haven't seen Zach around your place lately."

"No, I think he's been busy." Maggie tried to sound offhand and unbothered and was pretty sure she'd failed at both.

Liz's eyebrows rose. "Busy? He was a whole other kind of busy last week..." She gave Maggie a knowing smirk before bursting into laughter. "I can't believe you, girl! Snagging that hottie! I am *so* impressed."

"Liz." Maggie tried to give her friend a quelling look. "That was a freak event," she stated as firmly as she could. "One time only."

Liz's smirk disappeared as she nodded in understanding sympathy. "Honestly, knowing his reputation, Maggie, that might be just as well. You don't want to get hurt."

"Are you two talking about Zach Miller?" Annie burst out of the dressing room, looking like a fabulous Amazon in her scarlet pantsuit.

"Oh, *Annie*," Liz breathed. "You look gorgeous!"

Annie shrugged off the praise as she half-glared at them both. "Were you talking about Zach?" she demanded again.

"Um... yes," Maggie admitted. She was glad there was no one else in the boutique to hear more about her personal life. Had Annie heard what Liz had said about her "snagging that hottie"? Probably.

"Liz Cranbury, you should know better than to listen to this town's gossip when it comes to Zach's reputation," Annie declared, her hands fisted on her hips. "He might have been a bit wild in high school, it's true, but those days are long gone. Do you remember how he held down the store for over a *year* while his mother had cancer? When he was still a teenager, by the way. And how he and Jenna took that place over, when the Millers just upped and moved to Florida, with barely a goodbye. Not to mention how he's always willing to help anyone out, for just about anything? You turn around, and Zach's there, lending a hand—"

"If he's not on a date—" Liz murmured, shooting Maggie a laughing glance.

Annie rolled her eyes. "*I'm* going on a date. The boy's allowed to look for love. Aren't we all?" She glanced down at the pantsuit and then gave Maggie an approving nod. "Now this is something I can wear without feeling ridiculous. I'll take it!"

As Annie went back to change, Maggie browsed through the racks, looking for something to wear to the grand opening, her mind still on

Zach. It felt as if every interaction she had was pointing to the fact that she'd made a big, fat mistake. The question remained, though: what could she do about it? The answer was obvious—talk to Zach. Apologize. And she could do that, of course, but then the far thornier question remained about their kiss. What did she really want to do about *that*? And what if it wasn't up to her, anyway? It had been a whole week. Reputation aside, Zach had every right to have moved on, especially considering the way she'd behaved.

Recklessly, feeling the need to *do* something, Maggie took out her phone. As Liz rang up Annie's purchase, she opened WhatsApp and thumbed a quick message.

> I'm pretty sure I overreacted the other day. I'm sorry.

She pressed send before she could overthink it; she was already having palpitations at the thought of Zach reading the message.

"Now," Liz sang out, "we need to find something for you, Maggie!"

Two blue ticks appeared by her message. He'd read it already.

Maggie swiftly slid her phone into her pocket as Liz came toward her. "What are you looking for? Something special?"

"An outfit for the grand opening of the café," Maggie answered. Her fingers were still curled around her phone, waiting for the vibration to indicate that Zach had replied. "Good luck with your 'get-together,' Annie," she called as her friend started out of the store. "I want to hear all about it."

"And I want to hear all about you and Zach," Annie replied. "Because something seems to be going on there!" So she had heard the hottie comment, clearly. "Don't misjudge him the way everyone else has," she added, like a warning.

Okay, the universe was clearly sending her a message. Maggie's fingers tightened on the phone, willing it to vibrate. With a wave, Annie left the store, and Maggie turned her attention to Liz, who was pulling out silk blouses and tailored pants, not the kind of thing she wanted to wear to the opening of a boardgame café.

"I was thinking something more casual," she told Liz. "And colorful. And maybe a little... funky." She blushed as she said it.

"Colorful and funky?" Liz glanced at Maggie's outfit—a gray turtleneck sweater and dark blue jeans. She hadn't worn colorful and funky in a long time, but once she'd loved bright colors and whimsical prints. She'd put all those clothes away when Matt had got serious about his job, and she'd done her best to assimilate with the soccer moms of Greenwich, Connecticut—a well-heeled bunch, to be sure.

"Okay, let's see what we have in the colorful and funky department..." Liz murmured as she continued to riffle through the racks.

As discreetly as she could, Maggie slid her phone out of her pocket, just in case she'd somehow missed the vibration of a message. Nope. Nothing. Disappointment curdled her insides, and she slipped her phone back in her pocket. Well, what did she expect? Zach to snap back with a "sure, no problem"? She'd been too unkind for that, she realized. It was a bitter pill to swallow, the taste of her own insensitivity acrid on her tongue.

"What about corduroy?" Liz suggested. "I always think it's such a fun fabric, and this bright purple is pretty colorful, especially with the patch pockets." She held up a miniskirt in vivid purple with aqua-blue patches for pockets. Maggie might have worn something like that in college, but now as a respectable, middle-aged widow?

Except that wasn't who she was. It wasn't who she wanted to be anymore.

"I'll try it on," she told Liz, and took her hand off her phone to take the skirt.

"And let me find a top to go with it, maybe in that blue..." Liz said, hurrying away to look.

A few minutes later, Maggie was gazing at her reflection, quietly amazed at the transformation some new clothes—and color—could do. She might still have that skunk-like streak of white in her hair, but her face looked younger, less drawn, and the aqua top Liz had found brought out the blue in her eyes.

"Wow, that took ten years off you," Liz remarked, and then gave an embarrassed laugh. "Sorry, I meant that in a good way."

"I took it in a good way," Maggie assured her. She smoothed her hand down the skirt. With colorful tights and ankle boots, it would be the exact vibe she'd wanted for the opening of the store—fun, enthusiastic, a little bit whimsical.

"I'll take them both," she told Liz firmly. "And some tights."

Back at home, Maggie put her purchases away and then went to check on Ben—and Penny, who had definitely settled into their household routine. Her son was in front of the computer, morosely clicking on the message icon on the RainQuest app. A small sigh escaped her as she leaned against the doorway of the kitchen.

"Did you finish your schoolwork, Ben?"

"Yeah, a while ago." He sighed and slumped a little more in front of the computer. "Zach still hasn't messaged me. And he hasn't been on RQ at *all*."

"He's busy—" Maggie reminded him, knowing it was sounding like an increasingly feeble excuse.

"I know, but you'd think he'd still hop on once in a while. It makes me think he didn't ever want to play with me. Like, was he just doing it out of *pity*?" He pushed disconsolately away from the computer, spinning in his chair.

"Oh, Ben." It was, Maggie feared, time to be fully honest. "I think he's avoiding playing RainQuest because... well, because I'm afraid I might have been a little harsh with him," she admitted with a wince.

Ben glanced up at her, his gaze full of accusation. "So you *did* say something!"

"I might have lost my temper a little," Maggie felt compelled to acknowledge. "About the whole meme thing, I'm afraid."

"*Mom...*"

"I know, I know," Maggie said quickly, holding up one hand to stop the understandable torrent of dismay. "It was just, you'd told me you got the idea from him, and—"

"I mean I *did*, but I knew he was joking," Ben retorted, his voice full of disgusted defensiveness. "He even told me he wasn't suggesting such a thing, and that I shouldn't do anything like that, *obviously*."

Maggie had to bite her tongue to keep from pointing out that Ben hadn't mentioned those rather salient details during their discussion. In any case, she should have winkled them out, and even if she hadn't, she should have asked Zach about it before launching into her tirade.

"Why did you get so mad at him?" Ben complained. "He had nothing to do with it. I mean, not *really*."

"Well, like I said, I was in a temper," Maggie replied, although already she suspected that the reason was a bit more complex than that. If she were being entirely, and uncomfortably, honest with herself—and not necessarily with her son in this moment—some scared part of her had been looking for a reason to back away from Zach. As lovely as their kiss had been, it had also terrified her. And not just the kiss, but the intensity of her own feelings. She'd needed an excuse to escape, and the whole meme episode had unfortunately provided it. "I'm trying to make it right," she told Ben. "I apologized to him—"

Ben straightened, then leaned forward in his chair. "You saw him?"

"No," Maggie admitted, "I messaged him."

Her son rolled his eyes. "You know that's not the same thing. You told me that all the time when I wanted to be homeschooled. 'Nothing beats face-to-face communication,'" he mimicked in a falsetto that was definitely not how she sounded. At least she hoped not.

"And yet I let you do school online," Maggie reminded him. "But I was right. Face-to-face is always better." She was really shoveling in the humble pie today. Should she approach Zach directly? The thought made her insides fizz with anxiety and a tiny, treacherous bit of excitement. It had been over an hour since he'd seen her message, and he still hadn't replied. What did that mean? She didn't want to second-guess him, but it was hard not to. Hard not to fear the worst, that he just wasn't interested anymore.

"So are you going to talk to him?" Ben pressed.

"Yes, I will," Maggie agreed, with some reluctance. That was sure to be an awkward and uncomfortable conversation, but it was one she knew she needed to have. "Now, since Zach isn't playing RainQuest with you at the moment, what about teaching me how to play?"

Ben stared at her in disbelief. "You?"

"Why not?" Ben had asked her to learn before, but Maggie had always been reluctant. Now she knew she wanted to share in something that her son loved. "I'm meant to be running this boardgame café, after all," she reminded him. "I need to know how these games work for when you're not there. RainQuest is a boardgame as well as an online one, right? We stock it downstairs?"

"Yeah," Ben agreed cautiously, "but I didn't think it was your thing."

"Well, it isn't," Maggie admitted with a smile, "but it's yours, and that makes me want to know how to play it."

Ben swiveled around to face the computer. "Well, it's pretty complicated," he warned her, "but I guess I can teach you the basics."

Maggie smiled at his dubious tone, knowing already that she would find the basics challenging enough. She pulled out a chair and drew it next to Ben before settling down. "Okay," she told him. "Show me."

Ben started taking her through the fundamentals of the game, and after ten minutes, Maggie's brain hurt.

"So you have to choose a class, species, and occupation for your character, and all those things affect your... stats?" she clarified, trying to keep track of all the different options.

A smile tugged at Ben's mouth as he rolled his eyes good-naturedly. "Mom, I covered that ages ago. Keep up."

"Sorry..." Zach had told her what species she would be, she recalled, and she'd forgotten to look them up. What had they been? She racked her brain trying to remember, and then she saw it on the screen and pointed. "Ben, what's an... aasimar?"

"An aasimar? Why?"

"I've just never heard of it before."

"It's a planetouched humanoid descended from a celestial," he read off the screen, before clicking on the icon so Maggie could read the description.

Aasimar grew up cautious around others, sometimes misunderstood. With an inherent bent toward empathy for others, they can be easily hurt. They will openly strike at evil, but never if it endangers an innocent.

She swallowed hard. That all felt weirdly revealing, like Zach had seen something in her she hadn't even meant to show him. Was she easily hurt?

"And a shadar-kai?" she asked, recalling the other option Zach had given her.

Ben clicked on the relevant icon, and Maggie read the description.

Shadar-kai were originally trapped in the Shadowfell by the Raven Queen, unwilling to enter the Fortress of Memories. While they are hardier than other elves, thanks to the Raven Queen's curse they can be mournful, yet they also have strong magical abilities to resist evil and ultimately they can do much good.

Wow. Zach had really understood her and her grief in a way she was only beginning to understand herself. She felt both strangely vulnerable and also touched that he'd seen so much and found a gentle way to tell her. He'd wanted to know what she'd thought, she remembered. She wished she'd looked up the descriptions earlier. Maybe then she would have understood that Zach had far more depth to him than she'd so unkindly assumed, back when she'd confronted him and hurled all those hurtful things like burning arrows.

She checked her phone again; still no message.

"Mom?" Ben broke into her thoughts. "We're moving on now, okay?"

"Yes. Moving on." Maggie powered off her phone, not wanting the distraction. She felt like a teenaged girl, constantly hitting refresh on her messages, hoping her crush had texted. "Keep going," she told Ben, and he launched into a description of how potion making worked. Even though she wasn't really getting the game, Maggie enjoyed the way his eyes lit up and his voice filled with enthusiasm as he talked about it. He'd been so morose and unhappy for so many months—years, even—that seeing him look relaxed and confident was a huge boost. It gave her a needed certainty that moving to Starr's Fall had been the right thing to do, even if there was a long way to go before they were both fully settled there. And Zach was part of that; at least he had been...

She really needed to make it right between them.

"Mom, are you listening?" Ben broke into her thoughts.

"Yes," Maggie said quickly. "You were talking about, erm, potion making...?"

"That was, like, three minutes ago. I'm talking about combat now."

"Combat. Right." Ben looked at her dubiously and Maggie let out a little laugh. "I am trying, Ben."

"I know." He fell silent, his hands resting on the keyboard. "Dad was never interested in RainQuest," he remarked after a moment, his gaze on the computer screen. "Or me playing it." He paused, while Maggie waited, her breath held, her heart feeling squeezed. She and Ben had never talked this way about Matt. They hadn't talked much about him at all, a fact that only now filled her with a guilty unease. Should she have forced those conversations? Why hadn't they had them?

"Sometimes," Ben continued, still looking at the screen, "I felt like he didn't really like me playing it. Like, it was a little too weird and geeky for him, you know?"

"Oh, Ben..."

"Wasn't it?" Ben turned to look at her, his face full of bleakness. "Sometimes I think Dad wished he had a son like Tyler Gerard."

Tyler, the star lacrosse player who had bullied Ben relentlessly, simply for being different. "No, Ben," Maggie told him forcefully. "Dad would have never wanted that." She paused, needing to order her thoughts because it was so important she got this right. "I think sometimes he struggled with how to relate to you," she explained carefully, "simply because he wasn't into the kinds of things you were. But he loved you. He always loved you. I know that absolutely."

"Yeah." Ben didn't sound particularly mollified. "I mean, that's kind of a parent's job, right? But... I wish he'd *liked* me more."

"Oh, Ben." Maggie didn't know what to say to that. She couldn't deny it, not entirely, because she wasn't all that sure that Matt had liked *her*, even if he'd loved her, especially as the years had gone on and he'd become so focused on his ambition and making sure their lifestyle matched it.

"I'm not always sad he's gone," Ben blurted. He hunched down in his seat, drawing the neck of his sweatshirt over the bottom of his face as if to make himself disappear.

Maggie's heart ached with sorrow for her son. How long had Ben been keeping this secret? "That's okay, Ben," she said softly. She thought of what Laurie had told her; relationships, especially the most important ones, were never straightforward. "It's okay to have complicated feelings. You don't have to feel guilty about that." She rested a hand on his shoulder. "I'm glad you told me." A moment passed where neither of them spoke, and Maggie just let it be. Eventually she took her hand away and Ben sat up, pulling his sweatshirt back down and wiping his eyes like he had a speck in them, although Maggie knew better.

"Now," she said, with as much enthusiasm as she could muster. "Tell me again about the combat skills. My character can use a morning star but not a halberd?"

Ben glanced at her, a small smile curving his mouth. "Yeah, that's right," he told her. "I think you're catching on."

## 17

Maggie gazed at her reflection as butterflies swarmed and swirled in her stomach. The café's grand opening was in just under an hour and she had no idea if it was going to be a success, a complete flop or something depressingly in between and mediocre. What was occupying her thoughts even more than that was that she had no idea if Zach was going to come.

Two days ago she'd worked up the courage to go to Miller's General Store to see him. She'd stepped inside, browsing the aisles for a few minutes while she'd tried to look discreetly around for him, but he hadn't been anywhere to be seen.

Jenna had been behind the counter, though, and so when Maggie had taken a couple of cans of beef barley soup up to the cash register—bought only as a pretext to be in the store—she'd forced herself to ask casually, "Is Zach around? I haven't seen him in a while."

"Nope, he's gone into Hartford," Jenna replied as she scanned the soup. "Probably on another date."

Maggie had frozen for a moment before she'd murmured something nonsensical, then taken her soup and scurried out of the store. A *date*. Well, why shouldn't he, she told herself. He had every right. It wasn't as if *they* had been dating, after all. She recited all the reasons not to be hurt, but still, it had stung, more than a little.

Zach still hadn't replied to her message, and she hadn't seen him for nearly two weeks. It was the middle of March, spring getting closer every day, a time for fresh starts, and she clearly needed to have one when it came to Zach Miller. She told herself all this, and she did her best to make herself believe it.

Now, with the grand opening looming, Maggie doubted Zach would show up. While she understood why he stayed away, she was still disappointed, not just for herself, but for Ben. She wished Zach could show up for him, at least, especially since he'd read her apology.

A knock sounded on the door of the café, and Maggie's heart lifted. *Could it be...?*

Ben beat her downstairs, clearly hoping for the same thing. But when he unlocked the door, it wasn't Zach standing there with his crooked smile and gorgeous eyes.

"Lynn!" Maggie hurried forward to liberate a giant sheet cake from her sister's arms. "You're early!"

"I thought you might need some help setting up," Lynn replied. She glanced around the café as Penny leapt down from one of the sofas and wound her way between her ankles, tail high and swishing. "Wow, this place looks amazing. Great job, guys. And who's this?" She leaned down to pet Penny.

"Penny," Ben told her. "We just got her a couple of days ago."

"Seems like she's settled in."

"She has," Maggie confirmed. "Thank you so much for this cake. Ben, look." The cake had the logo from his banner printed onto the icing, complete with the die, the pawn, and the Sylvana figurine. Lynn must have gotten it from their website.

"Wow, thanks, Aunt Lynn!" Ben looked boyishly pleased. "That's really cool."

"What's really cool is this place," she returned. "I'm so proud of you both." Lynn straightened, giving Maggie a frank look. "Now, what can I do to help?"

Maggie had thought she was pretty organized, but now that the moment was approaching, it felt as if there were a million more things to do. The espresso machine needed to be turned on; the baked goods freshly delivered from The Rolling Pin put into the glass case; cups laid out; the floor swept one last time.

The three of them buzzed around the room, plumping pillows and restacking games, trying to make everything perfect. Ben put a mellow jazz playlist on for background music and got a few games out as "suggested plays." It was ten minutes to ten, and a few people were already milling around outside the store—Laurie and Joshua, Annie Lyman, Zoe Wilkinson, and a family with young kids that Maggie had never seen before. Her heart swelled with gratitude and affection for every single person there— this town really was making an effort. They were coming out for her, for Ben, and it meant so much.

Then she saw Zach.

He was in the back of the small crowd, wearing his usual t-shirt and plaid shirt combo with worn jeans and scuffed hiking boots, a paper bag tucked under one arm, his expression friendly but, Maggie feared, a touch reserved. Was she imagining the cool way he was surveying the scene, his eyes slightly narrowed, his expression unreadable?

She faltered in the middle of fanning some napkins on the counter, and then hastily put them in a pile before trying to catch Zach's eye to give him a welcoming smile. A smile that she hoped managed to convey, in the simple curving of her lips, how sorry she was, as well as glad that he'd made it. How she wanted to talk and hoped he did too. Even if all that could be communicated with a single smile, it didn't matter, because he didn't look at her once.

"Mom, it's two minutes to ten. Do you think we can open? There's, like, twenty people out there now." Ben's voice was full of excitement and only a trace of anxiety as he glanced outside at the growing crowd. "People want to come in!"

"I think we should do it," Lynn said, and Maggie nodded, tearing her gaze away from Zach, again.

"Okay," she agreed, "let's do it. Ben, do you want to do the honors?"

Her son's eyes widened with panic at the thought. "Me?"

"Yes, you," Maggie replied, smiling. "This was your idea, remember? I didn't even know what a boardgame café *was*." For a poignant second, she recalled the scene, ten months ago now—Ben lying on the hospital bed, his wrists heavily bandaged, spring sunshine pouring through the window, her heart as heavy as a bowling ball as she'd considered the total wreckage of their lives. "How can we make this better?" Maggie had asked him, needing him to answer, to *know*, because whatever it was, she was already certain she would do it. "What do you want to change about our lives?"

Ben's reply had been stark and wrenchingly honest. "Everything," he'd said simply.

Maggie had mentally staggered under that statement, the awful enormity of it, but then she'd forged ahead and asked him for details. With some gentle prompting, Ben had shyly started to paint a picture of the life he'd dreamed of—no more high school bullying, and in fact no more high school at all; he'd rather be homeschooled. He wanted to live in a small town where people knew and liked each other, open a boardgame café where he could help out and teach people the games he loved, especially RainQuest. He had, Maggie recalled poignantly, even mentioned having a cat.

And here they were, she thought with both pride and gratitude, living out that dream in just about every detail. She'd made it happen for Ben. They'd made it happen *together*, and so had Zach... who still wasn't meeting her eye.

"Go ahead, Ben," Maggie encouraged her son, forcing her fears about Zach to the back of her mind. "Open the door and welcome people in. This is your moment. Enjoy it!"

Ben gulped, then nodded, a sparkle coming into his eye that filled Maggie with joy as well as relief. "Okay," he said, like he was talking himself into it. "Okay." Then, straightening his shoulders in a way that made her feel a rush of fierce love and pride for her son, he went to the door and threw it open.

"Ladies and gentlemen," he called out in a booming voice that had Lynn smothering an affectionate laugh. "Welcome to Your Turn Next!"

A cheer went up and then people began to file in, exclaiming over everything—the sofas, the games, the baked treats, even Penny, who was curled up in the window seat, surveying everyone with the kind of haughty arrogance only a cat could possess. Within minutes, Maggie was too busy to worry about Zach; before he'd even come in, the family with little kids was asking if they had Candyland, and Maggie was bringing them over to the section of the bookshelf that Ben had organized for all the younger-player games. She glanced at the carving of a snake and ladder that Zach had made on the shelf's joint, and had to swallow the lump that had formed in her throat.

The next hour passed in a blur; Maggie manned the espresso machine while Lynn did the cash register—she had been intending to do both herself but quickly realized what an impossible job that was—and Ben acted as host, welcoming people in, recommending games, and helping people set up them up as well as learn the rules and strategies. Every chance she got, Maggie snuck a look at her son, who was so clearly in his element, relishing being the one with the know-how, making it all happen.

"The Dixit expansion pack is really worth the investment," she overheard him explain seriously to a family with teenagers who had come in and were sitting all together on the three-seater sofa. "Especially once you've played a few times. But if you're just starting out, go with the original cards, for sure. They're pretty wild."

"You know," Lynn said quietly, when there was a brief lull in the coffee orders, "I had my doubts about this whole venture, as I made abundantly clear, but looking at him here, Mags... you did the right thing. I've never seen Ben so happy."

"Thank you," Maggie whispered. Tears stung her eyes, and she blinked them back. It felt good not to just to hear her sister say that, but to see it and know it herself. They'd chased a dream and amazingly, thankfully, it had worked out.

Inevitably, her gaze moved to Zach. She'd been achingly conscious of him the whole time, even at her busiest—where he was in the room, who he was talking to, what he was doing. Every time he raked a hand through his hair and let it flop back onto his forehead, she noticed. The way he tilted his head back when he smiled. How he rocked back on his heels. His easy laugh as he cocked his head. Yes, she was aware of it all, because, she realized, she'd come to know him so well.

He was chatting with Annie Lyman now, over a game of bananagrams they seemed to have abandoned; they were clearly more intent on their conversation than forming a crossword with the tiles in front of them. He still hadn't looked at her.

"Have you talked to him yet?" Lynn asked quietly, following Maggie's gaze. "That's Zach, I'm assuming? The most gorgeous guy in the room?"

"Yes." Maggie let out a small, sad laugh. "And I tried." She paused, unable to tear her gaze away from him. "I think... I think maybe the moment has passed."

"The moment never passes, Mags," Lynn told her with a sternly knowing look. "Not unless you let it."

\* \* \*

By mid-afternoon, Maggie was exhausted, and the café was still humming with activity. People had left and others had come in, and Zach had stayed the whole time, moving from table to table, chatting with everyone and playing plenty of games. He'd talked to Ben at one point, and Maggie had strained to listen but with the conversation, music, and the veritable roar of the espresso machine, she hadn't been able to hear a word that had been said.

A few minutes later, Ben had come over, a long, emerald-green cape flung over his shoulders. "Look what Zach got me," he exclaimed as he turned around to let the cape swirl out. "It's a sylvan energy robe."

"A what?" Maggie answered with a laugh.

"It's from RainQuest," Ben explained in the tone of someone who thought she should have known this, which she supposed she probably should have. "He got it from a special gaming store in Hartford. Isn't that *awesome*?"

"It is very awesome," Maggie replied sincerely as she duly admired the cape. "You look like a grand maestro."

"I know, right?" Ben agreed, beaming. "It's perfect. He said I should wear it when I'm working the floor here. It can be my thing." He hesitated, the old anxiety once more shadowing his eyes. Maggie had been so grateful to see less of it in the last few weeks. "You don't think that's too... *weird*, do you?"

"Are you kidding me? It's exactly the vibe of this place. It's amazing,

Ben," she stated firmly. "Go ahead and strut your stuff." Ben grinned and Maggie watched, smiling, as he straightened his shoulders, threw his head back, and then returned to the floor of the café.

Most teenagers, she knew, wouldn't be caught dead in a sylvan energy robe, but she loved that her son was now able to wear it with pride—and that Zach had helped him gain that much-needed confidence. And, she realized, he'd bought it in *Hartford*... where he'd been the day she'd been trying to talk to him. Had he gone there specially, just for Ben? Maybe Jenna had been wrong about him being on a date...

Once again, she tried to catch his eye, but he wasn't looking at her. It had to be deliberate, she thought. He had not met her gaze once in all the hours he'd been in the café. The realization was both humbling and hurtful. He must still be so angry with her, she acknowledged bleakly. Either that or he'd become indifferent, which felt worse.

By four o'clock, things were finally starting to slow down, just a handful of customers left, and Maggie was dead on her feet. The opening hours of the café going forward were noon to six, and she half-hoped it wasn't as busy as this, because she already knew she wouldn't be able to manage it. Today, however, had been a very good one for business, and she was glad for all the support.

"I think I'll shut down the espresso machine," she told Lynn when there hadn't been any coffee orders for fifteen minutes. The only people left in the café were Zach, Ben, Joshua, Zoe, and Bella Harper. They were all playing the boardgame version of RainQuest, with Zach, Ben and Joshua the most committed, trying to explain to Bella and Zoe how it all worked, the board on the table in front of them with about a million tiny pieces.

"This is like, a serious investment of time and energy," Zoe remarked, shaking her head as she ran her fingers through her short, hot-pink hair. "I'm in awe. I'm also kind of intimidated."

"It does take a certain mental discipline as well as a commitment to the craft," Zach replied gravely, and Joshua nodded seriously. They fist bumped, their expressions appropriately somber, which made Maggie smile.

"I can see how it could be really cool," Bella said, only somewhat dubiously. She glanced at Ben. "Do you have the patience to teach us, though?"

"Oh." Maggie watched as her son's cheeks turned pink. "Definitely."

Zoe laughed as she shook her head. "I never knew this side of you," she told Zach teasingly. "An RPG gamer. You are so not who I thought you were, Zach Miller."

"Well, I'm glad you've come to your senses," Zach replied lightly.

Were they *flirting*, Maggie wondered with a lurch of something close to panic. Zoe was closer to Zach's age, and she was pretty and funky and fun. Why shouldn't they flirt? Why shouldn't they *date*?

Why were her insides knotted up with jealousy and agitation at the mere thought?

Maggie tried to listen to their continuing banter as she cleaned the espresso machine, but she was too far away to hear, and frankly, that was probably for the best. She did not need to add to her anxiety and obsession at this point, but she was determined to talk to Zach and give him a proper apology for the way she'd behaved. Maggie just hoped she managed to find an opportunity.

"This has been really fun," Lynn told her as she came back to the kitchen to help clean up. "And my cake went over well."

"Your cake was amazing," Maggie told her. They'd served it along with the free coffees when people had bought a boardgame, and it had definitely been appreciated.

"You've been amazing," Lynn returned, "and so has Ben." She paused, dishrag in hand, as she gave Maggie an earnest look. "Honestly, I'm so impressed by how you guys have pulled this off. You know I had my doubts—"

"Ye-es," Maggie replied with a good-natured eyeroll, and Lynn laughed.

"But I mean it. This has been a total success."

Maggie glowed from her sister's praise, but she still felt she had to be the voice of pragmatic pessimism. She'd already learned how much hope could hurt. "Well, this is just the beginning," she told her. "I mean, everyone comes out for the grand opening out of curiosity, and the free coffee—and cake! But as for the future..." She let the words trail away before finishing. "I just hope it really is a success. And that we can eventually turn a profit, because Matt's life insurance won't last forever."

"I think it will be a success." Lynn gave her arm an encouraging squeeze. "A big one. I have a good feeling about this."

Impulsively, Maggie threw her arms around her sister's shoulders and gave her a hug that Lynn laughingly returned. "Thank you, Lynn," she said, her voice muffled against her sister's shoulder. "That means a lot."

"I'm serious," Lynn said as she gave her another squeeze. "You've done well, Maggie. Really."

"Thank you."

"But," Lynn continued, and Maggie couldn't help but laugh because her sister always had a but, "you need to talk to Zach. I saw you sneaking looks at him all afternoon. Whatever is or isn't between you, you need to clear the air. Soon. Today, if possible."

"I know." Maggie quailed at the thought. Zach had absolutely *not* been sending her any positive overtures—no chitchat, no quick, smiling glance, no wryly arched eyebrow, *nothing*. What was she meant to take from the absence of all contact? Nothing good, she feared, but as she'd told Ben many times, just because something was hard didn't mean you didn't do it.

"I just need to find the time," she told Lynn.

Lynn nodded toward the group still sprawled on the sofa. "No time like the present."

"They're playing RainQuest." Even if Zoe looked like she wanted to be put out of her misery.

"But Bella's looking pretty into it," Lynn remarked with an arched eyebrow. "And into Ben, frankly."

"You think?" As discreetly as she could, Maggie glanced at her son and Bella, who was sitting next to him, heads close together as they chatted earnestly about the game. "Maybe..." She wasn't sure she was ready for Ben to be into girls, or girls to be into Ben, but it was an interesting and hopeful development.

"Go over there and ask him if you can talk," Lynn urged. "There's never going to be a perfect time, Mags."

"I know..." Maggie knew she did not sound enthused by the prospect.

She really did not want to ask Zach to have a private word in front of Joshua, Ben, Zoe, *and* Bella. But she knew she had to figure out something.

She finished tidying the kitchen, taking her time to give the espresso machine a *really* good polish, and then finally, knowing she could put it off no longer, she steeled herself to go over to their table and clear up the empty coffee cups and plates. As she stooped to collect the dishes, she glanced at Zach. As usual, he wasn't looking at her, but she was the closest to him she'd been all afternoon, so she could see the glint of stubble on his jaw and the way his lashes swept downward as he studied his cards.

"Having fun?" she asked lightly, making sure to look around at the whole group.

"My brain hurts," Zoe admitted. "But this café is such a cool idea. I'll definitely be coming back, although, sorry, guys, maybe not to play RainQuest."

"That's great to hear," Maggie told her warmly. "We've got plenty of other games."

"But I should probably go," Zoe continued, rising from her chair. "I closed The Latest Scoop for this, but I might open it for the evening now that it's getting warmer."

"If you call this warm, you really are a New Englander," Zach told her, and Zoe rolled her eyes.

"Aren't we all?"

Her departure invariably caused that of the whole group, and within a few minutes, with a scraping of chair legs and gathering of coats, Joshua and Bella had gone as well, although not before Bella had promised Ben she'd come back so he could keep teaching her the game. Ben was clearing up, and Zach started helping him. Maggie watched them for a few seconds before she took the dirty cups and plates back to the kitchen.

"Did you say anything?" Lynn whispered, and mutely she shook her head.

"*Maggie...*"

"I know." She took a deep breath. "I will." Resolutely, Maggie went back to the table. Ben was just putting the lid on the box, and Zach was reaching for his jacket. It was now or never. "It would be great if you could stay for a little while," she blurted. "I'd love to, um, talk with you." Cringe.

That had sounded so clunky and awkward, but how else could she have put it?

Zach looked, crushingly, like he was going to refuse. He had one arm already in the sleeve of his jacket, a look of resolute regret hardening his features. *Ouch*.

"Yeah," Ben chimed in. "You should totally stay, Zach. You aren't doing anything now, are you?"

Zach glanced at Ben, and then finally, *finally*, at Maggie. The look in his eyes was veiled, but also decidedly cool.

"I can stay for a little while," he said, the words aimed at Ben.

Maggie's spirits plummeted at that reserved, even reluctant, response, but then she told herself she'd just have to take what she could get.

"Great," she told him, and her voice came out in that high, slightly manic tone she'd once used with Ben. "Thanks," she added in a more normal voice. "I appreciate it."

Zach just nodded.

## 18

Zach had no idea what to expect as Maggie fidgeted and fiddled with her hair while Ben cleaned up the game and he simply waited, wondering what she wanted. Wondering also what *he* wanted, because ever since that talk with Jenna—and then Maggie had come blazing in with her assumptions and accusations—he'd realized he really hadn't known. He'd *thought* he'd known what he wanted out of life for years, but those two conversations had scattered all his certainties. It wasn't a nice feeling.

Nearly two weeks later, he was still reeling from the revelations, as well as the hurt. Maggie might have thumbed a quick text to assuage her conscience—and probably more for Ben's sake than his—but he was getting pretty tired of rolling over every time someone made an assumption about him. Jenna had shown him he needed to change. So, without realizing it, had Maggie.

"Let me help clean up," he told her, and she began a fumbling protest before she fell silent and then nodded.

"Thanks. That would be great." She turned to the kitchen and Zach followed her.

Ben had remained by the big sofa as he continued to put away all the elaborate pieces of RainQuest, while Lynn mumbled something about needing to check on something upstairs, and scurried away. Clearly she was trying to give them some privacy, and Zach wondered what Maggie had told her.

In the kitchen area he started loading cups into the industrial dishwasher.

"Another beast," Maggie joked with a nod to the big silver machine. "It scares me just as much as the espresso machine."

"It's just an appliance," Zach replied, and he saw Maggie wilt. If she'd been hoping for a bit of banter, he already knew he didn't have it in him. Not now.

Silently she started collecting cups from the countertops and handing them to him to load. They worked for several minutes in a silence that felt thick with tension. Zach had no intention of breaking it. Maggie had been the one who had said she wanted to talk, so she could talk.

"Look..." she began, just as Zach switched on the industrial dishwasher and the kitchen was filled with the noise of its mechanized roar. Maggie winced, and Zach gave an apologetic grimace. He hadn't meant to cut her off; it had just happened that way.

"Sorry," he said gruffly once the dishwasher had finished.

"It's okay." She cleared her throat. "All I really wanted to say was I'm sorry for what I said before, you know, back at the general store, about the whole meme thing. I shouldn't have rushed in with my assumptions the way I did." She swallowed, clearly forcing herself to meet his gaze. "I'm sorry."

She waited for his reply, and in truth Zach struggled to think of how to respond. How did he even feel? As far as apologies went, it had been decent enough, if a bit stilted. He didn't doubt she meant it, and yet it still felt like so little.

"Thanks," he finally said. "I appreciate that."

"Um, okay." Maggie looked disconcerted by his reply, or maybe by his lack of enthusiasm. "Well... I hope you're not still angry. I mean, I understand why you would have been before, but..." She trailed off, clearly longing for him to fill in the blanks the way he once would have. He would have *jumped* to make things easier for her. Smooth out all the bumps, make a wry little joke to pave the way a little more.

Trouble was, he just didn't feel like it anymore. Not with Maggie, and not with anybody in Starr's Fall. He was tired of trying to prove himself to this town. To anyone.

"I'm not angry," he told her. He'd been *hurt*, but he was getting over it.

"You don't sound like you're not angry," she replied unhappily. "Zach, I really am sorry…"

"I know."

She gazed up at him, her dark eyes full of misery and confusion. Zach felt a stirring of sympathy, and for a second he wanted to do nothing more than take her into his arms, kiss her the way he had before, and forget all this stupid drama. It wasn't who he *was*. At least, it wasn't who he had been.

But he was changing, whether he wanted to or not, and truth be told, he suspected that this kind of change had been a long time coming and was a good thing. But he was sorry for Maggie's sake, as well as his own. Whatever relationship they might have had felt like a what-could-have-been moment that had most definitely passed.

"Hey, I've finished cleaning up." Ben came into the kitchen, and then faltered. "Um…" He glanced between Zach and his mom, clearly taken aback by the unhappy silence that seemed as if it weighted the very air. "Who died?" he joked, his voice wobbling.

Maggie let out a huff of tired laughter. "Sorry, I'm just exhausted from the day." She turned to Zach, managing to look directly at him without meeting his eye, which took some skill. "Thanks so much for helping out, Zach." She could have been talking to any Joe Schmoe of Starr's Fall, a fact which irritated him even though Zach knew he'd been treating her the same way.

"Zach, why don't you stay for pizza?" Ben suggested eagerly. "My mom promised takeout tonight because she said she'd definitely be too tired to cook."

Ben sounded so hopeful that Zach hated to turn him down, but he was about to, for Maggie's sake, when she chimed in, "Yes, you should stay." She sounded wooden, but she wouldn't have said it unless she meant it, and maybe they did have more to say to each other.

"Okay," Zach said, and smiled at Ben. "But I'm not trying pineapple and black olive pizza."

"Come on," Ben laughed back, "you totally should. I bet you'll love it."

Zach kept up the banter with Ben as Maggie turned off the lights and they all headed upstairs. He had a feeling this evening was going to be painfully awkward, and also might tempt him to change his mind about Maggie, but he was determined to stay his course.

He wasn't going to be the stooge of Starr's Fall any longer, accepting everyone's insults with a smile, taking everything on the chin like none of it hurt. And he wasn't going to be the pathetic loser who was still sleeping in his childhood bedroom, taking orders from his big sister like he didn't have any ideas of his own.

No, what Jenna and Maggie had said to him had been a huge wake-up call. Zach Miller was going to be different... starting now.

* * *

As she came up the stairs, Lynn gave her a narrow-eyed look and Maggie just shook her head in response. She wasn't about to explain to her sister, in looks or whispers, what had happened between her and Zach... and in truth, nothing had. She'd apologized and he'd accepted her apology. End of a very brief, sad story.

She busied herself calling in their pizza order while Ben, Zach, and Lynn all deconstructed the details of the day. Ben was bubbling over with ideas—a chess tournament, rankings for various games kept on a scoreboard, a toddler hour with early-childhood games, bridge and Scrabble nights.

"Wait, do you play bridge?" Zach had asked with a laugh, and Ben had grinned, ducking his head.

"No, but I bet some people in Starr's Fall do."

"Henrietta Starr probably does," Zach agreed. "Her family founded the town and she's about ninety years old now. Laurie's friends with her. You might have seen her around."

"Yes, she came into Max's Place when I was there." Maggie recalled the elderly woman's acerbic dignity with a small smile. "She's quite the personality."

"She's got a tongue on her, that's for sure. She'll tell you what she really thinks." Zach turned to Ben. "You have the heart of a gamer and the mind of a businessman," he proclaimed. "Great combo, Ben."

"I think I'll go get the pizza," Maggie announced. "Too bad Slice of Heaven doesn't offer delivery service yet. Or that there aren't any other takeout places in Starr's Fall."

"And Slice of Heaven probably never will offer delivery," Zach told her, his eyes glinting in a way that *still* made her stomach flip. "Jake, who runs the place, got his license suspended after too many speeding tickets so it's pickup only for the foreseeable future."

"Oh, dear." Maggie felt her mouth tip up at the corners, but she still felt —and probably looked—miserable. She wished Zach hadn't agreed to stay, especially if it had been out of some kind of pity, for either her or Ben.

"Why don't I come with you to collect the pizza?" Zach suggested. He was already rising from the sofa and reaching for his coat.

"Sounds like a good idea to me," Lynn said in brisk agreement, with a stern look at Ben, who was clearly wondering why it took two people to get a couple of pizzas.

"Fine," Maggie replied, unable to summon a friendlier response. She felt too raw and fragile, which was alarming, because they'd barely spoken... but she supposed that was why she did.

They went back downstairs and out to her car in silence and had driven all the way down Main Street before Maggie finally worked up the courage to say something.

"So I guess this whole thing has kind of tanked anything more between us," she stated with an unaccustomed boldness that felt both reckless and welcome. She'd rather know, she decided, than keep skirting around what was becoming painfully obvious.

Zach stared straight ahead of him, his hands loosely clasped in his lap. "It depends on what you define as 'this whole thing,' I guess," he replied in a voice that was far too neutral.

"Well... me getting mad at you. And," she added, forcing herself to say it all, "jumping to conclusions about what you'd said to Ben—"

"It wasn't that," Zach interjected quietly, and there was a sorrow and a hurt in his voice that made Maggie wilt inside.

"What was it, then?" she made herself ask. "Because clearly something has changed, Zach. I mean... I know it was just one kiss, but it meant something to me."

"It meant something to me, too," he replied in the same even tone.

"Okay..." She wasn't sure where to go from there. What more could she say? "So what changed?"

Zach was silent for a long moment. Maggie waited, her hands gripping the steering wheel tightly, her stomach swirling with dread as the silence stretched on. What on earth was he going to say?

"Look, I know this is a cliché," he finally said, still staring straight ahead, "but it's not you, it's me. At least, it's *mostly* me. It's a little bit you, too, I think, even if you don't see it."

"What—"

He held up a hand. "Let me finish."

"Okay."

"As you know, I've dated a lot. And as you also know, this town sees me as some kind of player, who goes on dates and then dumps the women afterwards, like I'm just sowing my wild oats or whatever. But that's never how it's been. At least, mostly. Mostly, *I'm* the one who is dumped, because I go in too serious, I create all these expectations, looking for Miss Perfect, and she doesn't exist. Everyone ends up disappointed." He sighed and leaned his head back against the car seat. "That year staying at home with my parents when my mom had cancer really changed me. I didn't want to party and fool around and have fun anymore. I just wanted what they had —a stable marriage, a togetherness, and a purpose that they worked at *together*. At least, that's what I told myself. But my sister said something to me recently—right before you stormed into the barn, actually—and it made me realize how messed up it's all been for me. How I've become such a people pleaser, without even realizing it, because of the way my parents were—not with each other, but with me and Jenna."

They'd pulled into the darkened parking lot of Slice of Heaven, and Maggie parked the car and waited for more. Zach finally turned to face her, his face half-hidden in shadow although Maggie could still see how grimly resolute he was.

"I won't go into all the details about my childhood and all that kind of crap," he told her with an attempt at wryness, "but I've come to realize it was kind of unhealthy. And after you came into the barn and said all that stuff, I took a long, hard look at our relationship. I know we didn't really have one, but even in just our friendship, I realized I was the one doing all the heavy lifting." He held up a hand to stem any protestations she might have made, although in truth Maggie was reeling so much from what he'd said so far that she couldn't think of a single thing to say. "I'm not accusing you of anything," he told her. "I'm accusing myself. I should have stopped trying so hard a long time ago."

The bitterness in his voice surprised and alarmed her; she'd never heard him speak this way. It wasn't who he *was*. "Zach... there's nothing wrong with trying," she ventured cautiously. "Or being a nice person—"

"There is when it's solely to make people like you." Now he sounded as if he were full of self-loathing. "And frankly I think I've been in that mode for way too long."

She sat back, trying to digest everything he'd said. "When you said you'd done all the heavy lifting..." she began, and Zach gave a twitchy shrug.

"I'm not saying you should have done more, Maggie. Let's be honest, we didn't know each other that well, and I recognize that you and Ben have gone through a hard time, harder than I even realized, and so you were in a different kind of place. It's just... when you came into the barn and threw everything at me that everyone in this stupid town has insisted on believing for years, and you didn't even *ask* me, just bought into all the assumptions, even knowing how I felt about it all, because I'd *told* you..." His voice cracked, and Maggie had to close her eyes. When he put it like that, it made her realize, so wretchedly, how much she must have hurt him.

"I really am sorry," she whispered as she felt the hot press of tears against her closed lids. "So sorry, Zach."

"I know. And I am, too." Zach drew a quick, steadying breath. "But I'm done with proving myself to anyone anymore—to you, to my sister, to all of Starr's Fall. That's not who I want to be now."

"Zach..." Maggie knew she needed to be as honest as he had been, even though it felt like sticking pins in her eyes, every single word sharp and painful. "I threw all those accusations at you as an excuse," she told him, her voice wobbling all over the place. "I was scared. Scared of being in a relationship, of being vulnerable, of *feeling* so much…" She stumbled over the words, longing for him to understand. "Just scared in general. I didn't mean any of what I said to you, I promise. It was just the fear talking."

"I understand that." For a second, as he looked at her, Maggie felt the wild lurch of hope that maybe it was going to be all right. His lips curved into a small smile, and he even leaned forward a little, and she did too, almost as if they might kiss. She wanted to, felt that desire flooding her senses, making her yearn, and she thought Zach did, too…

Then he sighed and sat back. "But I'm not sure it really matters at this point, Maggie. I'm sorry, but…" He shook his head. "I just can't. Not now. Not till I figure out who I am, what I'm doing with my life."

Maggie nodded her understanding, even though she felt cut to the heart. She'd just bared her soul, and he'd said it was a moot point. "Like I said," he continued resignedly, "it's more me than you." He paused before adding, "Although I will say you should have told me how vulnerable Ben was, considering how much time I was spending with him—for his sake, not mine. If I'd known he'd been hospitalized for a *suicide* attempt… well, that's something I would have taken very seriously." He gave her a meaningful look that made her feel about two inches tall.

"I know I should have," she whispered. "*Zach*…" Her voice broke, and he reached out and tucked that single white streak of hair behind her ear.

"I still think you're amazing," he told her in a husky voice. "And gorgeous. And sexy." Maggie had to close her eyes to keep a tear from slipping down her cheek. She wasn't going to beg, but oh, she *wanted* to. Zach leaned forward and brushed a kiss across her cheek, his lips soft and cool as she inhaled the woodsy scent of him, and it made her ache all the more.

Then he leaned back and opened the car door. "Come on. The pizza will be cold."

Maggie didn't think she could have felt any more miserable as she followed him into Slice of Heaven. She could have dealt with his anger, she thought, or even his hurt; she could have survived a painfully honest conversation, if only it had *led* somewhere. But this felt like the dead end of all dead ends; there was no way forward, not just because of her, but because of him.

They'd only kissed twice, but it had felt like the beginning of everything. And it was only now that it was all over before it had really started that she realized not just how much she missed it, but how much she needed him. Zach Miller had been the best thing about her life in Starr's Fall, and she'd gone and completely ruined any chance they might have had together.

# 19

"Do you have Scrabble in this establishment?"

Maggie blinked in surprise at the sight of Henrietta Starr in the doorway of her café. She was dressed magnificently in a tweed skirt suit, a moth-eaten fox fur, head intact, draped around her bony shoulders, and a broad-brimmed hat trimmed with ostrich feathers perched on top of her head. Clearly she'd made something of an effort.

"Yes, we do have Scrabble," she replied warmly. "It's so nice to see you again, Miss Starr. Would you like to sit down? I can get you the game—"

"My dear," Henrietta Starr replied haughtily, "if you know the game at all, you must realize one cannot play Scrabble by oneself."

"That's true," Maggie acknowledged. Ben was upstairs doing his schoolwork, and she was alone in the café. Was the town's matriarch implying she wanted to play Scrabble with *her*?

Henrietta arched one thin, silver eyebrow. "Do you play?" she demanded.

"Er... I know how," Maggie replied. Scrabble was one of the few games she'd known how to play before opening the café, although not many had asked to play it. Over the last few weeks, while they hadn't had the flood of the customers they'd experienced on the first day, they'd still had a steady stream of gamers coming through the doors—families, teens, older couples, little kids. Your Turn Next had become something of a gathering point for the community, for which Maggie was very grateful.

"Would you like me to play with you?" she asked Henrietta, who sniffed in response.

"If you *must*, I suppose," she replied on an aggrieved sigh, "but by all means, please don't put yourself out on my account."

Maggie choked back a startled laugh. Laurie had warned her about Henrietta Starr's acerbic manner, but it was another thing to experience it herself. "I'd love to play," she stated firmly, and went to get the game.

Over the last month, she'd been doing her utmost to say yes to just about everything. Yes to bringing library books to Barb Lyman and chatting with Annie; yes to helping out with the spring festival that Starr's Fall Business Association was putting on; yes to her mother-in-law's surprising request to visit Ben next weekend; yes to finally getting in touch with some old college friends; and yes to playing Scrabble with ornery old ladies.

For too long she'd been hiding behind her grief and guilt, saying no to the world and everything in it because it had been easier. Safer, too, and ultimately more selfish. Her harsh words to Zach might have been a wake-up call to him, but his to her had been one, too, no matter what he'd said about it being him, not her. *Mostly*.

What Maggie knew was that she never wanted to be accused of not doing the heavy lifting in *any* relationship again. She didn't want to stew in the juices of her own emotions and not consider other people's, especially people she cared about, like Ben, or Lynn, or yes, Zach. Even if he'd chosen not to care about her. Accepting all that had been a bitter pill to swallow, but then most medicine was. And like most medicine, what Zach had said to her had been needed. She'd needed someone to shake her out of her determined stupor.

She and Zach had reached something of an equilibrium over the last month that Maggie accepted without truly enjoying. He played Rain-Quest online with Ben some evenings, and he came around to the café a couple of times a week, often for no more than a brief, friendly check-in, the same as Joshua Reed or Zoe Wilkinson would do, a quick hello, a swift smile, a perusal of the games, a teasing remark about her espresso-making skills. It hurt, the quickness of that smile that never reached his eyes, the friendliness that felt anodyne, but she understood it. Sort of, anyway.

Several weeks ago, he'd told her, in a matter-of-fact way that did not invite either questions or judgment, that he'd moved out from his parents' house and was renting a little log cabin on the edge of town, near the waterfall that had given Starr's Fall its name. He'd reduced his hours at the store and was considering some other options, although Maggie didn't know what those were, and, judging from his careful tone, she hadn't felt she could ask. Zach was clearly figuring himself out, and she knew she needed to let him do it.

Of course, Starr's Fall being what it was, none of these decisions had gone unnoticed. Maggie had lost track of the number of conversations she'd determinedly stayed silent through as everyone marveled and made conjectures about Zach's sudden life changes.

"Is it a crisis, do you think?" Liz Cranbury had asked, her blue eyes wide. "Is he in *trouble*? I feel like maybe I misjudged him." She'd leaned forward, dropping her voice to a loud whisper. "It's as if he's suddenly become *sensitive*, and no one ever knew. Did he ever say anything to you?"

"No," Maggie had replied firmly. "Not a word. And whatever he needs to do, well, he should do it."

She had, despite her own disappointments, come to believe that quite strongly. Zach needed this time, this space, to do whatever he needed to do to make a life for himself in this town... and Maggie wasn't a part of that. She had learned to accept it, but she still didn't like it. A thousand times or more she'd wished she had just *thought* for a moment before she'd rushed in with her accusations and angry judgments, even as she accepted that those had been no more than flimsy excuses for the far deeper fear she'd felt about her own feelings. It was all too late now, anyway, she reminded herself more than once, and really, that was just as well. Or it would be. Hopefully. Maybe.

"Here we are," Maggie sang out cheerfully as she forced her thoughts of Zach to the back of her mind. She took the lid off the Scrabble box and lifted out the bag of tiles. "I bet you're really good," she told Henrietta, whose lips twitched in response. Had that been a smile, Maggie wondered, or a sneer?

"I play tolerably well," she replied with dignity, which Maggie suspected meant the elderly woman was going to wipe the floor with her.

It soon became achingly apparent, however, that that was not going to be the case at all. After carefully arranging her tiles, and then drawing the lower letter to go first, Henrietta spent several minutes staring at her letters and then, very carefully, arranged the letters P-A-T. She straightened, clearing her throat, and then gave Maggie a beady look as if to dare her to say anything.

Maggie did not. She played I-L-E off the P to make pile and then smiled encouragingly at the older woman. "Your turn next," she quipped, but maybe Henrietta had forgotten the name of the café because she simply stared.

Then, after a few agonizing seconds, she made E-N-D off Maggie's E. The game continued apace, with each of them making pitiful, single-digit scores on every turn. Maggie felt the urge to both laugh and cry. Here was this dignified and clearly proud woman, playing the best she could, and daring Maggie to say anything about it.

Maybe that was all you could do when life came at you hard, Maggie reflected. Hold your head up high and try your best.

They were halfway through the tiles, the board a maze of three- and four-letter words, when Henrietta admitted stiffly, "I'm afraid my memory's not what it used to be. I once regularly scored seven-letter words in this wretched game." A sigh escaped her, long and trembling. "'Like the ghost of a dear friend dead/is Time long past.'" She glanced up, her lips pursed. "That's Shelley."

"Mary or Percy Bysshe?" Maggie asked, and Henrietta's nostrils flared.

"Certainly not Mary," she replied.

"I guess not," Maggie agreed, although to be fair she didn't really know. "But I gather the gist of that poem is that time flies." She smiled wryly. "And it kind of stinks."

Henrietta let out a rasp that was not quite a laugh. "Shelley had a *bit* more of a way with words," she replied, and placed T-A-B-L-E down to make her best word yet. Sometimes, Maggie thought, you just had to take what you were given and go with it. "You seem to be making something of yourself in this town," Henrietta continued as she replaced her tiles. "By all accounts."

"Oh, well..." Maggie couldn't tell by her tone if this was considered a good or bad thing. "We're trying, I suppose, to settle in. Starr's Fall has been a welcoming place."

"And something of a place to hide away," Henrietta replied with a narrowed, shrewd glance.

Ouch. How had this woman, who had never met her before, seen that? "Yes," Maggie agreed as she put down A-R-L-Y to make EARLY, the Y on a double letter space. "Sometimes in life you need to hide away for a little while."

"I hid away for about thirty years," Henrietta replied baldly. "Not that I recommend you taking that much time. You look like you're on the wrong side of forty already, if I'm not mistaken."

"You aren't," Maggie agreed with a laugh. Henrietta Starr looked like she was on the wrong side of eighty. "Who says it's the wrong side, anyway?" she added with some defiance, and Henrietta merely arched an eyebrow. Maggie decided not to press the point. "Why did you hide away?" she asked her instead.

"Well." Henrietta pursed her lips as she rearranged the tiles on her stand. "Typically, at first it was because I was hurt. And then it was because I was scared. And finally it was because I couldn't be bothered." She glanced up, the shrewdness in her pale blue eyes replaced by a compassion. "Try not to get to the third stage, if you can."

They finished their pitiful game of Scrabble without any further deep talk, and Henrietta left, promising to come again. "I also play bridge," she told Maggie. "But you need four players for that."

"I'm sure we can rustle some up," Maggie promised her. Alone in the café, she tidied up before sinking into the window seat next to Penny, who purred comfortably as Maggie sank her fingers into the feline's fur. Spring had finally sprung, and outside the late afternoon sun was sending buttery rays over the cherry trees that were reaching peak blossom, every single branch sporting a plethora of pink puffballs. The sky was pale blue, a few sparrows streaking across it. Maggie was content—mostly—but she wished she felt happy. She missed Zach, she knew. A lot.

A sudden, urgent tapping at the door had her turning. Laurie stood there, her face pale with anxiety.

"It's open," Maggie called as she rose from her seat. Laurie flung the door open and closed it behind her with a rattle of glass. "Laurie, what's wrong?"

"Nothing's wrong. Not exactly. I just..." She sighed and shook her head. "I heard from my mom again."

"You did?"

Laurie nodded. "I haven't told anyone yet. Joshua went to New York for some book thing and Jenna and Annie... well, they're my dear friends but they don't always get it, you know? Jenna thinks I should just cut my birth mom off totally and Annie can't talk about anyone's mom without getting grumpy or tearing up. It's so hard for her." Laurie shook her head, looking caught between misery and excitement.

"It is, but we're talking about you now," Maggie reminded her. "Let me make you a coffee and you can tell me all about it."

The story came out over lattes, complete with a frothed fern that Maggie was particularly proud of. Rose, Laurie's mother, had written her a letter—brief, to the point, asking her to meet.

"I couldn't tell the tone at all," Laurie admitted, her hands cradling her cup. "I mean, is she sorry for trying to pay me off or is she worried I might make trouble for her? It's been over six months. Why now?" She shook her head. "At first I was so happy that she'd reached out, but now... now I'm wondering if it's better not to meet. To protect myself, you know?"

Maggie took a sip of her own coffee. "I've generally found that protecting yourself doesn't work out too well. You get hurt anyway, and you also have to live with regrets, never knowing what could have been."

Laurie's eyes widened as she lowered her mug. "Okay, I have to ask... is this about you and your husband... or about you and Zach?"

Maggie grimaced in rueful acknowledgment. "What does this town know about me and Zach?" She'd been doing her best not to listen to the gossip, and so far she'd succeeded. Mostly.

"I think everyone is wondering," Laurie told her. "I mean, Zach spent so much time here, and then he just *didn't*, you know? And now he's having this complete life revamp—which I don't think is a bad thing, by the way

—and no one knows what's up with him." Laurie paused, her smile turning playful. "And no matter how much you tried to play it down, I could always tell you really liked him. Your eyes gave it away. They lit up at his name. They still do."

"They don't," Maggie cried, appalled that she could be so revealing, even now.

"They do," Laurie assured her. "And I'm not the only one who's noticed."

"Oh, heavens." Maggie pressed her hands to her now flaming cheeks. "That is seriously embarrassing."

"Only if you let it be. Zach's a good guy, Maggie." Laurie's smile faded. "Sometimes I've felt people here have given him a hard time. I'm a newbie, so I didn't live through his history, but it was all in high school, so..."

"There's nothing going on with me and Zach." Maggie cut her off before Laurie could give her the hard sell. "And that's not by my choice," she added quietly.

"Oh, Maggie..." Laurie reached for her hand. "What happened?"

"Nothing much," she confessed on a sigh. "I was stupid and scared—trying to protect myself—and Zach decided he didn't want to play those games anymore, which was totally fair. We're still friends, so—" She found she couldn't go on. There was a lump the size of a golf ball forming in her throat and Maggie had the horrible suspicion she was about to start bawling. "I really miss him," she finished on a sniff, and then had to wipe her eyes.

"Oh, Maggie..." Laurie said again, helplessly. "Have you told him how you feel?"

"Yes, basically, and he was... appreciative, I guess, but he said it didn't matter at this point, which it doesn't. Anyway." Now she had to wipe her damp cheeks. "Let's talk about you and your mom. Are you going to write her back?"

Laurie was quiet for a moment, pensively gazing into her coffee cup. "Yes, I am," she finally said. "And maybe you should give Zach another chance, too."

Maggie was already shaking her head. "I'm not the one who needs to give chances here, Laurie—"

"Give him a chance to reconsider," Laurie told her. "If you miss him that much, what, really, is the risk?"

Humiliating herself yet again, Maggie thought wryly, not that she even cared about that anymore. "I don't think so," she told Laurie. "Not yet, anyway. Zach needs some space. I need to give it to him. When he's figured out what he wants to do with his life..." She let that thought trail away into nothing. When Zach did that, she feared, he might very well walk away from her and Ben for good.

# 20

Zach stood on the porch of the log cabin, his coffee mug cradled between his hands as he watched the mist rise from the river in ghostly, gossamer strands and dawn sunlight filter through the haze of clouds. Although the air possessed a chill at this time of day, he knew it would be warm by mid-morning as the sun rose in the sky. It was mid-April, and spring had finally come to this corner of northwestern Connecticut, so the landscape was a glory of blossom and birdsong, damp earth and new leaf. Zach loved this time of year, after the frigid, deadening months of winter, when the whole world woke up again. Every breath felt like a fresh start, which was how he was feeling, now that he'd finally made some changes to his life.

None of it had been easy, mainly because changing so much as the color of your shirt in Starr's Fall could make the front page of its newspaper and feed the town's gossip mill for weeks. Moving out of his parents' house, more or less quitting his job, and no longer taking any crap about his personal life had been cataclysmic not just for him, but for everyone he knew, simply because none of them knew how to let people change.

Zach was going to make them do it, even if it involved a lot of kicking and screaming.

He took a sip of coffee, narrowing his eyes as he watched a heron land gracefully on the water, slate-blue wings outstretched. For some reason, the bird's inherent elegance made him think of Maggie. He missed her, missed what they'd almost had together, but at the same time he knew he'd made the right decision... for that time. He needed to figure himself out before he tried yet another relationship that would likely be doomed to fail. He cared too much about Maggie for that, and yet at the same time he recognized he very well might have missed his chance... something he was going to have to accept.

The memory of the look of hurt on her face when he'd given her that hackneyed it's-me-not-you line still had the power to make him wince. The trouble was, he'd meant every word. He just didn't know if Maggie believed him.

Over the last month, he'd made sure to drop by Your Turn Next every few days, checking in on both Maggie and Ben, keeping the conversation light, wanting to maintain their friendship. Although he always enjoyed seeing her, he didn't know if it was working or not. He felt a distance from Maggie that he didn't like, even though he knew he'd been the one to move away first. Whether they could move back toward each other one day remained to be seen...

Sighing, Zach turned away from the dawn beauty of the morning, swallowing the last of the coffee before he put the mug in the sink. This morning, he was enacting the next stage of his life plan, and he was determined to make Jenna agree to it.

He grabbed his jacket and keys and then headed out to his truck for the ten-minute drive into Starr's Fall. When he'd first told her he was doing it, Jenna had thought he was being "a little much"—leaving home and renting this log cabin out in the middle of nowhere—but the space had been good for him, better even than he'd expected. He'd enjoyed not being so close to Starr's Fall, where sometimes it felt as if life were being played out on a stage. He'd also been glad to take a step back from the store and reconsider what he really wanted to do with his life.

And now that he had a plan, he just needed to sell it—or really, state it —to his sister. Because this time Zach wasn't taking no for an answer.

He pulled into the parking lot of the store, the gravel crunching under the wheels. Usually he walked around to the back where their living quarters were, but this time he unlocked the front door and went through the store, feeling like it was a reckoning as well as a goodbye. He strolled down the aisles, running his fingers along the shelves of hardware supplies and grocery staples, including the argued-over soup. How many afternoons had he spent stocking these shelves? How many days stacking boxes or manning the cash register? All through high school, he'd done shifts whenever his parents had asked him, and then that year of his mom's cancer treatment, when he'd often been alone in here, wondering where on earth his life was going. The years since his parents had decided to retire, working with Jenna, hoping for something better.

None of it, Zach acknowledged, had been a waste, but he knew now he wanted more for his life than waiting and wishing. Today he was going to start going after it.

"Zach?" Jenna's voice seemed disembodied as it floated from the back of the store, where a door connected it to their living quarters. She came forward, pulling her cardigan more closely around her. "What are you doing here so early?" She pressed her lips together. "I thought you were taking a *break*."

"It wasn't a break," Zach replied evenly. Even though he'd stepped back from managing the store—or really, attempting to—he'd pulled his weight with shifts and grunt work, the same as he always did. "But I want to talk to you."

"Oh?" Jenna's eyebrows rose as she nodded. "Okay, well, this sounds serious."

"I'm serious, if that's what you mean. Let's go into the barn."

"The barn?" Jenna, Zach knew, hardly ever went into the barn, where they stored their inventory; she usually stayed in the store while Zach dealt with stock.

"Not the store's stock barn," he replied. "The other one."

"Okay..." Shaking her head, Jenna followed him out of the store, to the barns behind. While the first one was used for inventory, the one behind was crammed full of furniture his parents had collected over the years. They'd never done much with it, and a lot of it was junk, but antiquing had been one of their hobbies. Zach had lost count of the number of weekends they'd gone trawling through the countryside looking for treasures while he and Jenna held down the store.

Now he unlocked the door and slid it open. Sunlight streamed into the dim space, catching the dust motes dancing through the air.

"I haven't been in here since Laurie went through it months ago," she remarked. "And I think it must have been years before that. I half wonder if we should set fire to the whole thing."

"We definitely shouldn't do that," Zach replied. "Because I want it."

Jenna swung around to look at him in surprise. "What?"

"I want it," Zach repeated firmly. "All of it. This furniture has just been sitting here getting wood rot for decades. Mom and Dad don't want it—I already asked them."

Now her mouth dropped open. "You what—"

"I called them last night. They were fine with it." He met her gaze levelly. "And there's no reason why you shouldn't be, too."

Jenna gaped at him for a moment. "You talked with Mom and Dad?"

"Yes, on this thing called a phone?" He gentled his voice to keep from sounding too snarky because that wasn't how he felt at all. The conversation had been both good and healing, and he thought Jenna could probably benefit from the same. "They were actually really glad to talk to me," he told her, "and they invited me to come down to Florida for Memorial Day. You too. Said we should see each other more, even."

"What..." Jenna looked completely flummoxed, which was fair, because Zach had been pretty surprised by the suggestion himself, as well as gratified.

"People can change, Jenna," he said quietly. "They can have regrets as well as learn and grow. Even Mom and Dad."

"And you?" she asked him after a moment, sounding thoughtful. "Is that what this is about?"

"I've changed," Zach agreed. "But yeah. This is me moving on. Because the way things have been? Let's be honest. They haven't been working for a while, for either of us."

Jenna was silent for a long moment, her gaze downcast, face drawn in pensive lines. Then, to his shock, it started to crumple.

"Jenna—" He flung one hand out toward her. He couldn't remember the last time he'd seen his sister cry. She was always so strong, so indomitable.

"I'm sorry," she sniffed, gulping as she wiped her eyes. "I just feel like I've been a... a bad person. A bad *sister*, to you. Have I forced you out of the business? Our *home*?" She dropped her hands from her face as she looked at him bleakly. "Be honest."

"Maybe it felt that way at first," Zach answered slowly, "at least with the store. But this is a good thing for both of us, Jenna. This doesn't have to be some big split. You need to have full control of the store without feeling like you're cutting me out. And I need to do my own thing. Both of those are okay."

She was silent for a moment, absorbing what he'd said. "Hence, the furniture," she said at last.

He nodded. "Yeah."

She glanced around at the stacked furniture—sofas and armchairs, bureaus and desks, all piled haphazardly on top of one another. "So what are you planning to do with all this stuff?"

Zach sucked in a breath and then let it out slowly. "Well, it might sound a little crazy," he began cautiously, "but I want to start a furniture restoration business. Working on the bookshelves for the boardgame café made me realize how much I actually like that kind of stuff. And obviously, I'm not super experienced, so I'll have to start slow and work my way up, as it were, but... that's what I want to do." He nodded toward the furniture. "Start by refinishing this stuff, and then moving on to better-quality items, custom pieces. I've enrolled in a class on woodworking in Bristol. They have a whole series on making and restoring furniture." He let out a shaky laugh; it felt both invigorating and scary to tell his sister his fledgling dreams, ones that were only just starting to become reality. "So that's my plan," he finished.

Jenna was quiet for a long moment. Zach had no idea what she was thinking, but if his sister was true to form, she'd soon tell him. She stayed silent, though, and that made him nervous. Was his plan that outlandish, that ridiculous, that she couldn't bring herself to burst his bubble?

"I think that's great, Zach," she said finally, sounding so quietly sincere that he was rendered speechless. "But why not use the barn as your work-shop? I mean, if you want to, at least at the beginning. There's space here and it will cut down on costs, and..." She paused before smiling almost shyly. "And actually, it would be nice to work near each other, even if we weren't actually together, I mean, if you didn't want to be. I... I don't think I valued your input as much as I should have, I *know* I didn't, and I didn't realize that until you were gone."

Zach couldn't keep a huff of laughter from escaping him. "You didn't value my opinion at all really, Jenna, but that's okay. People can change, after all." He grinned at her. "Even you."

*   *   *

By late that afternoon, Zach had made a good start on organizing the furniture in the barn into stuff he could salvage and stuff he just needed to get rid of. He'd also tinkered with the start of a website and opened a few social media accounts. Miller's Woodworking and Furniture Restoration was now in its nascent form, and when Jenna had stopped by the barn to see how it was all going, she'd been quietly approving in a way she never had when they'd been working on the store together.

As he drove down Main Street back toward his cabin, Zach felt good about everything that had happened—his conversation with his parents last night as well as the one with Jenna this morning. The start of his own business, the steps he'd taken toward following his dreams.

Inevitably, his gaze swung toward Your Turn Next as he drove past. It looked empty save for a lone figure curled up on one end of the big sofa, her dark head bent. Maggie. Impulsively he pulled into a parking space on the side of the street and got out of the truck. He had no idea what he was going to say to her, only that it felt important to see her now, after he'd made so many strides. He realized he wanted to tell her about them all.

Bells jingled as he opened the door of the café, and Penny, curled up in Maggie's lap, looked up, her ears twitching. Maggie's ears didn't twitch but she looked almost as wary as the cat, even as she smiled. This was how it had been between them for the last month, Zach knew. Friendly but not the way it had been. The way he knew he still wanted it to be.

"Zach..." His name sounded like a question on her lips.

"I thought I'd stop by." He glanced around the café and saw it was indeed empty, save for Maggie sitting on the sofa. "Where's Ben?"

"Out with friends." She said this with a wry sort of pride. "Two boys from Torrington High School are into RainQuest, it seems. They came into the café today and they got to chatting to Ben... It was all about stats and combat strategies and I don't even know what." She let out a shaky laugh. "You'd probably have known what they were talking about, but I felt like they were speaking a foreign language."

"It kind of is," Zach agreed, smiling.

"Anyway... they invited Ben out to The Latest Scoop for ice cream, and amazingly, he agreed." She sounded both thrilled and fearful. "They're there now, but I'm practically counting the minutes, worried something might go wrong."

"That's understandable," he replied quietly, "after all you've both been through."

She nodded, looking down at the cat in her lap. "I know I should have told you about all that before. I'm sorry I didn't. It wasn't fair to you... or Ben. Starting over doesn't mean forgetting everything that went before."

"No." He thought of his own life. Maggie was right, change didn't mean forgetting. It meant remembering and then being different. "Maggie," he said sincerely, wanting to reach out and touch her hand but deciding not to, "that's great to hear, about Ben."

"It is, isn't it?" Her voice sounded shaky, and she let out a self-deprecating laugh. "I know it doesn't sound like that big a deal, but it feels huge."

"It is huge," Zach replied quietly. He sat on the opposite end of the sofa. "When did he last go out with kids his own age?"

"Honestly? Never. I mean, not since middle school, anyway, although I will say, Bella's been coming by a fair bit."

Zach's mouth twitched in a smile. "Has she indeed?"

"I am definitely *not* making a big deal of it." She sank her fingers into Penny's fur as a gusty sigh escaped her. "But... he never found his tribe in Greenwich, you know? I'm really hoping and praying he finds it here."

"It sounds like he might be beginning to."

"Maybe." She glanced up at him, her eyes dark and luminous. "You've been such a good friend to him, Zach. I hope you know that."

"I think I do," he told her with a small smile.

She let out another laugh, this one even shakier. "Hope feels so hard sometimes. To do it in the first place, and then also to risk the disappointment. I tell myself to be realistic about everything but sometimes I just want to *believe*."

She glanced at him again and then looked away quickly, and Zach wondered if they were talking about Ben—or something else, maybe even their own relationship... or lack of it. Did she miss him the way he missed her?

"Anyway," Maggie said into the silence, before he could think how to approach that topic, or decide if now was really the right time. "How are things with you?"

"They're... good." She raised her eyebrows, waiting for more, and haltingly Zach began to explain about his hoped-for woodworking business, the log cabin he had decided to rent long-term, the life he wanted to build. He could hear the excitement in his voice, and he wasn't embarrassed by it. This felt too important, too *good*, not to be unabashedly glad of what he was finally doing. "It feels like I'm getting my life on track," he confessed as he finished. "About time."

"Well, you're still so young," Maggie replied after a moment, and Zach just blinked, because she sounded like she was his grandmother and he'd just left high school or something. Was she trying to put some distance between them? He felt like there was plenty already. He didn't want more, and he hadn't thought she did, either, but maybe he'd got it wrong.

"Youngish, maybe," he finally replied lightly. Maggie didn't reply, just lifted Penny off her lap and took her empty coffee cup to the back of the kitchen.

"I'm really glad for you, Zach," she called back as she started tidying up, her movements brisk and decisive.

Slowly, Zach rose from the sofa and followed her back to the kitchen. He propped one shoulder against the doorframe as he watched her bustle about. What was going on here? He felt like the temperature in the room had gone down by about twenty degrees, and he wasn't sure why.

"Thanks," he said after a moment, unsure what else to say. "Seems like we're all having a new start."

"Yes." She took a deep breath, laid her hands flat on the counter. "In all kinds of ways." She paused before continuing, "Actually... I'm going out on a date this weekend." She lifted her gaze to meet his with a resolute defiance.

Zach went completely still, saying nothing. He felt like he'd been sucker-punched; he was breathless from the pain of it. So *that* was where this had all been going. Stupid him, for hoping otherwise. For thinking Maggie might feel about him the way he still felt about her. Maggie stared at him for another second, her expression still defiant, and then she turned away.

"Wow," he finally said, and his voice was toneless. He was amazed at how hurt he felt—not just because she was going out on a date, but also because she'd told him this way, like she was flinging it in his face, like she'd moved on a long time ago, and maybe she had. "Did you sign up to Tinder, after all?" he asked, his lips curving into a small, cool smile. "Good for you."

"Not Tinder," she replied stiffly as she turned back to face him. "He's a friend of a friend."

"Even better."

They stared at each other for a moment, and Zach had the urge to grab her by the shoulders, shake her and then kiss her. Or maybe just beg her to reconsider, the way he was, because he really didn't like the thought of her dating someone else at all, even as he recognized he had no right to object. A month ago he'd more or less told her he wasn't interested. Did he really want her pining for him now?

And yet... a *date*?

He opened his mouth to say—what? Don't go? But no. She had every right to find happiness—and he was done with trying to make people like him. He wasn't about to convince Maggie how she should take a chance on him. On *them*. If she wanted to go out on a date, fine. He wouldn't stop her. He dug his hands into the pockets of his coat, and his fingers closed around a small wooden figure he'd been keeping in there for months now. He'd never found the right time to give it to her, but maybe now he never would.

"Here," he said abruptly as he thrust it at her. "A memento."

"What..." She took the figurine, stared down at it in surprise.

"A shadar-kai," he said tonelessly. "In case you didn't know."

"I know," she said softly. She ran her thumb over the burnished wood of the tiny figurine—elven ears poked out of her long flowing hair, her slender body swathed in a robe, the expression on her face a mixture of defiance and fear. She looked up at him, her eyes luminous. "You said I was like a shadar-kai."

"Yeah." He felt exposed, then, for having made the figurine and then given it to her, especially since she was going on a date. "I should probably go," he said abruptly, and for a millisecond, her face crumpled. It was so quick Zach wondered if he'd imagined it, hoped for it, even. Then she nodded.

"All right. And—thank you." She nodded toward the figurine. "I'll... I'll treasure it, Zach."

He found he had to swallow past the lump in his throat. For a second, they simply stared at each other.

"Well..." Maggie cleared her throat. "I guess I'll see you around."

What a vague non-promise that was, he thought. Zach nodded back. "See you around," he echoed, and then he walked out of the café, feeling like he was walking out of her life. As the door slammed behind him, Zach thought that maybe he was.

## 21

"So what do *you* do?"

The question, Maggie reflected, would have meant more if it had come an hour, or even half an hour, earlier. As it was, she'd listened to Eric Roberts drone on about himself and his oh-so-important job as a corporate lawyer for most of the evening without him asking a single thing about her. It had been more than a little dull, and that was without taking into consideration the fact that she hadn't wanted to be here in the first place.

Eric Roberts had worked with Lynn before moving to Hartford a couple of months ago. He was mid-forties, divorced, okay looking, and probably an all-around good guy. Lynn had tried to talk him up, but Maggie had zero interest in him.

"I run a boardgame café," she told him as she took a sip of her wine. They'd met midway between Starr's Fall and Hartford, at a bistro on Route 4, air-kissing each other's cheeks before descending into awkward chitchat. And then Eric had started talking about himself and Maggie had more or less tuned out.

"A boardgame café," he repeated. He looked like he had no idea what to make of that. "What kinds of games?"

"All kinds," Maggie told him. "We're holding a gaming conference next weekend, actually, where people can play RainQuest for twenty-four hours straight." That had been, of course, Ben's idea. He and his new friends had arranged it all, and they had an incredible sixteen sign-ups so far. Slice of Heaven and The Rolling Pin were going to provide food, and Ben was livestreaming the event to other gamers. He had lots of other ideas, too—a Scrabble tournament, Saturday afternoon tutorials in new games, an evening trivia quiz.

"RainQuest? Is that, like, some kind of fantasy game? Like Dungeons & Dragons?" The disdain in Eric's voice was more than evident.

"Yes," Maggie replied coolly. "My son loves it." She lifted her eyebrows slightly, daring him to make some remark.

"Oh, well... I mean, boys like those kinds of games, don't they?" he stammered. "I was more into sports, myself, but I guess it's a phase some boys go through, especially if they're not athletic..."

"Actually," Maggie told him evenly, "RainQuest is an incredibly complex game with a lot of involved strategy. I'm not sure the average jock could get the hang of it." She paused while he goggled at her. "I play it myself now." Ben had helped her set up her own profile a few days ago. She was Maggie-kai, elven devotee of the Raven Queen.

"Oh, well..." Eric shrugged helplessly, and a long, tense silence ensued. The evening, Maggie feared, was going to go even more downhill, and that wasn't even about Eric. It was about *her* and the fact that there was only one guy she wanted to be with. Zach.

Why had she been so stupid *again* and said she was going on a date? At that point, she hadn't even agreed to Lynn's suggestion to meet up with Eric. But when Zach had started talking about his new life—the log cabin, the woodworking business—the enthusiasm in his voice... well, it had reminded her that he had so much life ahead of him and she didn't.

It had even been the kind of thing she'd imagined for him, minus the pretty little wife, but surely that would come one day, maybe even one day soon. And it wouldn't be her. It *couldn't* be her, because Zach deserved more than a middle-aged mom with grief and guilt issues. And so she'd pushed him away, because she seemed to be really good at doing that, and in the moment it had felt like the kindest thing.

Too bad she was regretting it now. Just as she was regretting this evening. It was, Maggie decided, time to call it quits.

"This has been fun," she told Eric, interrupting yet another monologue about one of his cases. "But I've got to get back to Starr's Fall."

"Oh." He looked startled. "I thought we could have dessert…"

"Sorry, it's a bit late for me." Maggie reached for her purse. "But let me pay my half."

Eric didn't protest, no doubt realizing that there was not going to be a second date. Ten minutes later, Maggie was out in the parking lot, sliding into her car with relief. She texted Ben to tell him she'd be home in half an hour; he was out with his new friends, something that thrilled her, but she'd still sensibly given him a 10 p.m. curfew.

The sweep of loneliness that she felt coming for her as she drove down the darkened road was different than those she'd endured after Matt's death. It wasn't grief so much as longing, a longing for Zach. She'd put the figurine he'd made for her on her bedside table. Every time she looked at it, her heart ached with both longing and loss. She could find him right now, she thought suddenly. She knew where his log cabin was. She could knock on the door and tell him she was crazy, crazy about *him*, and see what happened. Where it led.

Already Maggie knew she wouldn't. There were far too many reasons not to—for Zach's sake as well as her own, and also for Ben's. And yes, she was also chicken. She'd been rebuffed once before, and it had *hurt*. Laying herself out there again, and even more this time, did not feel like a good—or safe—thing to do.

And ever since Matt's death, she knew she'd had a big thing about being safe. Hiding away from life until Zach had forced her to take more than a few timid steps back into the land of the living. Not risking her heart, both because it hurt and also because part of her still struggled with wondering if she even had the right to such happiness. Did she deserve a second chance?

Everyone had issues, Maggie knew. Life—and people—were complicated. And her emotions were so tangled up that she didn't know if the reason she didn't knock on Zach's door was because she was afraid, or because she was being smart. Maybe a little bit of both.

As she pulled into Starr's Fall, the town's quiet peace felt like a comforting blanket being wrapped around her shoulders. The air was full of the smell of lilac as she parked the car and headed toward the café. Ben hadn't replied to her text, which would have once alarmed her, but now she knew he was out with his new friends and most likely having a good time. She was so, *so* glad her son had started to move on, but even that made her feel lonelier. She needed to move on, too... from Zach.

As Maggie came upstairs, Penny greeted her by winding her way between her legs, so she scooped up the cat into her arms and carried her into the darkened kitchen. She flicked on the lights and then sank into the chair by the desk, Penny purring in her lap. All around her the house settled softly into the darkness, and the sense of loneliness tugged at her, started to sweep her under.

She could have stopped by Laurie's, Maggie knew. Laurie was meeting her biological mother next weekend and was both anxious and excited about it, a potent emotional combination Maggie understood all too well. She could have driven over to the Lymans, checked in on Annie and Barb; Annie had started looking into hospice care for Barb, which was heart-wrenching for both of them. Or, Maggie reflected, she could have called on Henrietta Starr, who had recently invited her over for tea. She'd come in to play Scrabble twice more, and Maggie had enjoyed both games, as well as the old lady's acerbic wit. And there was Elaine, Liz, Zoe, Jenna... There were plenty of friends she could have called on rather than sit here alone in the dark, because right now there was only one person she wanted to be with.

The computer beeped, and Maggie turned to it, clicking on the mouse to see the purple and green screen of the RainQuest game come up. Ben must have left the house mid-game, and there was a message in his profile's chatbox, from the Zachanator.

Hey, you there?

Maggie's heart lurched, and then, having no idea of the ethics of the situation, she typed *Yes* before she deleted it and typed *Yeah* instead.

That sounded much more like Ben, although why she was trying to impersonate her son she had no idea. She just wanted to connect with Zach.

A few seconds passed and then Zach typed:

> Are you playing?

Maggie knew she wasn't nearly competent enough to attempt to play RainQuest, even though she had her own profile.

> No. Not right now.

Another second, and then simply:

> ???

Maggie let out a soft huff of laughter. How was she supposed to respond to that? And did she really want to pretend to be Ben for much longer? *Hold on*, she typed, and then she logged out of Ben's profile and switched to her own. As Maggie-kai, her heart thumping, she typed:

> Hi.

A long pause then, and finally Zach typed:

> Maggie?

A soft laugh escaped her.

> Yep.

> I already suspected it was you.

A small gasp escaped her.

> How?

> Because no teenager types in full sentences, with punctuation.

She laughed softly.

> Busted. I was sitting here alone in the dark and your message came up.

Another long pause. Her heart was starting to beat hard.

> Why are you alone in the dark?

And then, before she could start replying:

> I thought tonight was your big date.

> Nothing big about it.

And then:

> I wish I hadn't gone.

It felt like a confession.

> That bad, huh? I've been on a few of those.

He was keeping it light, Maggie realized, and so should she. They were just friends, after all.

> I could have watched three whole episodes of Is It Cake? instead. Talk about a missed opportunity.

Another pause, this one longer than ever. Maggie held her breath. Then he replied:

> If we're going to talk about missed opportunities…

Her breath came out in a rush. She waited. There was nothing more.

An entire minute passed, each tick of a second on the clock on the wall seeming to echo through the kitchen and right through her. Which one of them was willing to risk first? Say what they really felt?

Are we?

Maggie finally typed, like a dare.

Still no reply. She got up from her chair and went to put on the kettle. Made herself a cup of tea and let it steep for three whole minutes while Penny wound around her ankles. Still nothing from the Zachanator. A sense of disappointment so deep it felt like grief swept through her. He was going to leave it there, and so then would she. She didn't really have any choice, did she?

Taking her tea, Maggie sat down in front of the computer. She stared at the message inbox, willing the words to appear. *I miss you. I want to be with you. I'm sorry for what I said before. Let's start over.*

Was he thinking any of those things? Did he want to say them to her? Or maybe he'd moved on, and had gone back to playing RQ, their messages back and forth forgotten.

The only way she was going to read those words on the screen, Maggie realized with a lurch of panic as well as a surge of conviction, was if she typed them herself. And why shouldn't she? Surely risking and losing was better than sitting here alone in the dark, wishing she'd said something. Hadn't she told Laurie as much? There was no point in trying to keep yourself safe just so you'd have to learn to live with the regret. You got hurt anyway.

Maggie took a sip of tea to fortify herself, and then she started typing.

\* \* \*

Maybe he was being really stupid, but Zach *felt* like being stupid, or at least being bold. When he'd been typing to Maggie, he'd realized he hadn't wanted to have this kind of conversation by text. Some things were too important to skirt around. And while he'd certainly been burned by rushing in too fast before, this didn't feel fast anymore. It felt right... and necessary. He would tell her once and for all how he felt and if she backed away again, well then, fine. It would be over. But at least then he would know.

He parked his truck behind her car, climbed out, and headed to Your Turn Next. He raised his hand to knock but then, after a second's pause, he unlocked the door of the boardgame café instead. Maggie had given him a spare key months ago, when he'd first started working on the bookshelves. He'd meant to give it back, but he never had. Now he walked quietly through the café that they'd built together and then up the stairs. Then he knocked on the door to Maggie and Ben's apartment.

He heard her little yelp of surprise and smiled.

"Ben?" she called uncertainly. "Is that you?"

"Nope," Zach called back. Another yelp. Improbably, he found himself grinning.

He heard the sound of footsteps, and then Maggie threw open the door. She was wearing her purple skirt with the blue patches and her hair was tumbled about her face, including that streak of white. She looked flushed and discombobulated and entirely lovely.

"How did you get in?" she asked breathlessly. He held up the key. "Oh." She pressed her hands to her flushed cheeks and then dropped them. "You drove over here? Then I guess... I guess you didn't read my message?"

Zach frowned. "What message?"

"On the game chat thing. I typed... well... I guess you'll read it eventually." She let out an uncertain, embarrassed laugh.

His curiosity well and truly piqued now, he strode over to the computer, reaching for the mouse.

"Oh..." Maggie practically squeaked as he clicked it to light up the screen. "I don't... It's different when you're right here..."

"Isn't this what you're always having to tell teenagers?" he told her, mock-severely, as he turned around. He hadn't read the message yet, but he was now officially dying of curiosity. "Don't say something online you wouldn't say in person. I'm sure you've told Ben that at least a million times."

"Well, yes, but... I would say this in person," Maggie told him, "but that doesn't mean it isn't scary and potentially *very* embarrassing." She let out a little laugh that ended in a strangled sound as she ducked her head.

Okay, now he was seriously curious. Zach turned back to the screen and scanned her last message, his heart seeming to squeeze, expand, and turn over all at once as he read the words.

I think it's time I said all the things I've been wanting to say for a long time. That you're the kindest, truest, and I have to admit, sexiest guy I've ever met. I know I've backed away and said I'm not ready—and for a while I wasn't—but even when I was ready, I still acted out of fear. Fear of risking my heart again, because it was only after Matt died that I realized how broken it had become—not from his death, but from what came before. How broken our marriage had become, and how I'd become someone I didn't even recognize. I know that's a lot to dump on you now, but I wish I could have explained it before. Maybe I should have said it's not you, it's me?? Anyway... it's been hard to know how to stop acting out of fear, which is probably why I'm typing this rather than saying it to your face. And also because at this point I have no idea how you'll respond, but I've come to the conclusion that I need to say it anyway. You might have moved on, with your cabin and your woodworking and your brand-new life, and that's great. I really am genuinely so very happy for you, Zach.

She'd pressed send then, and then started to compose another message she hadn't yet sent:

But I guess I've realized that for me to move on, with or without you, I need to say all this. To tell you that I think I'm

It ended there. Slowly, Zach turned around. Maggie was gazing at him with wide eyes, her face pale, her fingers knotted together as she waited for his response to all that she'd typed.

"That you're...?" Zach prompted. "You didn't finish."

She swallowed hard. "You knocked on the door."

"So what do you think you are...?" he continued, wanting her to finish that very intriguing thought. "'To tell you that I think I'm...?'" he prompted again softly. "Maggie...?"

"You're making this very difficult for me," she whispered, her nervous gaze locked on his face. "Since you have not given me a *clue* about how you felt about all the rest, and I said quite a few things there."

"Well, I like that you think I'm the sexiest guy you ever met," Zach quipped, a grin tugging at his mouth as he took a step toward her. Happiness was unfurling inside him, spreading through him like he'd swallowed the sun. "But it actually means more to me that you think I'm the kindest." He reached for her clasped hands, gently prying her fingers apart so he could link them with his own, sliding their palms together. "And I appreciate everything you told me about your marriage and Matt, and we can talk about all that more later, but... to give you a clue, I could have typed a very similar message about you, pretty much word for word, but I decided to come over here in person and tell you instead."

Maggie's eyes widened as her fingers tightened on his. "So tell me," she whispered.

"Okay." Zach took a deep breath. "A few months ago you asked me why I was interested in you, and I gave you some answers. Those are still true, of course, but now I know so much more. I know how deeply you feel and love and how much you fight to protect those you love. I know you're willing to admit when you're wrong and forgive when someone else is. I know you can laugh at yourself but at the same time you feel for people deeply—"

"Like the aasimar," Maggie said, and he laughed softly.

"So you did read those descriptions."

"Yes, and it felt like you'd got right inside my head. Although I hope I'm not as mournful as the shadar-kai, even if you made one for me, and she's beautiful. I've kept her by my bed—"

"Shadar-kai are strong," he told her. "They've triumphed over their grief, just like you have."

"Grief really did a number on me," she confessed quietly. "Especially because it felt so complicated. Matt and I... well, like I said, our marriage was pretty broken. And I was kind of broken... Matt could be controlling, and I guess I let him control me. I became someone I didn't really like. We didn't have as strong a marriage as I wished we'd had."

Zach's heart ached for her, even as he realized he was unsurprised. "I think I sort of guessed that, by some of the things you said," he told her gently. "And didn't say. But I'm sorry for what you went through."

"That emotional astuteness I still need to credit you with," she quipped, and he laughed, tugging on her hand to draw her closer. She came, standing before him, her face full of both vulnerability and trust.

"If I'd finished that sentence," she told him, an honest matter-of-fact-ness to her tone, without any teasing or hesitation, "then I would have said that I think I'm falling in love with you." She stopped abruptly, waiting for his response.

Zach gazed down at her and felt a rush of love so strong and sweet it almost made him dizzy. She was everything he'd ever wanted—not the fairy-tale ending in itself, the way he'd once been looking for, but the life partner to walk by his side. How had he not realized that before? Never mind what they said in the movies, people didn't complete you. They *accompanied* you. They supported and strengthened, held and loved you, all along the way.

"Then you'd better keep up," he murmured as he slid his hands up to cup her face. "Because I'm pretty sure I *know* I'm already in love with you."

And then he kissed her, slow and sweet and deep, the way he felt. The way *she* felt. Amazingly.

As they broke apart, Maggie smiled, looking dazed but also still a little worried. "I'm still so much older than you," she blurted.

Zach laughed softly. "And, funny thing about age, you always will be."

"Zach…" she pressed, "doesn't that bother you? I mean, looking down the road… not to get all intense so soon or anything, but… I'm forty-one. If you want children… I know that's a lot to think about now, but I'm…" She trailed off, nibbling her bottom lip.

He considered this, knowing she needed—and deserved—an honest answer. "Maggie, I don't want to make any sweeping statements at this stage, except that I love you and want to be with you, and that is worth it to me. As for what the future holds… maybe we should just see what happens?" He pulled her back toward him. "Together."

She stared up at him for a long moment, taking in his words, and as her expression softened, Zach hoped she was trusting them. Neither of them could know what the future held, only that they could choose to face it together, with joy as well as gratitude, with courage as well as hope.

"Okay," she whispered, and he brushed a kiss across her lips just as they both heard the thundering of footsteps up the stairs. Before they could pull apart, Ben flung open the door, did a double take, and then fist-pumped the air as he crowed in delight, "Finally!"

# EPILOGUE
## TWO MONTHS LATER

"Settlers of Catan is a great game, but have you tried the expansion packs? The seafarers one takes a little getting used to, but I can walk you through it..."

Maggie smiled to hear Toby's friendly yet officious tone. Her most recent hire and one of Ben's best friends, he'd started working at Your Turn Next every Saturday, and would be upping his hours when school let out next week. And in September, Ben would be joining him at Torrington High School for tenth grade. Maggie was so grateful.

She was grateful for a lot of things—the success of the café, which had continued to serve as a community rallying point; the closeness of her friendships, especially with Laurie and Annie; how Ben was thriving, exceeding even her wildest expectations for what his life would look like in Starr's Fall.

Most of all, though, she was grateful for Zach. The last two months had been both wonderful and challenging—more than a few people had looked at them askance when they'd gone public with their relationship. They'd provided grist for the gossip mill for a solid three weeks, at least, but they'd made it through, and now she hoped they were stronger than ever. Maggie still sometimes worried about their age difference, but Zach seemed unbothered and so she tried to trust what they had now rather than catastrophize into the future, which she knew she could still be prone to do.

Zach's woodworking business was slowly but surely taking off; he'd renovated one of the old barns behind the store and set it up as a workshop and storefront. Maggie had been one of his first customers, buying a refurbished bookshelf to store yet more boardgames for the café.

It was all good, Maggie reflected, but that didn't necessarily make it easy. Life could still be hard—Annie's mom was now in a hospice, and when Laurie had gone to meet her biological mother, she hadn't shown up. Laurie had put a brave face on it, but Maggie could tell she'd been hurt. Then, a month ago, Henrietta Starr had had a fall and broken her hip, spending three weeks in the hospital before she was released. She'd been walking with a Zimmer frame since and wasn't able to come to the café. Every so often, Maggie went to her for a laborious but enjoyable game of Scrabble.

There was still her and Ben's grief to deal with, an emotion that sometimes felt inconvenient and uncomfortable, but was still there, and maybe always would be. No matter how happy she was, the future would always be uncertain. But, Maggie had come to realize, that was the nature of life—always changing, always unknowable, with the pleasure and happiness to be found along the way. She was learning to roll with the punches a little more, but occasionally she still needed to hide under her duvet and watch *Is It Cake?* for an hour or so, and that was okay, too.

The door to the café opened, and Maggie smiled to see Zach walk in. He still held the power to make her heart soar and her stomach flip.

"Hey." He gave her a deliberately sexy smile—something that had become a joke between them—as he leaned in for a kiss.

"Hey," Maggie replied softly. She brushed her fingers through his tousled hair, smiling as she did so.

"You off duty soon?" Zach asked. "I thought we could take a walk up to the waterfall and see the sunset."

"Now that sounds like a plan." She had come to discover just what a romantic Zach was at heart, and she loved it. "Think I can probably leave Toby in charge—there's only a few of our regulars booked for five."

Since Your Turn Next had opened, a few different people had made weekly bookings—two elderly couples who played Mahjong together; a couple of moms and their little ones who cracked open the Candyland. Maggie loved welcoming them all every week.

"Okay, sounds good," Zach said with a smile that made her stomach flip—again—just as his sister stormed into the café, looking thunderous. Zach's eyebrows lifted as he shot Maggie a bemused glance.

He'd told her that since he'd started Miller's Woodworking and Furniture Restoration, he and Jenna had been getting along better than ever. She listened to his ideas and even took his advice, more than she had been, at least, and they'd enjoyed each other's company more, too. It had definitely been the right decision to branch out, he'd concluded, and Maggie had to agree. Everyone seemed happier... except right now Jenna did not seem happy at all.

"What's wrong?" Maggie asked as Jenna blew out a frustrated breath, her eyes sparking with anger.

"I have just had the most *annoying* customer in the store," she declared. "Right before closing, and demanding I stock *salmon*, of all things! And then saying he'd never shop there again because it was such a waste of space. He's just moved here, and honestly, I hope I never see him again."

"Seems unlikely," Zach murmured, and Jenna mock-glared at him. At least, Maggie thought it was mock.

"I know, I know, this is a small place, but that's exactly my point. Where does he think he is? New York City? Honestly, he was so *entitled*, it just..." She trailed off, shaking her head, her face flushed, her eyes still sparkling.

"Is that where he's from?" Maggie asked.

"Apparently." Jenna flung her hands up in the air. "We didn't exactly have a heart-to-heart conversation, considering how rude he was."

Maggie glanced at Jenna thoughtfully. Her friend definitely seemed agitated, but there was a sparkle in her eye, too, which made Maggie wonder if this guy, whoever he was, happened to be good-looking. She knew what it was like when you unexpectedly ran into someone who made your heart beat faster...

"Did you get his name?" she asked.

"Jack Wexler. He's some city bigshot, or so he says."

Zach smothered a laugh. "He *said* he was a city bigshot?"

"Well, no, obviously not," Jenna replied impatiently, "but he acted like one. Honestly, I hope I never see him again."

"I think," Zach whispered under his breath, "the lady doth protest a little too much."

Fortunately, Jenna didn't seem to hear him. She glanced around the near-empty café with a rueful grimace. "Sorry to storm in here like this," she told Maggie. "I was so mad about it that I went for a walk and then I saw you guys..." She smiled sheepishly. "All right, I'm calmer now. He's a jerk, end of story."

Or the beginning, Maggie wondered. Whoever this Jack Wexler was, he'd clearly got Jenna pretty worked up. She wondered why he'd moved to Starr's Fall... and if it would work its magic on him the way it had on her and Ben.

"Anyway, I should go," Jenna said. "I'm meeting Annie for dinner at The Starr Light."

"Have fun," Zach replied, still looking bemused by the whole exchange. As Jenna left, he turned to Maggie. "Now that was interesting..."

"You know Jenna. She has opinions." Maggie smiled. "Now, about that waterfall walk... are you bringing a picnic?"

"And a blanket, and a bottle of wine. What do you take me for?" He pulled her close for a quick kiss.

"A mind-reader," Maggie teased. "I think I'm good to go," she said, and slipped her hand through his.

Zach gave it a squeeze as they walked out of the café.

"Maybe we'll run into this Jack Wexler guy," he remarked as they climbed into his truck. "Do you think he's as much of a jerk as my sister makes out?"

"Probably not," Maggie replied with a laugh. "But I'm not sure *she* thinks he's so much of a jerk, really."

"She did seem a little worked up, and not necessarily in an angry way," Zach agreed musingly. "I wonder why he moved to Starr's Fall."

"Maybe Starr's Fall will work its magic on him," Maggie suggested with a smile. "It certainly did on me."

"And me." Zach grinned at her before starting the truck, and Maggie smiled back, her heart full of gratitude and love. Zach knew the power of this place just as she did.

"And I'm glad it did," she murmured as she leaned her head back against the seat, and they drove off into the sunset to find a little more magic of their own.

* * *

## MORE FROM KATE HEWITT

In case you missed it, the previous book in the gorgeous, romantic Starr's Fall series, *Coming Home to Starr's Fall*, is available to order now here:
www.mybook.to/CHStarrsFallBackAd

# ACKNOWLEDGEMENTS

It's been so fun to be back in the world of Starr's Fall again! Thanks must go to my editor, Isobel, who gives me wonderful advice and also encourages me to trust my instincts. Thanks also to everyone on the Boldwood team who work so tirelessly to make my books a success. I must thank my son Ted for his gaming advice, especially in regards to gaming slang, and to Rachel Lilly, who made the beautiful map of Starr's Fall. Lastly, and most importantly, thank you to my readers, who read my books and wonderfully let me know how much they enjoyed them!

# ABOUT THE AUTHOR

**Kate Hewitt** is a million copy bestselling author of historical, contemporary and romantic fiction. An American ex-pat, she lives in a small market town in Wales with her husband and five young(ish) children, along with their two Golden Retrievers.

Sign up to Kate Hewitt's mailing list for news, competitions and updates on future books.

Follow Kate on social media here:

f facebook.com/KateHewittAuthor
X x.com/author_kate
O instagram.com/katehewitt1
BB bookbub.com/authors/kate-hewitt

# ALSO BY KATE HEWITT

**The Starr's Fall Series**

Coming Home to Starr's Fall

Playing for Keeps in Starr's Fall

# Boldwood

Boldwood Books is an award-winning fiction publishing company seeking out the best stories from around the world.

**Find out more at www.boldwoodbooks.com**

Join our reader community for brilliant books, competitions and offers!

Follow us
@BoldwoodBooks
@TheBoldBookClub

Sign up to our weekly deals newsletter

https://bit.ly/BoldwoodBNewsletter